A CATERED
ST. PATRICK'S DAY

Books by Isis Crawford

A CATERED MURDER

A CATERED WEDDING

A CATERED CHRISTMAS

A CATERED VALENTINE'S DAY

A CATERED HALLOWEEN

A CATERED BIRTHDAY PARTY

A CATERED THANKSGIVING

A CATERED ST. PATRICK'S DAY

Published by Kensington Publishing Corporation

A Mystery with Recipes

A CATERED
ST. PATRICK'S DAY

ISIS CRAWFORD

KENSINGTON BOOKS
www.kensingtonbooks.com

KENSINGTON BOOKS are published by

Kensington Publishing Corp.
119 West 40th Street
New York, NY 10018

All Kensington titles, imprints and distributed lines are available at special quantity discounts for bulk purchases for sales promotion, premiums, fund-raising, educational or institutional use.

Special book excerpts or customized printings can also be created to fit specific needs. For details, write or phone the office of the Kensington Special Sales Manager: Kensington Publishing Corp., 119 West 40th Street, New York, NY, 10018. Attn. Special Sales Department. Phone: 1-800-221-2647.

Kensington and the K logo Reg. U.S. Pat. & TM Off.

Library of Congress Control Number: 2011937866

ISBN-13: 978-0-7582-4740-7
ISBN-10: 0-7582-4740-0

First Hardcover Printing: February 2012

10   9   8   7   6   5   4   3   2   1

Printed in the United States of America

For my Bruegger's buddies.
You make the day start better.

Acknowledgments

As always, for Dan, who always comes up with a solution to my problem.

Chapter 1

It was a little after nine o'clock in the morning and Bernie and Libby Simmons were rolling out pie dough in the kitchen of their shop, A Little Taste of Heaven, when the call came in. Ironically, they had just been congratulating themselves on how peaceful everything had been in the last four months.

There'd been no crimes committed in Longely—at least none that they'd been called on to investigate—the shop was running smoothly, no strategic piece of equipment had broken, their staff was showing up on time and were not exhibiting the usual drama to which they were prone, and the shop's sales figures were more than respectable. In fact, it looked as if they could get a new delivery vehicle soon.

"It's almost boring," Bernie had told her sister as she went over to the cooler and took another portion of dough out. Their dough had so much butter in it that it had to be refrigerated until it was ready to be rolled.

Libby sprinkled a little more flour on the counter and flipped the piece of dough she was working onto its other side. "As Mom would have said, 'Bite your tongue.'"

Bernie rolled her eyes and brushed a speck of flour off

the black silk shirt she was wearing. She made it a point of honor to cook in clothes that she would wear outside the kitchen, unlike her sister, who preferred jeans, sweats, and T-shirts.

"What's wrong with saying that?" Libby demanded, noting her sister's expression.

"I didn't say anything was wrong with saying that," Bernie protested with mock sincerity.

"You rolled your eyes. It's the same thing."

"I just think it's a silly expression. I thought so when Mom used to say it and I think so now. It's like believing that knocking on wood will bring you good luck and walking under a ladder will bring you bad luck."

Libby gave the dough on the counter two more outward strokes with her rolling pin before slipping her rolling pin under the perfect circle she'd created and transferring the dough to the pie pan. She allowed herself a moment to admire her handiwork before speaking.

"You mean that's not true?" she asked her sister as she crimped the pie's edges.

Bernie closed the cooler door, put the dough she'd retrieved on the table, and gave it a couple of good whacks with her rolling pin to soften it up. "You're kidding, right?"

"No, I'm not," Libby said even though she had been. She was in a crabby mood and got a certain amount of satisfaction out of pushing her sister's buttons.

"It's a superstition."

"Well, sometimes there are reasons for superstitions," Libby pointed out. "Walking under a ladder isn't the smartest thing to do—something could drop on your head. And that thing about breaking a mirror bringing seven years bad luck . . ." Libby's voice trailed off. She'd lost her train of thought. Damn. She hated when that happened.

Bernie peeled the wax paper off the dough. "And why is that?"

"I forget," Libby confessed. Then, as she moved the salt aside to make more room on the table, she remembered. "Because mirrors used to be very expensive. Like salt."

For some reason, today's shop feature, four-leaf-clover-shaped sugar cookies with green icing in honor of Saint Patrick's Day, sprang into Bernie's mind. "What about four-leaf clovers? Why are those good luck?"

"Because they're rare and rare connotes valuable," Libby said.

"They could just as easily be bad luck. Unusual is not necessarily good," Bernie mused. "Now if that were true," she said, thinking of all the cookies they'd baked and the cupcakes they'd decorated with four-leaf clovers, "we'd be out a fair chunk of change. No one would buy them."

Libby put her rolling pin down and went to pour herself another cup of coffee. It was an organic Guatemalan light roast. When she'd told her dad that was what she was giving him this morning, he'd snorted and said, "What happened to a plain old cup of joe?" And maybe he was right. After all, Starbucks had switched to Pike Place. Maybe she and her sister should try and find a signature brand of coffee to sell in the shop.

"On the other hand," Bernie continued when Libby got back, "we do touch the kitchen witch for luck every morning before we start working."

"Is that habit or superstition?" Libby asked.

Bernie thought for a moment, then said, "Learned behavior. We saw Mom do it every morning so we do it too."

"She did, didn't she?" Libby said in a softer voice.

Bernie nodded her head. "Without fail."

Their mom had gotten the kitchen witch at a local craft fair when she'd first opened the shop and it had been hanging over the kitchen window ever since. It hadn't been particularly well made, so now the witch was tattered and shabby looking. Libby had resewn her seams and restuffed one of her arms and her hat several times, but both she and Bernie were loath to get a new one. She was irreplaceable in their eyes.

Funny how things go, Libby thought as she added a smidgen of heavy cream to her coffee and watched it swirl around in the cup, turning the liquid from an almost black brown to a pleasing shade of tan.

"Changing the topic . . ." she said after she'd raised the cup to her lips and taken a sip. "I have a question about the coffee." But she never got a chance to ask it because Bernie's cell went off.

"I wonder what Brandon wants," Bernie said as she reached for it. "He should be asleep by now."

"Maybe he forgot to tell you something," Libby suggested.

"Maybe," Bernie said. But she couldn't think of what it could be that couldn't wait.

She knew that Brandon had closed the bar last night, which meant that he hadn't gotten home until after three in the morning, which meant he hadn't fallen asleep until around five because it always took him a couple of hours to wind down. It was now a little after nine. He should be snoring up a storm at this moment, not calling her.

Especially since the day was going to be nuts at RJ's, it being the day before Saint Patrick's Day, which meant that they would be serving green beer this afternoon. Couple that with the fact that it was Friday and you got chaos. They couldn't pay her enough to work behind the bar this weekend, Bernie decided. Not that anyone had asked her. In fact, she had absolutely no desire to go anywhere near RJ's until Saint Pat's Day was over. She could do without the puking and the fights and the crowds.

"Hi," Bernie said to Brandon as questions swirled through her mind. "What's going on? Is everything okay?"

"No," Brandon told her. His voice was hoarse. "It's not okay. It's not okay at all. Come around to the back of RJ's as soon as you can." And he hung up.

"What's going on?" Libby asked.

Bernie shook her head. "He wants us to meet him at the back of RJ's."

"Why?"

"He didn't say." Bernie hit speed dial.

Libby put down her coffee mug. "What are you doing?"

"Calling him back." This time the call went straight to voice mail. Bernie looked up. "He shut off his phone."

"He never does that," Libby said.

"I know." Bernie bit her lower lip. "Listen, can you take care of the pies? I'm going to see what's up."

The shop had a standing order for ten pies for Friday night for the after-theater event at the Longely playhouse.

"Don't be silly. I'm coming too," Libby told her sister. "Mrs. Saks isn't picking up her order until five o'clock. We've got plenty of time to finish up before then."

Bernie gave her sister a quick hug. Okay, they did bicker a lot, but Libby was always there when she needed her. "Maybe it's not that bad," she said as she rewrapped the dough ball in a fresh sheet of wax paper and plopped it back in the cooler. The crust would be a bit tougher from being overly handled, but there was nothing she could do about that now.

Libby dusted the flour off her hands. "You don't really believe that, do you?"

"No," she said softly. "I don't."

In the first place, Brandon had sounded really tense. In the second place, he never turned off his phone. And in the third place, Brandon was never one to ask her for help if there was any other possibility. He was a guy guy, and as such thought that he should be able to handle anything that came along by himself. They'd once been lost in the Adirondacks for a little under two hours and not only had

Brandon refused to ask for directions, he wouldn't let Bernie ask either.

"I don't know what this is about, but whatever it is, it isn't good," Bernie conceded. "It isn't good at all. " She started to punch in Brandon's number again and then stopped. What was the point? "I guess we'll find out when we get there."

"Guess so," Libby said as she and Bernie slipped on their coats, walked out to the front of the shop, and told their counter people that they were leaving for a little while, and would, hopefully, be back shortly.

On the way out the door, they fielded comments from Mrs. Gupta and Mrs. O'Conner as to the spiciness of the ginger chicken and the type of apple used in the shop's trout, apple, walnut, and frisée salad, fended off a Coca-Cola salesman and another salesman who wanted to sell them a new POS machine, and took delivery of a load of kale and beets from one of the local farmers. Ten minutes later they were finally underway.

Neither of the sisters spoke to each other as they drove through the streets of Longely. They were both too nervous for chitchat. It had been a relatively mild winter and patches of green grass were visible among the brown thatch on people's lawns. And Libby thought she could spot a few of the willow trees starting to bud. Spring would be here very quickly, she realized, which made her think that she and Bernie had better start planning their spring menu.

They always changed things up for each season, although they were careful to keep some of the perennial favorites. Libby was about to tell Bernie they'd better get going on that, but looking at the expression on her face, Libby decided that this wasn't the right time or place to bring the subject up, so she just sat back and watched the houses and the shops go by. Even with the economic downturn, Longely was still a prosperous community, something

Libby was unendingly grateful for, and the houses they passed were all freshly painted and neatly landscaped.

RJ's was located about three miles away from A Little Taste of Heaven. Unlike the shop, which was situated on Longely's main street, RJ's was located on the edge of an old strip mall that contained a hardware store, a cleaner's, a beauty salon, a Rite Aid, a small diner, and most recently a dog-grooming place. The bar was a community fixture. It had been in existence for twenty years and Bernie and Libby had hung out there when they were younger, eating chicken wings, drinking beer, shooting pool, and playing darts.

They still hung out there and enjoyed an occasional game of pool, but that was as much a function of Bernie's boyfriend Brandon working behind the bar as anything else. It remained a very popular place however, especially on Saint Patrick's Day. Longely might not have a parade like New York City did, but they did have green beer at RJ's, and that was good enough for most people.

Bernie drove around to the back and parked the van. Earlier in the week, she'd broken out her new Marc Jacobs knee-length double-breasted navy spring coat, the one she'd gotten on sale at Barneys last fall, while Libby was still wearing her old beat-up winter parka, mostly because she'd been too lazy to go down to the basement and dig out her spring jacket, which actually wasn't in much better condition than her winter one was.

"You should get rid of that thing," Bernie told her as she reached out and touched it. "It's so old the material is starting to fray."

"It's my good luck jacket," Libby protested.

"It's an offense to the eyes," Bernie countered. She was about to add something to the effect that even the Salvation Army wouldn't take it when she caught sight of Brandon.

"Over here," he called, waving the sisters in his direction.

Brandon was standing next to the first of ten large kegs of beer. Bernie knew that the kegs contained green beer and that they had been, as was the custom, dropped off by a trucker yesterday and that they were due to be wheeled into the bar and tapped with a great deal of ceremony sometime later that afternoon. At least that was the way things usually went, but she had a feeling that this time things were going to be different.

"So whazz's up, Holmes?" Bernie asked as she walked toward Brandon.

Brandon took a step to the side and pointed to one of the kegs. "Check it out."

Libby and Bernie moved closer.

"I take it this is not about the quality of the beer?" Bernie asked him.

"I wish it were," Brandon replied.

Bernie took another step forward. Now that she was closer she could see a body bent over the barrel Brandon was pointing at. From the looks of what she could see of him, Bernie decided that the person was obviously male.

And obviously dead.

Unless he didn't need to breathe air. His legs were visible, but his chest and head were floating face down in green beer.

"Maybe he was drinking and fell in," Bernie suggested.

"And maybe the cow really did jump over the moon," Brandon told her.

"There is a chance it could have been an accident," Bernie countered.

"A very small chance," Brandon allowed. "An infinitesimal chance."

"Yeah. I don't really think so either," Bernie admitted.

"Do you know who it is?" Libby asked Brandon.

Brandon nodded. "Unfortunately, I do. It's Mike Sweeney."

"Mike Sweeney of the Corned Beef and Cabbage Club?" Libby asked. "That Mike Sweeney?"

"Yup. That's the one," Brandon said.

"He's such a jerk," Libby blurted out. She clapped her hand over her mouth when she realized what she'd said.

"Now he's a dead jerk," Brandon replied.

"I guess drinking green beer didn't bring him much luck," Bernie observed.

Brandon rubbed his chin with the knuckles of his left hand. "I never believed that one."

Bernie reflected that he looked exhausted. "Have you called anyone besides us?" she asked.

"I called my boss first."

"Naturally," Bernie said. "That's who I would have called. Who needs the cops anyway?"

"Well, it *is* his place," Brandon said defensively.

"That's true," Bernie conceded. "So what did he say?"

"He said to hold off calling anyone until he got here."

"Then why did you call me?" Bernie asked.

"I was hungry for your body."

"Seriously," Bernie said.

Brandon moved his eyebrows up and down. "I was hungry and I thought you'd bring me a corn muffin and some coffee."

Bernie stood up on her tiptoes and kissed his nose. "That's very sweet, but I don't believe you."

"About the coffee? I definitely need some."

"That I believe," Bernie told him. "You look as if you're ready to fall asleep standing up. But I don't believe you called so I could bring you a muffin. For one thing, you didn't ask."

"I thought you'd know, being as you say you can read my mind."

"You could have gotten something at the diner, which is—what?—two steps away?"

Brandon made an attempt at a smile and failed. "His stuff isn't nearly as good as yours," he pointed out.

"Seriously," Bernie repeated, wondering what Brandon wasn't telling her.

Brandon sighed. "Seriously, I called you because I wanted you to see how everything is before people start mucking around with things."

"Are you talking about people in general or is there someone specific you have in mind?"

Brandon ran his hand through his hair, which Bernie noticed was standing out in all directions, then zipped up the hoodie he was wearing. "Just in case," he said instead.

"Just in case what?" Bernie asked.

Brandon crossed his arms over his chest and frowned. "Just in case," he repeated.

"Now you're not making any sense," Bernie told him.

Brandon didn't say anything. Instead he shifted his weight from one foot to the other.

Bernie studied him for a moment. "Are you afraid you're going to get arrested?" she asked gently.

"It had crossed my mind," Brandon admitted.

"Why don't you tell Auntie Libby what happened," Libby coaxed.

Brandon jammed his hands in his pockets and pressed his lips together.

"After all," Bernie pointed out, "isn't that why you called us down here in the first place?"

"I guess you're right," Brandon said.

And so he did.

Chapter 2

The story Brandon told Bernie and Libby went like this: The night before had been on the dead side at RJ's. At six o'clock there had been twenty people in the bar and that number had dwindled down to twelve by ten o'clock. At 12:50, six more people had departed, leaving only the guys from the Corned Beef and Cabbage Club drinking at the bar.

By one o'clock Brandon had started washing the glasses, wiping down surfaces, and prepping for the next day. Now, all the time he was doing that, the guys from the Corned Beef and Cabbage Club were pestering him to bring in one of the kegs and crack it open so they could have an early taste of the green beer.

"Not that it's great stuff," Brandon commented.

"We know," Bernie said. *Cat piss* were the words that came to mind when describing it, and although she'd called it that before, she didn't say that now.

"I mean," Brandon continued, "even though I told them there was no friggin' way that was going to happen, they just wouldn't let it go. Finally I had to tell them to shut up or get the hell out and they chose to leave."

Bernie buttoned her coat. The sun was deceptive. It was

chillier outside than she thought it would be. "So these six guys . . ." she prompted.

"Five guys and a girl," Brandon corrected.

Bernie raised an eyebrow.

"Her name is Liza," Brandon said.

"Liza Sepranto?" Libby asked.

Brandon nodded.

"That's new," Libby observed.

"Not really," Brandon told her. "She's been hanging out with them for a while."

"I guess we've gotten out of touch with those guys," Libby observed.

"We've never been in touch," Bernie reminded her sister.

"Believe me, either way it's no great loss," Brandon said.

"Okay. So they left willingly. What happened next?" Bernie asked, getting back to the matter at hand.

"Well, I finished cleaning up and I was cashing out when I heard a noise in the back."

"How long after they left was this?" Bernie asked.

Brandon thought. "Probably twenty minutes. Maybe half an hour at the most."

Libby dug a piece of dark, single-origin chocolate out of her parka and ate it. Chocolate helped her concentrate. "What kind of noise?"

Brandon shrugged. "People talking. Something heavy being moved. Anyway, I opened the door and took a look. And don't you know it, there was Mike Sweeney trying to open up one of the barrels. So I go out there and we get into it."

Bernie shuddered, visualizing the worst. "How badly did you get into it?" she asked, knowing Brandon's temper and his strength.

"Bad enough," Brandon admitted. "I was pissed, so I decked him. He was just lying there. For a moment, I was a little worried, but then he kind of came around and Duncan and Liam picked him up and dragged him off. No foul, no harm."

"That was lucky," Bernie observed.

Brandon shrugged. "I guess it was. Anyway, I locked up and went home and went to bed. And that was that. Until now, that is."

"Why are you back here so early?" Libby asked.

"Bad luck," Brandon said. "Shorty was supposed to open, but he's in the ER down in Mount Sinai with a kidney stone, so he woke me up and asked if I could be a pal and come down and take care of things for him." Brandon frowned. "If I find out he's lying to me, he's in deep trouble. Anyway, I threw on some clothes, jumped in my car, and here I am. When I came in, the place looked exactly the way it had when I'd left. Then I opened the back door to air the place out and that's when I saw Sweeney."

"How do you know it's Sweeney?" Bernie asked. "Did you turn him over?"

"No. I haven't touched him." Brandon smoothed down his cowlick with the palm of his hand. "I know it's Sweeney because I recognize the pants and those friggin' shoes of his."

Bernie and Libby both looked down. Sweeney had on saddle shoes.

"Evidently they're the latest thing in trader land," Brandon said. "I heard him bragging to Duncan about how they cost him five hundred bucks."

"Leave something long enough and it becomes fashionable again," Bernie commented.

Libby pointed to her jacket. "So I guess I should keep this."

Bernie snorted. She was about to reply that the jacket hadn't been worth keeping when Libby bought it, when she heard the sound of a car entering the parking lot. A moment later, a Lexus barreled into the back lot and squealed to a stop a few feet in front of them. RJ's owner, John Mulroney, got out of his car and waddled over. "What the hell happened?" he demanded, even though Brandon had already told him when he'd called him.

Mulroney was a little guy, about five-foot-six, and almost as wide as he was tall. Bernie could see from the way he was moving that any sort of motion at all exhausted him. Brandon stepped aside so Mulroney could see the barrel and Sweeney floating in it.

"Jeez," Mulroney said. "Who is that?"

"Mike Sweeney," Brandon answered. "Remember?"

"Yeah. Yeah." Mulroney swallowed. "I don't suppose there's any chance that he got really drunk and passed out and that he's still alive."

"Not unless he's grown gills," Bernie said.

Mulroney looked up and the flesh under his chin jiggled and his face got red. He seemed to be noticing Bernie and Libby for the first time. He turned to Brandon. "What the hell are they doing here?" he demanded. "I thought I told you not to call anyone."

Libby put on her game face. "Sorry. We were wandering by and we stopped to say hello," she said brightly. "We were just keeping Brandon company until you came."

"He's a big boy. He can take care of himself," Mulroney growled. He took a handkerchief out of his vest pocket and mopped his brow, after which he turned to Brandon and jerked his head in the sisters' direction. "These two are the busybodies who always get themselves involved in things they have no business getting involved in, correct?"

"I wouldn't go that far," Bernie said.

Mulroney ignored her.

"And our chief of police doesn't like them," he continued.

Brandon suppressed a smile. "Hates them, actually."

"That's a bit of an exaggeration," Bernie said.

"Not really," Brandon replied.

"All of you be quiet," Mulroney snapped before Bernie could reply.

"That's rather rude," Bernie said to him.

"Ask me if I care," Mulroney spat out as he glared at Brandon, Libby, and Bernie.

Bernie thought it was a good glare as far as these things went and she could see why some people she knew might be intimidated by him. Then her gaze drifted to Mulroney's tie. It was red and white check with black dots in the middle of the red checks. Bernie was thinking it was one of the worst ties she'd seen in a while when Mulroney started talking again.

"Listen," he continued, "the only thing I care about is getting this thing squared away so we can get RJ's ready for this afternoon."

"I'm not so sure that's going to happen," Libby observed, assuming that "this thing" Mulroney was referring to was Mike Sweeney's death.

"And why is that?" Mulroney demanded.

"Why do you think?" Libby asked him. The man was either incredibly callous or incredibly stupid. Or both.

"I don't have a clue," Mulroney said.

"Call me crazy, but the last I knew," Libby told him, "murder investigations take precedent over business openings."

"Murder?" Mulroney's eyebrows came together. "Why do you assume Sweeney's death is a murder?" he said, his voice rising. "It looks like an accident to me."

"You're kidding me, right?" Bernie said.

Mulroney straightened out the lapels of his camel-hair coat. "Not at all. Obviously, Sweeney snuck around to the back and opened the keg. Then when he went to drink some beer, he slipped, hit his head on the barrel, and passed out. No one was there to pull him out, so he drowned." Mulroney patted his tie. "Hell, it could even be suicide. I heard this guy Sweeney had a lot of problems.

Maybe he decided to end it all. Yes, the more I think about it, the more I'm sure that's what happened."

"It would be a novel way to do it," Bernie said. "Is that the story you're going to tell the police?"

"I'm not going to tell," Mulroney italicized the word *tell* with his fingers, "the cops anything. They'll come to that conclusion on their own." He shrugged. "If you'd been in the bar business as long as I have, you would have learned that a lot of weird stuff goes on. One thing I will say, though. Sweeney was a pain in the ass when he was alive and he's a pain in the ass now that he's dead. That's indisputable." He turned to Brandon. "Has the linen guy come in yet?" he asked him, dismissing Mike Sweeney in one sentence.

Bernie was offended. Even though she hadn't liked Sweeney, he still deserved better than being treated like an inconvenient piece of trash.

"Well, has he?" Mulroney repeated when Brandon didn't answer immediately.

Brandon looked at his watch. "He should be here in another ten minutes or so."

"Good," Mulroney said. "Why don't you go inside and get busy, while I wait for the police."

"So you're really going to try to get this place open for business?" Libby asked Mulroney.

"On one of the busiest days of the year? What do you think?"

"I think yes," Libby said.

Mulroney bared his teeth in what passed for a grin and clapped. "Very good. Now, I think it's time for you girls to get moving. Brandon and I have a lot of work to do."

Libby looked at Bernie, who gave her an imperceptible nod, and started moving toward the van.

"Later," Bernie said to Brandon.

"Definitely." And he made a fist and held it up to his ear, mimicking a calling motion.

"What do you think?" Libby said to Bernie once they had turned out of the parking lot.

"About what?" Bernie asked as she waited for a car to pass before she got into the left-hand lane.

"About Sweeney's death being a homicide."

"Oh, without a doubt," Bernie said. "I think that somewhere between three and nine in the morning someone killed Sweeney. Now whether he was drowned in the keg or killed somewhere else is a question the ME will have to answer."

Libby looked up from studying a small rip in her jacket pocket. "I think he was killed here. It makes more sense. Why kill him somewhere else and drag the body to the back of the bar? Sweeney was a big guy. It would have been quite a job."

Bernie readjusted the van's rearview mirror. "Unless someone was sending a message."

"To whom and for what?"

"Don't know," Bernie answered. "It was just a thought."

Libby looked at Bernie. "So if Sweeney was killed in back of RJ's," she said, thinking aloud, "that means that he came back with someone else and that he and that someone most likely had a fight and one way or another the someone we're talking about got Mike Sweeney's head in the barrel."

". . . Or knocked him out first and then held his head underwater . . ."

"Beer . . ."

"A liquid . . ."

"Whatever. But either way is the same. Mike Sweeney drowned."

"Agreed," Bernie said. "There is one thing I am sure of, though. It's that Mulroney is going to call in all his favors. . . ."

"Which are considerable," Libby interjected. "Marvin

told me he's a big supporter of the Chamber of Commerce."

"Yes, he is, and he's going to use his considerable influence to convince the authorities to process the scene as quickly as possible. In fact, I think if we weren't there, Mulroney might have moved the body to the Dumpster in back of A La Carte. Don't get me wrong—eventually it would get figured out, but in the meantime RJ's would be open. And that's the important thing to Mulroney."

"Lucy would crucify us if we did something like that," Libby asked.

"So would Dad, but evidently Mulroney thinks he can get away with Sweeney's death being a case of accidental drowning. You heard him. Hell," Bernie said as she turned the van onto Oak Street, "I wouldn't be surprised if Mulroney used that barrel of beer."

"You think that's why Brandon called you?"

Bernie thought about her answer for a moment before replying. "I think he wanted us as witnesses. I think that Brandon was afraid that Mulroney would want him to relocate Sweeney's body to a less troublesome place and that he precluded that by having us there."

"I think you may be right," Libby said. "It'll be interesting to see if RJ's opens today."

"Bet you five that it does," Bernie said.

Libby nodded. "You're on."

When Libby went upstairs to their flat to tell their dad what had happened, he added five dollars to the pot, making the odds two to one against her.

"High finance," Sean said, chuckling as he pushed his money onto the center of the coffee table.

"So you think Lucy can be bought?" Libby asked her dad later in the day.

They were eating their lunches, which consisted of egg

salad sandwiches, coffee, and ginger-spice cookies. The egg salad was made with homemade mayo, finely chopped fennel, minced scallions, a tiny dab of mustard, and, of course, perfectly boiled eggs. Which were always harder to achieve than people thought.

Most people tended to overcook them, making the yolks rubbery. It was the simple things in life that turned out to be the most difficult to achieve, Libby thought as she savored another bite of her sandwich. A properly boiled egg, an omelet, a perfectly roast chicken—these were miracles. Which made Libby think about the oatmeal-whole-wheat bread the egg salad was resting on.

It was everything a bread should be, easy to make, a good keeper, had a good crumb, made excellent toast, and, most importantly, was quite tasty. The ingredients were simple, consisting as they did of old-fashioned oats, whole wheat and white flour, salt, yeast, a small amount of molasses, and a hint of cardamom.

The grain had been ground fifteen miles away in a newly opened gristmill. To be honest, Libby wasn't sure she could taste the difference between the flour bought in the store and the flour made there, but she bought it there anyway because she wanted to support the business.

She liked the idea of knowing who her suppliers were and where the ingredients she was using came from, and on a practical level it made quality control easier. Customers seemed to like the idea as well, since they lined up to buy the loaves as soon as they came out of the oven, which was why they baked the bread seven days a week.

Sean, normally a white-bread kind of guy, chewed on his sandwich and thought about the fact that even he had to admit that this bread was excellent. Then he shifted gears and considered how to answer his daughter's question about the moral probity of Lucas Broadbent, Longely's chief of police, known as Lucy to his detractors, which were legion.

"I'll take that as a yes," Libby said when her dad didn't immediately respond to her inquiry.

"That's not true," Sean replied after he'd swallowed. "I don't think Lucas can be bought. At least not outright," Sean added. "And I should know, having worked with him for a number of years. But Lucy is nothing if not a political animal and a man who always puts what's good for him first."

Sean took a sip of his coffee and put the mug down. "So therefore, I do think he can be influenced to treat Mike Sweeney's death as a possible accident. He's got a fair amount of wiggle room here. After all, it wasn't as if Sweeney was shot through the heart, so the cause of death isn't that obvious." Sean took another bite of his sandwich and washed it down with a swig of coffee. "They're going to have to do an autopsy to find that out.

"And today's a big day business-wise for RJ's, and Mulroney was a big contributor to his campaign when Lucy ran for re-election, so you do the math. My guess is that Lucy will wrap up the investigation as quickly as possible. Which," Sean said, thinking of recent cases, "he has a tendency to do anyway."

"True," said Bernie as she walked through the door. She went over to the table, grabbed half a sandwich, took a bite, and swallowed. "But let us not forget that Sweeney was a rich, connected guy, so this is not the kind of crime that can be swept under the rug for long."

"I didn't say it was going to be," Sean protested. "I just said the CID will wrap things up pretty fast."

As it turned out, Sean was right. RJ's opened early that afternoon. The death of Mike Sweeney was conveniently not reported in the local paper for two days and even then it was downplayed. The local paper called it a "possible tragic accident" and simply noted that the incident was under investigation.

Then, the story was swept off the paper altogether by

the tale of a local accountant who had swindled several rich seniors out of significant sums of money and contributed said money to an orangutan preserve in Indonesia. When caught, the accountant had explained that he thought the orangs were more deserving than the people he had taken the money from. Knowing the people he had taken the money from, Bernie was inclined to agree.

Whenever Libby or Bernie asked Sean's friend Clyde, who was a policeman in the Longely PD, about the status of the investigation, they were told that the investigation was proceeding apace. Bernie figured that that was code for nothing was happening, so she was surprised when the police arrested Duncan Nottingham for Mike Sweeney's murder two weeks later.

Then, an hour after Duncan's arrest, Duncan's aunt, Bree Nottingham, turned up on Bernie's and Libby's putative doorstep asking—no, demanding—help for her nephew. That, on the other hand, didn't surprise Bernie at all.

Chapter 3

Bree Nottingham, real estate agent extraordinaire and social arbiter of Longely, settled herself on the sofa in the Simmonses' apartment. All three of the Simmonses were there as per Bree Nottingham's request, even though it had meant that Libby had had to leave Amber in charge of taking the apple, walnut, cream-cheese muffins out of the oven at the proper time, something Libby wasn't quite comfortable with Amber doing, since Amber tended to have a somewhat casual attitude toward time, not a good thing when it came to muffins.

But, given the circumstances, Libby wasn't about to say no to Bree or make her wait. How could she? So she tried to impart to Amber the importance of getting the muffins out when the timer went off. Then she dutifully put some cookies on a plate, put the pot of oolong she'd been brewing on a tray, added sugar, lemon, and cream, as well as the appropriate silverware to the tray, and carried it up the stairs with Bree trailing behind her.

Libby's sister and father had just learned about Duncan from the local TV news program ten minutes ago and had been discussing the arrest when they heard the two sets of footsteps on the stairs.

"It's Bree," Bernie said, hearing her voice. She reached over and clicked off the TV.

"I was wondering how long it would take her," Sean mused. "After all, Duncan is her favorite nephew."

"He's her only nephew," Bernie pointed out right before Libby and Bree walked in.

Seeing her, Bernie reflected that Bree looked a little less well groomed than usual, although Bernie would not have gone so far as to call her disheveled. Disheveled would have been understandable under the circumstances, but Bree was far from that. She was just less than perfect. One of her nails had a chip in the polish, her eyeliner was askew, and the stocking on her left leg had the beginning of a run in it.

Actually, Bernie could never imagine Bree being disheveled. Not even a little mussed up. Even if there was a category 4 hurricane, Bernie was positive that Bree would have the proper gear. She'd probably turn out for it in a tailored, color-coordinated, French raincoat, with her waterproof mascara and bright red lipstick firmly in place.

Bernie noted that Bree was wearing one of her signature Chanel suits. She had five of them, and Bernie reflected that outside of Bree she had never known anyone who had one Chanel suit, let alone five, especially since they were custom made and cost, the last time she'd asked, twenty-five thousand dollars each. Who knew that one of those suits was almost as expensive as the van they needed to get?

Maybe the suits were even more now. This one was a black and white flecked tweed, with black ribbon piping around the jacket, and was, as the expression went, to die for. Every time Bernie saw it, she fell in lust, and while she wouldn't have swapped her firstborn for it, she would have had to think about that for a while.

Underneath, Bree was wearing a white, crew neck cashmere sweater, with a triple strand of the obligatory pearls

in place. Black suede three-inch pumps completed the out-
fit. Bernie thought they were vintage Manolos but she
couldn't be sure. Although, maybe they were Dior. Bernie
was trying to decide when she became aware that Bree was
talking to her.

"It's outrageous, don't you agree, Bernie?" Bree demanded as she played with the clasp of her handbag. A
Hermès. "I simply can't believe they arrested Duncan. He
had to surrender at the police station. It was either that or
they would come and get him. Appalling. Absolutely appalling."

"Not to mention humiliating," Bernie said.

Bree gave her the fish-eye and Bernie quickly corrected
herself and told Bree she absolutely agreed, although she
didn't. If Duncan had been poor he wouldn't have had options. The police would have come in the middle of the
night and dragged him out. Money definitely had its perks.
Maybe it couldn't buy happiness, but it sure could buy a
lot of other things. Bernie pushed the plate with spice
balls, sugar cookies, and lemon bars across the coffee table
to Bree.

"Have one," she urged.

"I couldn't," Bree said. "I'm much too upset to eat."
But she took a sugar cookie anyway, broke off a small corner, and began eating it.

She was one of those people, Libby reflected as she
watched her, who always nibbled on things. Just like a
mouse, Libby thought uncharitably, but then maybe that's
why both of Bree's thighs were as big as one of hers. Come
to think of it, she'd never seen Bree eat a piece of chocolate. How terrible was that! Libby wondered if you could
be a minus zero dress size. If anyone was, it was definitely
Bree. She didn't seem to have a body. But then Libby
thought that maybe she was just jealous. She probably
hadn't been that thin since the day she was born. If then.

While Libby was pouring tea for herself, Bernie and

Bree having declined the offer, Sean sat in his armchair, looked at Bree, and waited for her to talk. He was one hundred percent sure that he knew why she was here—she wanted to request their help—but he wanted Bree to say it herself. Even though it was a little thing, it mattered. Especially with someone like Bree, who tended to take over everything.

He took another bite of one of Libby's lemon bars, a sip of tea, and waited some more. He chewed and swallowed. Nothing. He finished the lemon bar and dusted the powdered sugar off his hands. When Bree still hadn't said anything, he decided it was time to nudge her along.

"Duncan is out on bail now, isn't he?" Sean asked her. "He was never really incarcerated. Isn't that correct?"

Bree sniffed. "That's correct, but that's not the issue. The issue is that my nephew should never have been arrested in the first place."

"If you say so," Sean said, goading her to get a response.

Bree jammed her purse into the sofa. "I most emphatically do say so. He would never, ever have done something like that."

"You mean murder Mike Sweeney?" Libby said.

Bree glared at her. "No one in my family has ever gotten so much as a parking ticket up until now. My sister is so upset she had to be sedated." Bree's face collapsed for a moment, then she got hold of herself. "It's just not possible. Duncan is a good boy. He's never engaged in any sort of wrongdoing—not even when he was in high school. He's always been a model citizen."

Sean knew that this was most emphatically not the case from firsthand experience with Duncan in a variety of situations, including, but not limited to, field parties, brawls outside of the Slurp and Burp, mailbox bingo, a couple of stolen cars, and curfew infractions. However, he elected not to bring up the long list of misdeeds Duncan had committed in high school and college. At least not at this moment.

"There must have been cause, otherwise the police would never have arrested him," Sean gently said instead.

Bree sat up straighter. "The police have no evidence. Everything they have is circumstantial and I want you to prove that that's the case. I want you to prove my nephew didn't kill anybody. That he's innocent."

Bernie exchanged glances with her father and her sister. That's what her father had said and what she'd thought Bree had wanted to speak to them about when she'd walked in, and it looked to Bernie as if she and her dad had been right. Unfortunately. Because from what the news anchor had been saying, the case looked fairly tight. Although, Bernie reminded herself, they'd just heard the DA's side of things. Still, to arrest someone who was as well connected as Duncan meant that the DA had to have some fairly solid evidence.

"Well . . ." Bernie began.

"You have to," Bree pleaded, cutting her off.

"Maybe," Sean said carefully, "your lawyer could suggest some experts to help in the investigation." He was sure that Bree's lawyers had their own investigative team and would prefer to use their people.

Bree crossed and uncrossed her legs before leaning forward. "It's true we have experts, but I want you three working on the case as well. Which is what I told my people."

"And what did they say?" Sean asked.

Bree waved her hand dismissively. "Who cares what they said."

"I care," Sean said.

Bree gave him an incredulous stare. "Of course, they said yes. I'm paying the bills, aren't I? What matters is what I want and I want you. You know the people and you know the area."

"But what if Duncan is guilty—?" Sean began.

"He's not," Bree snapped before Sean could finish. "I refuse to entertain that possibility. I already told you that. Just find that girl who he was staying with and we'll be all set."

Sean's ears pricked up. There'd been no mention of a girl on the news. "Girl? What girl?"

"Liza."

"Liza who?"

Bree frowned. "I'm not sure. Stevens. Stephens. Something like that. The only thing I do know is that she's trailer park trash and I don't have any idea why Duncan was hanging around with her."

"I think you mean Liza Sepranto?" Bernie said.

"That's the one. See," she said to Sean, "this is why I want the three of you on the case." Bree tugged her skirt back over her knees, then stood up abruptly. "It's settled then. Duncan is staying at the guest house in back of my house. When you want to talk to him just come on by. I suppose you'll want a retainer. . . ."

Libby began to say that they'd like to talk things over among themselves first, but Bree cut her off after the words "We'd like."

"Don't be ridiculous. You know you're going to do it," Bree said. Then she reached in her purse, took out an envelope, and placed it on the coffee table. "There's ten thousand dollars in cash in there, which I trust will be enough to get things rolling. I believe in paying fair value for what I want and I want you people for this. And now, if you'll excuse me, I have a massage to go to."

As Bree walked down the stairs Libby reached for the envelope and opened it up. "She's right," she said after she'd counted the money. "There's ten thousand dollars in cash here. So what does everyone want to do?"

Sean was quiet for a moment. Then he said, "Nothing like being steamrolled, I always say."

"She is good at that," Libby agreed.

"We can still say no and return the money," Sean suggested, thinking as he did that he needed a cigarette.

"I don't think it would hurt to talk to Duncan," Bernie said. She got up and started pacing around.

"Well, I don't have anything on my agenda," Sean said. "I'm concerned that Bree won't want to believe what we find out if the results are negative. I mean he wasn't an angel when he was a kid. To put it mildly."

"No one in that group was," Bernie pointed out.

"That's for sure," Libby said. "But they all went away. Maybe they changed."

"You think people can change?" Bernie asked.

"Of course they can," Libby replied. "Look at you."

Sean laughed and held up his hand to forestall Bernie's reply. "I say we vote."

Bernie pushed a lock of hair out of her eyes. "I vote yes. Anyway, I'm curious about the whole thing."

"Curious about what?" Sean asked. "The who? The why? The what? The how?"

"All of the above," Bernie said as she snagged another cookie. "When you think about it, the murder doesn't make much sense."

"Most don't," Sean pointed out. "People lose control and do dumb things. That's just the way things are."

"No," Bernie amended. "I'm talking about the manner in which the murder was committed."

Sean leaned forward and took a ginger ball. As he bit into it and the softness of the buttery dough melded with the sugary bite of the candied ginger in his mouth, he reflected that he had to stop eating so much because he was starting to develop a gut. Also, the extra weight would make it difficult for him to walk.

"I guess," he said, "it's time to call up Clyde and bribe him. Do two apple pies and a box of chocolate-chip-walnut cookies seem excessive for some information?"

Libby shook her head. "I'll throw in a linzer torte as well if he wants."

Sean got on his cell and dialed Clyde's number. When Clyde answered Sean relayed his request. "You're a cheap date," he told Clyde, listening to his answer.

"What does he say?" Bernie asked.

"He says if you'll give him a dozen sticky buns instead of the linzer torte we have a deal."

Libby laughed. "He's on."

Sean nodded and told Clyde.

"Call me back in ten minutes. I'll be home by then," Clyde told him.

Sean gave him fifteen. He looked serious when he got off the phone.

"So what did he say?" Libby asked.

Sean took another swallow of tea before replying. "He said that Duncan had threatened to kill Sweeney at a party two days before Sweeney died."

"Why?" Bernie asked.

Sean put his teacup down. "Clyde's not sure. He's hearing this all secondhand. But this thing he is sure of. Duncan's alibi, Liza Sepranto, has disappeared—or at least the police can't find her to confirm Duncan's alibi."

"Sucks for him," Bernie said.

"Maybe she just doesn't want to get involved," Libby suggested.

"Maybe," Sean agreed. "In any case, we should really try and find her."

Libby jumped up. She was anxious to see if Amber had taken the muffins out on time. If they stayed in too long, they got flat tops, and muffins with flat tops just wouldn't do in A Little Taste of Heaven. Her customers expected muffins with gently rounded tops and that's what Libby intended to give them.

"Okay. I'm in too, although you realize that we're being bought," she commented.

Bernie grinned. "And about time! I'm glad someone's finally recognized our worth."

"Bernie," Libby wailed.

"I'm kidding," Bernie said. "Actually I disagree with you. I don't think Bree is wrong for leaving us the money. Heaven only knows, she has enough of it, and if she wants to spend it in defense of her nephew, I think that's very nice of her. Most people get paid to do what we do anyway."

"But she's so blatant about it," Libby complained.

"Oh puhleeze. Bree's always blatant. Look at her clothes. But she's right. We *do* know the players. We *do* have contacts. We might be able to find out things that other people can't. I don't think it'll hurt to scout around and see what we come up with."

"Agreed," Sean said. "It's not as if we're being asked to manufacture evidence."

Libby drew a chocolate kiss out of her pants pocket, unwrapped it, and put it in her mouth. This whole thing with Bree was stressing her out. "But what if we don't get the results Bree is looking for? What if we can't find Liza or we find her and she refuses to confirm Duncan's alibi?"

"Come on, Libby," Bernie replied. "We've already discussed this."

"Your sister is right," Sean said to Libby. "I don't understand your problem."

"Actually, I think I do," Bernie said. "Libby is afraid that if we don't find evidence to exonerate Duncan, Bree will get angry at us and we'll lose her business. Isn't that right, Libby?"

Libby nodded. "That's it in a nutshell."

Bernie started putting the cookies and the tea things back on the tray. "You do know that conversely we'll lose Bree's business if we refuse to take this case."

"So what you're saying, Bernie, is that we really can't say no."

Sean interrupted. "I think you're both missing the point here," he said sharply. "What happens if Bree is right? What happens if Duncan is innocent?"

"I thought you said you thought that he wasn't," Bernie said to him.

"Well, now I'm saying that I think this case merits looking at," Sean replied. "So are you in or out?" Sean asked Libby.

Libby ate another chocolate kiss. "I already said I'm in," she said.

"Good," Bernie said.

"I just have a few caveats."

"Libby, you always have caveats," her dad pointed out.

"So how do you want to proceed?" Libby asked, acknowledging the truth of her father's observation by not saying anything on that subject.

Bernie picked up the tray, realized her skirt had gotten twisted, put the tray back on the table, and untwisted her denim pencil skirt before answering Libby. The skirt was a little loose and the zipper tended to meander around her side, but she hadn't had time to get it to the dressmaker yet. "I think," she said when she'd stopped futzing around with her skirt, "that we should go talk to Duncan first and then we should go talk to his buddies."

"And maybe their girlfriends and wives," Libby said. "Women always tend to be chattier."

"Definitely chattier," Bernie said.

Sean laughed. "I wasn't the one who said that. And I think that I," said Sean, "might go talk to Pat Dwyer."

"Pat Dwyer?" Bernie said. "Who the hell is Pat Dwyer?"

"He used to be Mulroney's partner and he's Liza's stepfather. Like I've always said, it's a small town."

Bernie tapped her fingers on the side of the sofa. "Who else do we know who knows the Corned Beef and Cabbage Club guys?"

"It's not exactly as if we travel in their circle," Libby pointed out. "We didn't even in high school."

"True," Bernie said. "They were definitely too hoity-toity for us."

"Yes," Libby agreed. "They were going skiing in Aspen over Christmas vacation and we were working in the shop. Not that that was a bad thing," she quickly added in deference to her dad. She didn't want to hurt his feelings.

"I never thought it was," Sean commented.

Everyone was quiet for a moment.

Then Bernie said, "If anyone knows who they hang with, Brandon probably does."

Sean nodded. "I bet you're right. Maybe Marvin and I will drop by RJ's later and ask him."

"And there is someone else we should talk to," Bernie observed as she picked up the tray again in preparation for going downstairs.

"And who would that be?" Libby asked.

Bernie was immediately sorry she had spoken. "Forget it," she said.

"Seriously, Bernie. Who is it?" Libby asked.

Bernie hesitated for a moment and then said, "Orion."

Libby took a deep breath and let it out slowly. She knew hearing his name shouldn't bother her after all this time, but it still did. "I doubt that," she told her sister.

"No. Truly," Bernie said. "He works for the same hedge fund Liam does."

"How do you know?" Libby demanded.

"Missy told me."

Libby put her hands on her hips. "And how does she know?"

"Come on, Libby, stop it," Bernie said.

"Well, I'll tell you one thing. I'm not talking to him."

"No one asked you to," Bernie said.

"Just so we're clear," Libby said.

"You know," Bernie told her, "it's really time you lightened up on this."

"Really?" Libby said.

"Yes, really."

Sean held up his hands before his daughters could get into it. "Peace," he said. "I'll speak to him if need be."

"Good." Libby smiled at the thought. Her dad would not be nice, but that was okay with her. In fact, it was more than okay. Even though she knew she was the one who had allowed Orion to treat her like crap, it didn't matter. She still wanted to see him suffer. Bernie was right. It was time to let it go. She wanted to, but she just couldn't.

Bernie looked from her sister to her dad and back again. Everything seemed to have settled down. Thank God. "Okay. So when does everyone want to get started on this project?" she asked.

Sean rubbed his hands together. "What is it they say about there being no time like the present? I think I'll call Marvin and see if he can give me a lift to Pat Dwyer's office."

"Maybe Marvin's busy," Libby told her dad. Since Marvin was her boyfriend she felt the need to protect him from her dad, who could be a bit overwhelming at times.

"I'm sure if he is, he'll tell me," Sean replied. "After all, he *is* an adult. Anyway, he likes to do this kind of stuff. It's sure better than embalming people."

Which Libby had to admit was true. Marvin did like sleuthing, and in her estimation pretty much anything was better than embalming people.

"And we"—Bernie pointed to herself and Libby—"should go talk to Duncan."

"As soon as I'm done with the muffins," Libby replied.

Bernie snorted. "You don't know that Amber's going to burn them."

"You're right. I don't," Libby conceded, mostly for the sake of keeping the peace.

But Bernie wasn't fooled. "Why are you always so negative?" she asked.

"I'm not negative," Libby told her. "I just believe in planning for the worst and hoping for the best."

As it turned out, this time Libby was correct.

Amber had taken the muffins out of the oven ten minutes too late, which resulted in flat tops and burnt bottoms. Libby and Bernie had to make a couple of new batches before they left the store.

"See," Libby said to Bernie as she weighed out the flour. "I told you."

"Stop gloating," Bernie told her.

Libby tried, but she didn't try very hard.

Chapter 4

Two hours later the sisters finally walked out of the shop. It was a nice, sunny day with a clear hint of spring in the air. Bernie and Libby both paused to admire the blue sky with the lacy clouds drifting overhead before they jumped in the van and headed over to Bree Nottingham's guest cottage. Although in Bernie's opinion guest cottage was too humble a word for the structure Duncan was now residing in. She'd seen houses that were smaller.

"I wonder why Duncan is living at Bree's," Libby mused as she and her sister motored down Route 42 to the Apple Green Estate—the Apple Green Estate being the name Bree had given her house. "I mean it's not as if he doesn't have his own place."

Bernie shrugged as she took note of the trees. Soon they'd be greening up. April was almost here. "Maybe it's a condition of his bail," she suggested.

"Maybe," Libby said before turning her attention back to the road, which was always busy no matter what time of day it was. Cars wove themselves around the van, which was chugging along at its top speed of forty miles an hour.

"I'm going as fast as I can," Libby shouted at one of the myriad drivers who honked at her before finally passing the van on a clear stretch of road. "We definitely need a new vehicle," Libby said to her sister through gritted teeth.

"Agreed," Bernie said, still looking out the window. Recently, she'd noticed a lot of empty spaces in the retail operations at the strip malls that lined the road, more than she ever remembered seeing in all the time she'd lived here. Which made her nervous. Their shop was doing well and Longely's Main Street was doing well. . . . But still . . . things seemed so much more tenuous these days. Shops that had existed forever were gone. She shook her head to clear the dark thoughts away.

Ten minutes later, Libby muscled the van onto Wycoff Lane, a small road that led into the residential area that harbored some of the more affluent people in Longely. The houses here were big, most dating from the early 1900s, and were still in excellent repair. Bernie admired the variety of styles as they motored on toward Bree's residence. The houses were a mix of colonial, Greek revival, and Tudor. Almost all of them were fronted by large expanses of closely cropped lawn and extensive landscaping. They were showcase houses, built to be seen and admired.

Bree Nottingham's house was at the end of the lane. The mansion had once been the home of railroad tycoon B. C. Wiley, before he had fallen on hard times and ended up drinking himself to death on the Bowery in New York City. Bree had rescued and restored the structure to its former splendor. Cozy it was not.

The place contained seven bedrooms, each with its own bathroom and fireplace, as well as a huge living room and dining room, a mirrored ballroom, a library, a small indoor lap pool, a gym, a projection room that was now used for private screenings, and an extremely well-appointed kitchen. Whenever Bernie and Libby worked out of it,

Bernie always felt as if she was working in a showcase. Literally.

Everything in the kitchen looked brand new, mostly because it was. Bree kept updating it with the newest, most expensive appliances. Not that it really mattered, because they were rarely used. Every time Bernie worked here, it was clear to her from the condition of the counters, the pots, and the stove top, that no one ever cooked in the kitchen, except for them. But then why should anyone? Bernie had reflected. There was no need. Left to her own devices, Bree never ate anything except salads and baked chicken and diet strawberry Jell-O.

The guest house, on the other hand, had a much warmer feeling. Even though it was more than spacious, it was still a three-bedroom bungalow, with living room furniture that looked as if it had been sat on and floors that were slightly scuffed. Bernie loved the large bathroom/sauna with its skylight, and the kitchen, a definitely low-tech kind of place because Bree didn't deem it worthy of her scrutiny. In addition, there was an outdoor hot/cold shower and a changing area.

The cottage sat about twenty feet away from the pool, and whenever Bernie saw the pool she thought of the pools of the rich and the famous she'd seen when she'd lived and worked in LA, pools with grottoes and nymphs and angels, and large ferns trailing their leaves into the water.

Now the ferns were gone, having been brought into the greenhouse to winter over, the pool was drained, and Bernie thought the angels and nymphs looked slightly sad—maybe they were just waiting for summer to come— as the van shuddered to a stop in front of the cottage. Bernie and Libby had just gotten out of the van when the cottage door opened and Duncan Nottingham stepped out to greet them. Or maybe not.

Libby decided Duncan didn't look happy to see them.

He looked annoyed—as if he'd been in the middle of something that they'd interrupted. She knew that some of her friends considered Duncan attractive, but she wasn't one of them. His teeth were too white, his hair was always too perfectly combed, and his clothes were always too perfectly matched for her.

He really was Bree's nephew. Like her, Duncan was also thin, too thin for Libby's taste. She preferred her guys like Marvin—a little bit sloppy, a little bit too earnest, a little bit overweight. She liked Marvin's love handles. They gave her something to hang on to in those important moments.

Duncan's frown grew as he took a step forward. Definitely not happy to see us, Libby thought. Which was interesting because she would have imagined it would have been the opposite. But obviously she'd been wrong.

"I figured you'd be along soon," Duncan said to them. "My aunt told me she'd hired you, although frankly I don't see how you're going to do much good." He stifled a sneeze. "I told her you were going to be a waste of money, but she insisted on going ahead and getting you guys anyway. But at least I persuaded her to hire some professionals as well as . . ." Duncan stopped talking, allowing his sentence to trail off.

"Some local yokels," Bernie said, finishing the sentence for him.

Duncan threw up both his hands. "Hey, I didn't say it, you did."

"Charming as always," Libby remarked. Now it was all coming back to her. She'd forgotten what an asshole he could be. Her dad would say that he was acting like a jerk because he was scared, and maybe her dad was right. But it didn't matter. Duncan's attitude still put her teeth on edge.

Duncan shrugged. "Hey, I'm just telling the truth."

"So I take it this means you want us to go?" Libby asked him.

Duncan studied the geese flying overhead for a minute, then looked back at Bernie and Libby. "No. I don't. Whatever gave you that impression?"

Bernie crossed her arms. "Your welcoming manner."

"And your smile," Libby added. "You lit up when you saw us, don't you agree, Bernie?"

"Without a doubt, Libby. Who could resist something like that?"

Duncan sighed. "Okay. I get the point and I'm sorry. But how about cutting me a little slack. This has just been a bad day for me. I'm not used to being arrested. . . ."

"Unlike some of your other brethren traders," Bernie couldn't resist saying.

Duncan hung his head. "I guess I deserved that. No. I want you to come in and help me out."

"Could that be," Bernie said, "because your aunt is paying your bills and you don't want to piss her off?"

"Something like that," Duncan admitted as he stood aside and motioned Bernie and Libby in.

"So why are you here?" Libby asked as she stepped inside the living room.

The room was decorated in early southwestern. The colors were all pale pinks and blues and greens. There were Georgia O'Keefe prints on the walls, Native-American rugs on the floor, and distressed wood furniture. The result, Libby decided, was not displeasing.

Duncan turned toward Libby. "What do you mean, why am I here?"

Bernie noted that he looked puzzled. "My sister means, why aren't you staying in your own place?"

Duncan's eyes narrowed ever so slightly. "My lawyer thought it would be better if I stayed here."

"Your lawyer or your aunt's lawyer?" Libby shot back.

"Well, it's my aunt's lawyer if you want to be OCD about it, but I prefer to refer to List as my lawyer since he's working on my case."

As Libby looked at Duncan, she got the clear feeling that he was lying. When she looked at Bernie she could tell that her sister thought so too. But instead of saying anything, Bernie nodded absentmindedly and sat down on the sofa. Libby followed suit, sitting a little to the right of her.

"I'm not going to ask if you want any coffee or anything, because I don't have any food in here yet," Duncan told them while he plopped himself down in the armchair across the way.

"Bummer," Bernie said as she leaned over and picked up the books sitting on the coffee table. "Interesting titles," she said as she started going through them. One was a travel book about Costa Rica, the second was a travel book about Belize, while the third was a travel book about Brazil. Obviously, there was a theme going here.

"Planning on going on vacation?" Bernie asked Duncan, indicating the books with a nod of her head. "Or just engaging in some wishful thinking?"

Duncan sneezed again and shifted his weight from one side of the seat to the other. Then he changed the position of his legs, resting the ankle of his right leg over the knee of his left leg. "I was planning on going away for a week or two," he told Bernie. "But obviously that's not a possibility now."

"Obviously," Bernie said as she put the books back where she'd found them. "You know, I'm told you can buy a Belizian citizenship for twenty thousand dollars."

Duncan flushed. "Why would I care?"

"I didn't say you would," Bernie replied.

"Then why did you say that?" Duncan asked.

Bernie shrugged. "I suppose just to have something to say."

"I thought you were saying I'd be interested in doing something like that."

"Would you?"

Duncan snorted. "Most definitely not."

Bernie leaned forward. "Okay," she said. "Enough with the dancing around. Tell us what happened that evening."

"I already told everyone," Duncan objected.

"We're not everyone," Libby pointed out.

"Point taken," Duncan said, and he began to talk.

Bernie and Libby both noted that even though Duncan had initially been reluctant to say anything, he seemed to relax as he talked. There were no hesitations. No pauses. He was absolutely clear in his recitation. As if he'd rehearsed it, Bernie and Libby both thought. Or being more charitable, maybe it was because by this time Duncan had told the story so many times.

He took them through Brandon throwing the Corned Beef and Cabbage Club out of the bar and about Brandon coming out and finding Sweeney trying to pry open one of the barrels of beer.

"Brandon was pissed, man," Duncan recounted. "He just clocked him one. Right in the jaw. Sweeney went down for the count."

"But he came back up?" Bernie asked, trying to keep the anxiety out of her voice. Although she hadn't said anything to anyone, she was anxious that the defense might try to prove that Mike Sweeney had a concussion, which was a contributing factor in his death.

"Yeah," Duncan said. "He was fine. Don't worry."

Bernie smiled.

"Sweeney was a hardheaded son of a bitch," Duncan told her. "I'll give him that. I mean I told him not to do that. I told him he was making too much noise. I told him to wait, but hey—when Sweeney got an idea in his head, he went for it and there was nothing you could do to stop it."

"And then what happened after Sweeney got up?" Libby inquired.

"Nothing happened," Duncan replied. "We went home."

"We?" Bernie asked.

"Liza Sepranto and I."

"You two an item?" Libby asked. Somehow she couldn't see the two together. Bree was right about that. Duncan was ultrapreppy and Liza was Jersey Shore.

"We're friends," Duncan said, emphasizing the word friends. "Good friends."

"We get it," Bernie said. "How'd you get home?" Libby asked.

"How do you think?" Duncan sneered. "I got in my vehicle and drove Liza and myself back to my place. Then we went upstairs and passed out."

Bernie raised an eyebrow. "Weren't you afraid of getting a DWI?"

"Nah. I know most of the cops, and anyway I drive better drunk than some people do sober."

Arrogant son of a bitch, Libby thought as she asked him if anyone could swear that he and Liza entered his apartment complex and hadn't come out again until after nine.

"Nope." Duncan's tongue darted out and licked his lower lip. "Didn't see anyone. Guess they must have been asleep when we came in. I didn't meet anyone when I parked my car and we didn't meet anyone in the elevator either."

"And in the morning?" Bernie asked.

Duncan shook his head. "Guess they'd all gone off to work."

"It's unfortunate your building doesn't have a doorman," Bernie observed.

"Isn't it though?" Duncan snapped back. "Well, the next time I'm accused of murder I'll make sure and rent a place that has one."

"Rent?" Bernie asked.

"Sublet actually. Why? Do you have a problem with that?" Duncan asked.

"No," Bernie replied. "I'm just surprised. I thought you'd have a co-op."

"I sold mine last year."

"And you didn't buy another?" Bernie asked.

"No. It doesn't make economic sense right now. Do you want me to explain why?" Duncan asked in a condescending tone.

"Not really," Bernie replied. "What I want you to do is tell me where Liza took off to."

Duncan gave a half shrug. "I don't know. She was gone when I got up and I haven't seen her since."

"Have you tried getting in touch with her?" Libby asked Duncan.

He gave an exasperated snort. "What do you think? Of course I looked. As have the police and my lawyer. She's just disappeared."

"Why would she do that?" Bernie asked.

"Haven't a clue," Duncan said. "Maybe she got nervous and split."

"That seems like an odd thing to do," Libby observed.

"She's an odd girl," Duncan said.

"Any idea where she'd go?"

"None," Duncan said. "Believe me, if I did I would have told the police."

"Would you have?" Bernie asked.

Duncan scowled. "Why? Don't you believe me?"

"No. I'm not sure I do," Bernie told him.

"But I do," Libby said, jumping into the conversation before Duncan had a chance to reply. "How about the other people in the group?" she asked. "What did they do?"

Duncan shrugged. "As far as I know, everyone drove themselves home and went off to nighty-night land."

"Including Sweeney?" said Libby, thinking back to what Clyde had told them.

"Yeah, including Sweeney," Duncan replied.

"I thought he left with you," Libby said.

Duncan leaned over and pulled up one of his socks. "Whatever gives you that idea?"

"The police."

"Well, that's one of the many facts they've gotten wrong," said Duncan as he pounded his fist into the palm of his other hand.

"Wasn't anyone concerned about Sweeney getting behind the wheel of a car?" Bernie asked.

Duncan gave her an incredulous look. "Why?"

Libby opened her eyes wide. "Duh. Because he had been knocked out cold."

Duncan shook his head at the apparent idiocy of her statement. "Duh yourself. He was knocked out all the time on the football field. It never bothered him before, so why should it have bothered him then?"

"Good point," Bernie said. "Did you see Sweeney leave?"

Duncan shook his head again. "Liza and I were the first ones out of there."

"May I ask why?" Libby inquired.

Duncan leered. "What do you think?"

"Besides that," Bernie said.

Duncan rubbed his hands together. "Frankly, I'd had enough, and to be honest with you I didn't want to be around if Sweeney pulled any more stuff."

"Which he was prone to do?" Libby asked.

Duncan studied the palms of his hands for a moment before looking up and replying. "Yeah. You could say that."

"So Sweeney either did or didn't go home," Bernie said, thinking out loud.

"No, he went home all right," Duncan interrupted. "Liam said he saw him drive away."

Bernie leaned forward. "And then for some reason he came back and sometime between three and nine in the morning, someone drowned him in a barrel of green beer. Is that correct?"

Duncan looked down at his fingernails. "That's what they tell me."

"They?" Bernie said.

"The lawyers and the cops."

Libby shifted her position on the sofa to get more comfortable. It was a great-looking sofa, but it was too deep for her. "And what do your friends tell you?"

Duncan looked Libby and Bernie directly in the eyes and said, "They don't know anything either."

Bernie smiled. "Amazing, how no one knows anything, isn't it, Libby?"

"Absolutely, Bernie," Libby replied.

"Ask my friends," Duncan cried, doing a passable imitation of outrage.

"Don't worry," Bernie told him. "We intend to."

"Be my guest," Duncan told her, giving both Libby and Bernie a sullen look.

"And there's nothing more you want to add to what you've already told us?" Libby asked him.

Duncan shook his head. "Persistent, aren't you? I told you I was asleep."

Libby sat back. She frowned. "Then why did the police arrest you?"

"Because they're idiots."

"Aside from that?" Bernie asked.

"They claim they found my wallet near the barrel Sweeney was drowned in, but that was because I must have dropped it there earlier in the evening. Also my fingerprints were on the steering wheel of his car, but that was because I'd started his car earlier in the day when it had stalled out."

Interesting, Bernie thought. Clyde hadn't told her dad anything about that. She wondered if Clyde was holding out on him or he didn't know. She'd vote for the latter possibility.

"So all the police have is circumstantial evidence?" Bernie asked.

Duncan nodded his head vigorously. "That is correct."

"And you have no motive for killing Sweeney?"

"No. Absolutely not. I mean I've known the guy since high school."

"And you were good friends?"

Duncan shrugged. "We drifted apart a little when we went to college, but then we reconnected when everyone moved back. No. I feel terrible. Absolutely terrible. Mike was the greatest guy in the world. I can't imagine who would want him dead."

"So you didn't threaten to kill Sweeney at a party two days before he died?" Bernie asked.

Duncan passed his hand over his face. "I was pissed, okay? And I was drinking. When I drink I say things. But I don't mean them."

"Why were you pissed?" Bernie asked.

Duncan looked down at his hands. "I don't remember."

"Really," Bernie said.

"Yes, really," Duncan replied. He took his cell out of his pocket and looked at it, checking for messages. "You know, I appreciate your coming by and I hope I've been some help, but I really have to go."

"Because you have miles to go before you sleep?" Bernie asked.

Duncan gave her a blank look.

"It's a riff on a line from Robert Frost," Bernie explained.

"Who's that?" Duncan asked. "Some rapper?"

"No," Bernie shot back. "A player for the Jets."

"Really?" Duncan said.

Bernie just shook her head in disgust. "No. Not really. He's a famous American poet."

"Whatever," Duncan said.

Libby decided that he was clearly bored with the conversation. She didn't say anything. She just watched Duncan for a moment. Then she leaned back, reached in the pocket of her hoodie, took out a chocolate kiss, unwrapped it, and popped it in her mouth. "I have a question for you before we go," she said to Duncan, after the chocolate had dissolved on her tongue.

Duncan planted his feet on the floor, leaned forward, clasped his hands, and rested his arms on his knees. "Yeah? Make it short, because I really have a lot of stuff I have to do."

"So you've said."

"Well, it hasn't seemed to make any difference," he snapped at Libby.

"I'm just curious about one thing."

Duncan's left leg started jiggling up and down. "I'm waiting," he said when Libby didn't say anything else.

"How come your aunt is paying for your lawyer?" she asked, even though she was pretty sure she already knew the answer. She was just curious to see what Duncan was going to say.

Duncan gave her a blank look. "That's it?"

Libby nodded. "That's it."

"I don't get the question."

"The question is simple," Libby went on. "From what I hear, you're a very rich man, a man who could easily afford the one hundred thousand dollars, even the two hundred thousand it costs to mount a defense, let alone post a bond for bail, and yet your aunt is doing it. And not only is she doing it, but she's letting you live in her guest cottage as well."

"That's because the lawyers thought it would be better," Duncan replied, a sullen tone creeping into his voice.

"Why is that?" Libby asked, noting as she did that Duncan had stopped tapping his foot.

Duncan glared at her. "Ask them if you're so interested. See, I knew hiring you was a mistake." He started to get up. "I think we're just about done here."

Libby stayed where she was. "You know what I think?" she said. "I think that if we asked around we'd find that you're living in your aunt's guest house because you're behind on your rent. In fact, I bet we'd find you're in the process of being evicted. Am I right?"

"My money is tied up right now," Duncan told her stiffly. "Not that it's any of your business."

"And that's why your aunt is paying for your defense as well?" Bernie asked.

"I'll pay her back," Duncan said. "She knows that. I'm just not very liquid right now."

"So what happened?" Bernie asked him.

"What do you mean 'what happened'?" Duncan demanded.

"I mean what happened to your money?"

Duncan adjusted a button on his shirt. "You wouldn't understand," he told her. "It's very complicated."

"You're probably right," Bernie said. "I don't understand all this high finance stuff." She turned to Libby. "Correct me if I'm wrong, but wasn't Mike Sweeney involved in the finance business?"

"I believe he was," Libby replied.

"And didn't he trade something like derivatives?"

"Right again," Libby said.

"And aren't those very volatile?" Bernie asked.

Libby nodded. "Indeed they are, Bernie. In fact, a lot of people have lost enormous sums of money on them recently."

Duncan scowled. "Hey. Spare me the finance lesson here. I know what derivatives are, thank you very much."

"I bet you do," Libby said sweetly. "And I'm also going to bet that that's why you don't have any money right now. And I'm further going to bet that Mike Sweeney is responsible for your present predicament. And I'll go even further and say that that's what the argument was about at the party and that's why you said you wanted to kill him. And that, coupled with your wallet, is why the police arrested you. You have a really good motive for wanting to kill Sweeney, that motive being that he lost all of your money for you."

"That's a crock," Duncan told her.

Bernie jumped in to the conversation. "It doesn't seem that way to me," she said. "Judging from your reaction, we seem to have hit the mark."

"A lot you know," Duncan said.

Bernie looked up at Duncan. "Then enlighten us," she challenged him.

"Let me tell you something," Duncan said, glowering down at her. "Sweeney might have screwed me over, but that was nothing compared to what he did to the other guys. I'm not married. I don't have dependents. And anyway, I'll make the money back easy enough. I made it the first time and I'll do it again. Sweeney got a little more complicated than he should have. It happens." He paused to take a breath. "I don't know why I'm talking to you guys about this. I thought you were hired to help me."

"We are," Bernie said. "And we will."

"This is what you consider helping?" Duncan demanded. "You two are worse than the DA."

"We just need to know all the facts," Libby explained.

Duncan put up his hands. "You already know them."

"I think there's more," Bernie said.

"There isn't," Duncan said. "I've already told you everything I know."

"No, you haven't," Bernie said.

Duncan didn't say anything. After a minute had passed Bernie motioned for Libby to get up.

"Fine," she said to Duncan. "If you want to waste your aunt's money, that's fine with me. If you want to go to jail, that's your business not mine."

"I'm not going to jail," Duncan retorted.

"I think maybe you are," Libby answered.

"No friggin' way," Duncan shot back.

Libby zipped up her sweatshirt. "Here's something to think about. Given your connections in this town, I don't think the DA would have moved to have you arrested if he didn't have a good case, a case he thought he could win. Are you sure there isn't anything else you want to tell us before we go?"

"Yes," Duncan said.

"Fine," Libby said, and started for the door. Bernie followed. They were almost there when Duncan called out to them.

"Stop," he said.

Libby and Bernie both turned.

Duncan was standing there looking down at the floor and plucking at the hem of his shirt.

"We're waiting," Libby said when Duncan didn't say anything.

Duncan looked up and bit his lip. "It's just that this is hard," he said.

"No doubt," Bernie said.

"It makes things look worse."

"Did you kill Sweeney?" Libby asked.

"No. Of course not," Duncan cried. Then he went back to looking at the floor.

"You don't seem so sure," Libby said.

Duncan didn't say anything. The sisters waited.

"Okay, okay," Duncan finally said to them after a moment had gone by. "Truth . . ."

"Truth," Bernie replied.

"The truth is I don't know, because I don't remember anything," Duncan said.

"I don't get it," Libby said.

Duncan waved his arms in the air. He looked on the brink of tears. Suddenly Libby felt bad for him.

"I don't remember anything. The last thing I remember is having a drink at RJ's and the next thing I know I'm waking up in my bed the next morning with a hangover you wouldn't believe."

"How many drinks did you have?" Bernie asked him.

"One. A beer."

"So you blacked out at the party when you threatened to kill Sweeney?" Libby asked.

"Yeah. But that was because I had five Singapore Slings and a couple of shots, and anyway I was lying."

"About remembering?" Bernie asked.

Duncan looked away. "Yeah."

"Go on," Bernie said.

Duncan rubbed his hands together and looked down at the floor. "I say things when I drink. . . ." His voice trailed off. "But as to this blacking out thing—that's never happened to me before. Not after one drink." He lifted up his head, looked Bernie and Libby in the eyes, and put his hand up. "I swear." He turned to Libby. "Do you believe me?"

"Yeah, Duncan, I do," Libby told him. "So bottom line, what you're telling us is that you have no idea about what happened that night?"

Duncan shook his head. "Not really. No. Everything is a blank. And believe me I've tried to remember."

"And all that stuff you told us?" Libby asked.

Duncan shrugged. "I made it up. I mean I didn't know what else do to. How bad would the other have looked?"

"Pretty bad," Libby admitted.

Bernie tapped her fingers against her pants leg while she thought. Finally she said, "So this has never happened to you before."

"That's what I just said. I mean one beer. Come on. I

can pound five of those down without breaking a sweat," Duncan said before lapsing into silence again.

"Do you think someone could have slipped something in your beer?" Libby said slowly.

Duncan looked at Libby as if she'd gone crazy. "No. Absolutely not."

"It's just a thought," Libby told him.

"A far-fetched one if you ask me," Duncan said.

"But it does explain things," Bernie said.

"I refuse to believe it," Duncan said. "Anyway, who would do something like that?" he asked.

Libby shook her head. "Someone you were drinking with that night?"

"I was drinking with my friends."

"Maybe they're not," Bernie observed.

"I can't believe it," Duncan said.

"Or won't believe it," Bernie interjected.

"That's the same thing," Duncan told her.

"Not really," Bernie answered. "Think about it."

Duncan shook his head violently from side to side. "It's not possible."

"Okay, let me ask you a question," Libby said. "Have you had a drink since that night?"

"Yes," Duncan said. "More than one."

"And have you passed out?"

Duncan was quiet for a moment. Then he said, "That doesn't prove anything. It doesn't," he insisted, reading the expressions on Libby's and Bernie's faces.

Libby shrugged. "Have it your own way," she told him. "It's true we can't prove what happened, because we can't do a chemical analysis at this point, but it's the best explanation for what happened."

"I think my sister is on to something," Bernie told Duncan.

He looked from Libby to Bernie and back again. "I don't know."

"It doesn't mean it happened," Bernie said gently. "But it would be a good avenue to pursue."

Libby didn't say anything. She could see Duncan struggling to come to grips with the idea.

Duncan sighed. He studied one of the Georgia O'Keefe prints on the far wall. A moment later, he looked back at Libby and Bernie and asked, "So what are you going to do?"

Bernie smiled. "We're going to do what we do best. Bake muffins."

Duncan laughed.

"No. Seriously. We're going to snoop around and see what we can find out," Bernie said. "And in the meantime, I'd keep away from my friends in the Corned Beef and Cabbage Club if I were you. At the very least, don't go drinking with them. And if you do go drinking with them, take your drink to the can with you when you go."

Duncan made a face. "That's gross."

"But effective."

"I still can't believe it," Duncan said as he sat back down.

When Bernie and Libby left he was sitting on the sofa with his head in his hands.

Chapter 5

"That would really suck if it's true," Bernie said to Libby when they were outside the guest house.

"Yes, it would," Libby agreed as she fished the car keys out of her backpack. "It would give things a whole new twist."

"It would, wouldn't it though?" Bernie observed. "I'm calling Dad and seeing what he thinks." And she whipped her cell out of her bag and punched his number in.

He answered on the twelfth ring. As she waited for her dad to pick up Bernie pictured him looking for his cell and cursing when he couldn't find it.

"We need to get our house phone back," Sean said when he finally answered. "This is ridiculous."

"You're right, Dad," Bernie agreed. "We do. And we will."

"Why did we ever get rid of it in the first place?" Sean asked, slightly mollified.

"Because you wanted to save money," Bernie said.

"I've changed my mind," Sean told her. "Now tell me how your talk with Duncan went."

So Bernie did. By the time she'd finished talking with him she and Libby had reached the van.

"What did Dad say?" Libby asked as soon as she heard Bernie say good-bye.

Bernie lowered the phone. "He said it was an interesting hypothesis and that we should pursue it."

"And?"

"That we're out of crunchy peanut butter and we should pick some up."

"He didn't say anything else?"

"Like that it was a brilliant idea?"

"Something like that," Libby said.

Bernie laughed and wrapped her scarf more tightly around her neck. It was bright red, with orange flowers sewn on in random places, and she loved it. "Good luck waiting for that to happen," she told Libby as she climbed in the vehicle. Once she was seated, she called Brandon.

"I want to talk to you about what happened the night that Mike Sweeney was killed," she told him.

"Well, hello to you too, gorgeous," Brandon replied.

Bernie chuckled. "Flattery will get you anywhere."

"This I already know. That's why I use it."

"What's a good time to come over to the bar?"

"I always have time for you, sweetheart," Brandon told her, doing his best Bogart imitation.

"When do you have time to talk?"

"As opposed to other activities in the storeroom."

"That would be a good trick," Bernie said, thinking about how packed full of supplies that place was.

Brandon laughed. "Now would be a good time. We're not into the evening rush yet."

"And when does the Corned Beef and Cabbage Club usually come in?"

"If they come it'll be within the next half an hour or so."

"Great," Bernie said. "See you soon." And she hung up, slipped her cell phone back in her bag, and leaned back in her seat.

"You think that someone actually slipped some sort of knockout drops into Duncan's beer?" Libby asked as she started up the van. She'd suggested it as a lark.

The engine coughed, then fell silent. "Drats," Libby muttered. She tried again. This time the engine spluttered for thirty seconds before quitting. On the third try, the engine finally turned over.

Bernie patted the dashboard. "You go, girl."

"I think it's time to start shopping around for a new vehicle," Libby observed. Then she corrected herself. "A new, used vehicle."

Bernie put a finger to her lips. "Sssh," she told Libby. "Not so loud. You don't want to hurt Mathilda's feelings, do you?" she asked as she buckled up her seat belt.

"Definitely not." Libby patted the dashboard. "Sorry, Mathilda," she told the van. "We're not going to put you out to pasture. We're just going to insure you have a comfortable old age." She turned to Bernie. "Is that better?"

Bernie nodded. "Much. We are nuts."

"Some people talk to their pets, we talk to our van," Libby said as she backed into a bush at the end of the driveway, before putting the car into drive and doing a U-turn. One of the van's wheels slipped off the pavement onto the gravel. "Not a big deal."

"You know, I know what you and Marvin see in each other," Bernie said suddenly, changing the subject.

"And that is?"

"You both drive the same."

Libby got all four tires back on the pavement. "Ha ha ha. Very funny."

"I'm serious."

"I'm way better than he is."

Bernie waved her hands in the air. "Okay. Maybe that was a slight exaggeration."

"Slight? At least I stop for stop signs."

"I'll grant you that."

Libby opened her window and readjusted the side-view mirror. "You realize you still haven't answered my question."

"About the roofies in Duncan's drink?"

"Yeah."

Bernie gave an exasperated sigh. "I already said I think it's a real possibility," she told Libby as she pulled over to avoid hitting Bree's brand new BMW, which had suddenly appeared out of nowhere. "In fact, I think it's more than possible. I think it's probable. You have to stop second-guessing yourself."

"I know, I know," Libby replied. And she did know. It was one of her worst habits.

Bree waved and Libby and Bernie waved back.

"Nice car," Bernie commented.

"I don't think I'd want to drive something like that," Libby said. "Too showy."

"Well, I wouldn't mind at all," Bernie said wistfully. "But I don't think it's going to happen."

"At least not in this life," Libby said. "You think Bree knows about Duncan blacking out?" she asked her sister as she got back on the road.

"It wouldn't surprise me," Bernie replied. "She has a way of knowing everything and admitting nothing."

"Especially to herself."

Bernie reached over and clicked on the radio. She got static. She tried another station. Same thing. She gave up and clicked it off. "Maybe that's why Bree came right over. I wonder if Duncan's told his lawyer about blacking out?"

"I don't think so."

"Me either," Bernie said. "He had a hard enough time admitting it to us."

"Yeah. But if we suspected it, the lawyers certainly should have."

"We should tell them just in case," Bernie said.

"Really, we have nothing to tell except our suspicions," Libby said.

"Maybe we should hold off for a little while."

Libby nodded in agreement.

"I'll tell you one thing though. If what we're talking about is real, it certainly makes everything a lot more complicated."

"It does, doesn't it?" Libby said.

The sisters fell silent for a moment. Then Libby spoke. "You know what this means if it's true?" she said.

"That we should have asked for more money?" Bernie asked.

Libby ignored her.

"Okay. It means that someone is trying to set Duncan up," Bernie said.

"Well, whoever did this certainly didn't nominate him for the Citizen of the Year award," Libby mused. She slowed down to take the turn onto Bradley. "Now the question becomes who hated Duncan and why."

"Maybe," Bernie said, tapping her fingernails on the dashboard—she really had to get a manicure—"the question is who hated Mike Sweeney and Duncan? Or here's another possibility. Is Duncan just some random stooge who was picked to take the fall?"

Libby frowned. "I don't know about that. You've really got to dislike someone to do something like this to him."

Bernie shrugged. "Maybe. Or maybe the person who did it doesn't have any feelings one way or another. Except anger."

A shiver ran up Libby's spine. "That's very cold."

"I didn't say it wasn't," Bernie replied.

Libby stopped at a stop sign. "Well, Duncan did say he was drinking with Liza, so if anyone put anything in his beer, she's probably the one."

"Which might be why she disappeared."

"That would be my guess," Libby said. "I hope Dad's friend comes through with her whereabouts," she added as the car behind her honked. "I'm going. I'm going," she said as she went through the intersection.

"I hope Dad's friend comes through too," Bernie said. "But even if he doesn't, all is not lost, as they like to say in the movies."

"True. I'm sure Liam or Pat or Connor knows where she is. The trick will be getting them to tell us," Libby reflected.

Bernie grinned. "And it will be a good trick. Because the more thought I give this, the more I realize that this was a two-person job. I mean think about it. Even if we assume that Liza doped up Duncan, she didn't kill Sweeney. She couldn't have. He's way too big."

"Maybe she doped him up too and led him to the barrel. . . ."

"And he just meekly put his head under?"

"To take a drink. She could have suggested that to him."

"She still wouldn't have had the strength to hold his head under. Drugged or not, he would have started struggling when he ran out of air. That's a basic instinct."

"So we're looking for at least one guy," Bernie said. "Maybe two."

"You're postulating a conspiracy here between Liza and one of the guys at the very least," Libby said.

"Yes I am," Bernie allowed.

"Which would mean advance planning."

"True. Which," Bernie said slowly, thinking out loud, "is very different than two guys getting into a fight and one of them killing the other on impulse and then running off."

"So which is it?" Libby asked her sister.

Bernie shook her head. "That is the question, isn't it?"

"Yes it is," Libby replied.

"I don't know. I guess we have to keep both possibilities in mind."

"Or here's another thought," Bernie said. "Maybe someone didn't slip anything in Duncan's drink. I mean he could be lying about that. That's another big if."

"He could be," Libby agreed. "But do you think he is?"

Bernie thought back to the talk they'd just had and to the expression on Duncan's face when he'd told them he didn't remember anything. "No," she said. "I don't think he's lying. He really didn't want to tell us. I think he was incredibly embarrassed to have to admit something like it. It made him look like an idiot, and that's something that Duncan doesn't like to do."

"Still," Libby said as she turned into RJ's parking lot, "we do have to consider the possibility."

"Never discount anything," both sisters chorused together, echoing one of their dad's mantras.

They looked at each other and burst out laughing.

"So what would make someone commit that kind of crime," Bernie asked Libby when they stopped.

Libby parked the van and turned off the ignition. "That's simple," she said. "Money."

"Or revenge," Bernie said.

"Or both," Libby said.

Chapter 6

The only three people sitting in RJ's when Libby and Bernie walked in were Otis, Megan, and Bruce. This made the place look bigger than it was. RJ's had an allowable occupancy of two hundred, but on good days it ran way over that number.

The place would fill up later in the day as people stopped by to get a drink on their way home from work, but for now the balls on the pool table were racked, no one was playing darts, and the TV was on mute. The only sounds were the occasional cackle from Megan laughing at one of her private jokes and Otis humming to himself while he downed his second gin.

Bernie and Libby nodded to them as they moved on to their customary seats at the other end of the cherrywood bar. The countertop was Mulroney's pride and joy and he never tired of telling the story of how he'd salvaged it from a bar in Vermont before the tax people had come and closed the place down.

Bernie knew that Mulroney wouldn't have approved of Otis, Megan, and Bruce sitting there and drinking. They weren't the type of clientele he wanted, but since he was never there at that hour of the day it didn't matter. Even though Longely didn't have any town drunks, that designation being totally unPC—these days people had drinking issues—Otis, Megan, and Bruce came as close as anyone in town to filling that particular bill.

Brandon always let them sit there and drink until the commuters came in, at which point he shooed them out, since they tended to be somewhat odiferous if you got close enough. Otherwise, everyone complained about their smell and their generally unkempt appearance.

Over the years Bernie had noticed that Otis, Bruce, and Megan didn't seem to mind their unofficial curfew. They always left willingly and Bernie thought they were just grateful to Brandon for letting them stay in RJ's in the first place—since most of the other bars in Longely wouldn't let them through the front door—as well as for the fact that Brandon could be relied upon to spot them a couple of bucks now and then when things got really tight.

"My heroines," Brandon called out as Libby and Bernie sat down on the bar stools near the window. He'd been restocking in preparation for the evening rush and had seen their reflections in the mirror hanging over the back shelves when they'd entered. He went over to the cooler and got them both bottles of root beer.

"Good stuff," he said, pushing the bottles across the counter after he'd opened them. "Artisan."

"Be still my heart. What did they do?" Bernie asked. "Go out and collect the roots?"

"Yes, and they were wearing capes and carrying willow baskets when they did it," Brandon told her. "Unless you want something a little harder. I figured it was too early for anything else, but I could be wrong."

"You? Never," Bernie said in mock horror.

"Let's not exaggerate." Brandon put a bowl full of unshelled peanuts between Bernie and Libby. "It has happened once or twice."

"Maybe even three times," Bernie said teasingly. "No. This will be fine, thank you very much. Nice bottle," Bernie said, picking it up and studying it before putting it back down. "Old fashioned."

"That's the idea," Brandon told her.

"You know," she said, "back in the old days root beer had a kick."

Brandon leered. "So do I."

Bernie took a sip from the bottle. "Are you comparing yourself to a bottle of root beer?"

Brandon wagged his eyebrows. "I'm much better than that. If you want I'll prove it to you."

"Thanks, but I think I'll have to take a rain check on that," Bernie told him. "We're here on business."

Brandon put his hands to his heart. "I'm crushed," he said.

"That'll be the day," Bernie told him.

"You don't think I'm crushable?" Brandon declared. "Do I not bleed when you prick me . . .?"

"Enough," Bernie cried, holding up her hand. "No mangled Shakespeare, please."

Brandon sniffed. "If you feel that way, fine, but I'll have you know I was in Macbeth in college."

"Yeah. In the stage crew. Don't even pretend that your feelings are hurt," Bernie told him.

Brandon smiled. He put his elbows on the bar and leaned in toward Bernie and Libby. "So I'm just guessing here, but I take it I owe the pleasure of your visit to Mike Sweeney's unfortunate demise? Although I have to say, if you're a drunk, maybe that's the way to go."

"I don't know about that," Libby said. "I think his death falls under the 'be careful what you wish for' category."

"It's probably not a good way to die," Brandon conceded. "Drowning is drowning. They ran the story on the news earlier."

"Yeah, I saw it," Bernie said. "They gave it a lot of play."

"Hometown boy kills hometown boy. Pretty unusual stuff up around here." Brandon stifled a yawn. "Sorry. I have to start getting to bed earlier. How's the investigation going?"

Bernie nodded. "Slowly. Very slowly."

"I've got to say I'm a little surprised. Duncan was never one of your . . ."

"Biggest fans?" Bernie asked, finishing Brandon's sentence.

"Exactly," Brandon said.

"Duncan didn't hire us," Libby said.

"So who did?" Brandon asked.

Libby took a sip of her root beer. It was surprisingly good. No. It was great. She took another sip and thought about the old soda fountain on Main Street, and that got her wondering about whether or not they should serve root beer floats in the summer. She thought it would be easy enough to do. Maybe they could even make and sell their own ice cream. She'd have to remember to talk to Bernie about that. But that was for later. Right now she had more pressing concerns—like the Sweeney investigation.

"Bree hired us," she told Brandon, getting back to the matter at hand.

"Ah," Brandon replied. "The duchess must not be pleased about the situation her nephew has gotten himself into."

"You could say that about her royal highness," Bernie said, thinking back to Bree's behavior in their flat.

Brandon leaned over, grabbed a handful of peanuts out of the bowl, and began shelling them. "Well, over the years she's spent a lot of time and money keeping Duncan out of trouble. I'm not so sure she can do it this time."

"I guess we'll see what we can turn up," Bernie said noncommittally.

"You think there's a chance that Duncan didn't do it?" Brandon asked.

"That's what we're trying to find out," Bernie said. She took a peanut out of the bowl, shelled it, and popped it into her mouth.

As he did likewise, Brandon said, "You know the cops were around a while ago asking for Liza."

Bernie reached for another peanut and cracked the shell between her thumb and forefinger. She decided that what she liked about peanuts in the shell was that you had to eat them slowly. "So what did you tell them?" she asked.

"I didn't tell them anything because there's nothing to tell," Brandon replied. "I haven't seen Liza since the night Mike Sweeney died."

"Have you heard anything?"

"About her?"

"No. About my dad."

Brandon shook his head. "Not a peep. It's like she's disappeared from sight."

"Was she in here a lot?" Libby asked.

"She'd stop in at least three or four times a week with the other potato heads."

Libby wrinkled her forehead. "Potato heads?"

"He means Sweeney and Liam and those guys," Bernie explained. "So," she said to Brandon, "I don't suppose that by any chance you heard any of those guys saying anything about her?"

Brandon straightened up. "What are you implying?" he asked Bernie.

Bernie rolled her eyes. "I'm not implying anything."

"You most certainly are. You're implying that I eavesdrop on my customers, a suggestion I find abhorrent in the extreme."

Libby giggled. "Like you're not the gossip queen."

"Queen?" Brandon squeaked. "You're calling me a queen now?"

"Okay, a king then," Libby said.

Brandon tried to look offended. "That's terrible."

Libby giggled harder. "I'm sorry," she finally managed to get out.

"I didn't think it was that funny," he said when Libby stopped laughing. "Seriously," Brandon said.

Libby tried to look repentant. "You're right."

Bernie decided it was time to intervene. "Okay, Brandon," she said. "Let me ask you another question. Do you think it's possible that Liza put some kind of knockout drops in Duncan's drink?"

"For real?" Brandon asked.

Bernie nodded.

"It's a theory we're exploring," Libby added. "So what do you think?"

"I think it's certainly possible; anything is possible. But there's no way I can tell you for certain. I wasn't really paying attention."

"There weren't a lot of people in here that night," Bernie observed.

"I know, but I was busy cleaning and then I was reading the newspaper for a little while. I wasn't watching Liza, Duncan, or Sweeney. I mean she was sitting between both guys, but . . ." Brandon shrugged his shoulders.

"But what?" Bernie asked.

"I remember Duncan and Sweeney both hit the head a couple of times. I suppose Liza could have put the stuff in Duncan's beer then."

"Was Duncan acting weird?" Bernie asked Brandon.

"Weird as in how?"

"Weird as in spacey," Libby said.

"No more than usual." Brandon straightened up. "Of course, that's the beauty with roofies. People act the way they usually do. They're just more suggestible. Of course, the same holds true of Oxis."

"Oxis?" Bernie asked.

"Oxycontin," Brandon said. "The painkillers."

"I know what they are," Bernie told him. "But I didn't know they did that."

Brandon shrugged. "Evidently they have that effect on some people."

"Who knew?" Bernie said.

Brandon laughed. "Not me, that's for sure. At least not until Spike told me."

Libby cleared her throat. Bernie and Brandon looked at her.

"So you didn't notice anything odd about Duncan's behavior?" Libby asked again. "Anything at all?"

Brandon shook his head. "Nope. I can't say I did, but then, like I said, I really wasn't paying attention." He was about to say something else when the front door banged open and the remaining members of the Corned Beef and Cabbage Club rolled into the bar.

Brandon nodded toward them. "Apparently it's your lucky day. Now you can ask the guys about Liza yourselves."

Chapter 7

Bernie watched as Brandon ambled down to serve Liam, Patrick, and Connor. "Hey," he said. "You guys are early today. Did they finally decide to fire you losers?"

"Cute," Liam said. "In answer to your question, no. They have not decided to fire us. We have declared this day an official day of mourning for our fallen brother. We would all like black and tans," he told Brandon as he, Pat, and Connor bellied up to the bar.

As Bernie studied them, she realized that the guys all looked the same—big and burly with fair skin, light brown hair, and hazel eyes. Duncan was thinner than the rest of them by a wide margin. But Mike Sweeney had been the same size as the other three. Now she remembered that he, Patrick, Liam, and Connor had all been rugby players, whereas Duncan had not. Probably hadn't wanted to mess up his perfect features.

So given that, the question was how had Duncan held Sweeney's head under when Sweeney outweighed him by a good fifty pounds? She supposed he could have. Anything was possible. But it would have been a real struggle, something that would have been much easier for Liam, Patrick, or Connor to do, unless of course Duncan had knocked him unconscious first.

But according to Clyde the ME said that hadn't happened. And even if it had happened, it still would have been very difficult to drag Sweeney over to one of the barrels, lift him up, and hold his head under. Bernie was still trying to work out the scenario as she got off her bar stool and walked over to the guys.

"Hi," she said to them. "Let me buy you this round."

"We won't say no," Liam told her, not hiding the fact that he was looking her up and down.

She turned to Brandon. "Put their drinks on my tab."

Brandon nodded. "Will do."

"Thanks," Patrick said. He was wearing a blue and green tie. He leered at her. "You're looking good since you got back from Cali. Real good, if you don't mind my saying so."

"Yeah," Liam joined in. "I was just thinking that myself."

Connor grinned. "What do you want with that lug," he asked Bernie, nodding in Brandon's direction, "when you can have one of us?"

"Or all of us," Liam said.

Brandon scowled and started toward them, but Bernie held him off with a look. "Have any of you guys seen Liza?" she asked, ignoring their comments.

"Why do you want to know?" Liam demanded. "You want to make it a foursome?"

"Fivesome, wet brain," Connor said to Liam. "Learn how to count."

Liam shrugged. "That's not my best ability."

"Hey," Brandon growled. "Let's show some respect here."

"Don't you have a sense of humor?" Liam asked him.

Brandon got red in the face. "Not in this case."

"Lighten up," Liam told him. "We're only goofing."

"Just so you know," Brandon said.

Liam put both hands in the air, palms outward. "I get it. I get it."

"Good," Brandon said. He came over and slammed the men's drinks in front of them. Then he moved a short distance away, leaned on the back of the bar, crossed his arms over his chest, and glowered as Libby got down from her seat and walked over.

"Your sister's boyfriend is pretty touchy," Patrick said to her.

"Listen," Libby replied. "Why don't you stop being a jerk?"

Patrick took a gulp of his beer and put his bottle back down. "Well, I'll say one thing for you. You're certainly direct."

"And feisty too," Connor said.

"I like that in a woman," Liam added.

Libby ignored them and went on with what she was saying. "We need to find Liza."

"Good for you," Liam told her.

"My sister and I are working for your pal Duncan. Liza has information that could be valuable to his defense."

"Hurray for you," Liam said.

"It would be real helpful to Duncan if we could find her," Bernie said.

"Well, we all want to be helpful to Duncan, don't we?" Liam asked Patrick.

Patrick nodded. "Absolutely."

"Without a doubt," Connor said.

Liam turned to Patrick. "Have you seen Liza?"

Patrick shook his head.

He turned to Connor. "Have you?"

"Nope."

He turned back to Bernie and Libby. "And I know that I haven't. Any more questions?"

"Yeah," Bernie said. "Where do you think she went?"

Liam shrugged. "How would I know?"

"You're her friend, aren't you?" Libby asked.

Liam took another sip of his drink before replying. "In a manner of speaking."

"What manner of speaking is that?" Bernie asked.

"Listen," Liam said, "she's a drinking buddy. That's it. You want to know any more you'll have to ask Duncan."

"We already have. He doesn't know anything. That's why we're here."

"Well, you could have saved yourself the trip," Patrick said. "Because we haven't seen her since that night."

Bernie took a deep breath. "Does she take off like this often?" she asked.

Connor shrugged. "Often enough. She's not what you would call the most stable of people."

"Not at all," Liam agreed.

"Do you think Liza would put knockout drops in Duncan's drink?" Libby asked.

Liam burst out laughing. "You're kidding me, right?"

"No, she's not," Bernie said.

"Why would she do that?" Patrick asked. "That is by far one of the stupidest things I have ever heard."

"Well, Duncan says he was set up for Mike Sweeney's murder and that he doesn't remember anything after the first beer he had that night, hence the assumption that Liza put something in his drink. Unless you did."

Connor untied his tie, then pulled it off, folded it up, and put it in his breast pocket. "I'm not even going to dignify that with an answer," he scoffed. "Duncan's nuts, and if you believe him, you're nuts too."

"So you think that Duncan killed Mike Sweeney?" Bernie asked him.

"I didn't say that," Connor said sharply.

"Then who do you think did?" Bernie asked.

"How about a pissed off leprechaun," Liam said. "I understand they have very bad tempers when aroused."

Libby took a step closer. "Maybe one of you killed Mike Sweeney," she said.

"Maybe one of us did," Patrick agreed. He grinned. "Good luck proving it though."

"So you want Duncan to take the fall for this?" Bernie asked.

"Duncan will be fine," Liam said. "He'll come out of it smelling like a rose."

"A wild Irish rose," Patrick added.

"You don't seem very sad about Mike Sweeney's death," Bernie observed.

"Of course, I'm sad," Liam said. "We just grieve in our own ways."

"And what way is that?" Libby asked.

"It's obvious, isn't it?" Liam asked.

"Not to me," Libby said.

"We drink," Liam said. "And now, if you'll excuse me I think it's time for Connor and Patrick and me to get down to the serious business of mourning." And he turned around and faced the bar.

Bernie studied the three men for a moment. Then she said to Libby, "Come on. I think we're through here."

They were going out the door when Liam's wife, Kylie, brushed by them. She stormed over to Liam, slapped him across the face, and marched back out.

Libby looked at Bernie and Bernie looked at Libby. They both thought the same thing. An angry wife? This was too good an opportunity to waste. By the time they were out the door, Liam's wife had gotten into her silver Infiniti and was backing out of the parking lot.

"I'm driving," Bernie said, as she and Libby ran for their van.

Chapter 8

The Infiniti was a quarter of the way down the block by the time Bernie had muscled the van out of the parking lot.

"Hurry up," Libby cried. "You're going to lose her."

"I'm trying," Bernie told Libby as she gained on the Infiniti. "I'm not exactly driving a BMW here, you know."

The Infiniti turned onto Randall Road and so did the sisters. By now they were three car lengths behind Kylie. Fortunately traffic was heavy, otherwise Kylie would have left them in the dust.

"I wonder what Kylie was so pissed about," Libby said.

"It'll be interesting to talk to her," Bernie observed.

"Do you think she will? Talk to us?" Libby asked.

"Not a clue," Bernie said. She kept her eyes on the silver Infiniti.

"She might just tell us to go to hell," Libby said.

"She might," Bernie agreed. "But then again, she might not."

"Which we won't know until we try."

"Exactly," Bernie said.

"And she did seem really, really angry at Liam," Libby continued.

"Indeed she did. That was not a love tap she gave him. So she might be more disposed to talk about things she'd otherwise prefer to keep hidden."

"Anger does that to people," Libby observed.

"Like you," Bernie said.

"And you, Bernie."

"I never said it didn't, Libby."

The sisters were silent for a moment. Bernie concentrated on Kylie's car, while Libby thought about how they were going to talk to Kylie when they caught up with her.

"I think she's going to the mall," Libby said as the Infiniti turned off onto Ash.

"Oh goody," Bernie said. "We can get you some clothes while we're there. I love multitasking."

Libby frowned. She hated shopping, especially shopping with her sister. She made her try things on. "We won't have time."

Bernie grinned. "Trust me, Libby. There's always time to shop."

Neither sister said anything else until after Bernie had parked the van and they'd walked into the mall. During the weekend the place was packed, but this was a weekday afternoon and no one was around. After five minutes of looking, Bernie and Libby spied Kylie at Banana Republic. She was browsing through a rack full of pencil skirts in various patterns.

"Hi," Bernie said to her.

Kylie turned. She was holding a black and white tweed pencil skirt in her left hand and a brown and white checked one in her right. Bernie reflected that Kylie was one of those natural blondes who are stunning when they're eighteen and faded by the time they're thirty. At twenty-five she was well on her way to the negative side of the equation. Of course, Bernie thought, the fact that Kylie wasn't wearing any makeup didn't help matters.

Neither did the fact that she'd gained about thirty

pounds since Bernie had last seen her, a sure sign that things were not going well. Hence the muffin top spilling over the top of her skinny jeans. Some people, Bernie decided, should not wear skinny jeans. No. Cancel that thought. Most people shouldn't wear skinny jeans. They didn't do anyone any favors.

"I think I'd go for the black and white tweed," Bernie told Kylie. "You'll get more wear out of it."

Kylie spun around. "I just saw you in the bar," she said.

"I know," Bernie gushed. "Life is just one big coincidence, isn't it?"

Kylie frowned. "And now you're here."

Bernie smiled her winningest smile. "So it would seem. Great minds with a single thought and all that." She leaned in. "My sister and I are going shopping."

Kylie glanced at Libby and frowned. "I so don't believe that. What do you want with me?"

Bernie kept smiling. "Would you believe we're here to give you some fashion advice?"

"Right." Kylie put both skirts back and moved to the next rack.

Bernie moved with her, while Libby stayed slightly in the background.

"They are a little pricy for what they are," Bernie noted. "I used to like Banana more two or three years ago."

Kylie didn't say anything.

"Okay, you got me," Bernie conceded. "We followed you here."

Kylie stopped at a display of cardigans. She lifted up a bright pink sweater, held it to her, then put it down and walked on. "There's a shocker."

"We want to talk to you about Liam."

Kylie moved on to the rack of white blouses. Libby and Bernie followed.

"That's nice," Kylie told Bernie as she looked through the merchandise. "Because I don't want to talk to you.

About anything. So if you don't mind, could you please leave me alone?"

And Kylie pulled a long-sleeved, white cotton blouse with a Peter Pan collar off the rack, walked over to the mirror, and held the blouse up in front of her. She studied her reflection in the mirror, cocking her head first to one side and then to the other.

Libby moved closer. Kylie ignored her.

"It must be hard," Libby said softly, "going through what you're going through with Liam."

Kylie turned to face her. "How do you know I'm going through anything?" she demanded.

"You looked pretty upset to me back in the bar," Bernie told her.

Kylie frowned, walked over, and hung the blouse back where she'd found it.

"How long have you been married?" Libby asked.

"A year. A year and a half," Kylie said, still looking at the blouses.

"Not that long," Bernie commented.

"Long enough," Kylie replied. There was no mistaking the bitterness in her voice.

"He wasn't what you thought he'd be?" Libby asked gently.

Kylie shook her head and avoided eye contact. She pulled out a blouse and put it back. Bernie and Libby waited for her to start talking. They knew that she would. It would just take a little time, and they could wait.

"I mean I knew Liam had issues," Kylie said when she did start to speak. "But he always treated me nice. He took me to Puerto Rico. He took me on a cruise. He bought me jewelry. He got me a car. He even paid for our wedding."

"Where was that?" Bernie asked.

"The South Street Seaport down in New York City."

"It must have been lovely. And expensive," Libby observed.

"It was," Kylie agreed.

She stopped talking. Bernie and Libby didn't say anything. They waited some more.

Finally Kylie turned and faced them. "We were going to get this house out on Randall Road," she explained.

"Nice," Bernie said.

Randall Road was a big fancy development with houses that started at $750,000 and went up from there.

"But not anymore," Kylie said.

"Is that why you slapped him?" Bernie asked.

Kylie nodded. "That son of a bitch didn't even have the decency to tell me that we couldn't do that anymore. I had to find out from the bank manager. I mean how embarrassing is that?"

"Very," Bernie said. "What happened?"

Kylie's body stiffened. "Mike Sweeney is what happened. I told Liam not to give him our money. I told him Sweeney was a loser. But he didn't listen. Obviously. Because, after all, what do I know?" She jabbed herself in her chest with her thumb. "Being a female and all. Some of that was my money too. He had no right to give it to Sweeney to invest in one of his crazy schemes. Absolutely none." Kylie waved a finger in the air. "I will never, and I do mean never, have a joint checking account with anyone ever again."

"I take it Sweeney and Liam were friends?"

"Friends?" Kylie pondered the question for a moment before replying. "Yeah," she finally said. "I guess you could say that. Most of the time. Although I never got it."

"How so?" Bernie asked.

"I mean would you be friends with someone who stole your car and wrapped it around a tree?" Kylie asked the sisters.

"Not hardly," Bernie and Libby said together.

"Me either," Kylie said. "But Sweeney would do something like that and Liam would rant and rave about it and about how he was going to find Sweeney and kill him and then the next thing I knew they'd go back to being friends again. I mean go figure."

"They must have had something in common," Bernie observed.

Kylie snorted. "Yeah. That stupid Corned Beef and Cabbage Club. All they did was sit around and drink and talk about how much money they were going to be making. But as far as I could see, no one was doing very well. Not after 2008."

"Including Mike Sweeney?" Bernie asked.

"Especially Mike Sweeney," Kylie said. "He screwed everyone over. In fact, I think he got Duncan fired. Maybe that's why Duncan killed him."

Libby took two chocolate kisses out of her pocket and offered one to Kylie, who took it after protesting that she shouldn't.

When Libby and Kylie had both finished unwrapping the kisses and popping them in their mouths, Libby said, "Duncan is saying he was set up."

"And I'm the Queen of England," Kylie retorted.

"Maybe Liam was pissed at Sweeney for losing all his money."

"Is Duncan saying that Liam set him up?" Kylie asked.

"No," Bernie said. "He's saying that Liza did."

"That skank?"

"Is that what she is?" Bernie asked.

"Yeah. She's the queen of the skanks, if you ask me."

"Do you think she could have set Duncan up?" Libby asked.

Kylie laughed. It wasn't a pleasant one. "I think she could do anything. Especially if there's money involved."

"Are you saying what I think you're saying?" Bernie asked.

"That she used to work in a strip club somewhere downtown in the city? That she sleeps with anyone who has pants on? And some that don't? Yeah," Kylie said, finishing up. "That's exactly what I'm saying."

"Who is everyone, Kylie?" Libby asked.

"Duncan. Mike. Patrick. Connor. And God knows who else. She probably slept with Brandon as well. "

"That I doubt," Bernie said. She could feel her face start to flush.

Kylie spread her hands. "Chill. All I'm saying is that if something walks and talks Liza has made a play for it, be it male or female. She probably does other species too."

"What about Liam?" Bernie asked her.

Kylie's voice tightened. "What do you think? Why should he be different from anyone else?"

"When was this?" Bernie asked.

Kylie's face turned beet red.

"Come on," Libby coaxed. "It can't be that bad."

"Oh yes, it can," Kylie said.

"Tell us," Libby said.

Kylie shook her head. "I don't want to."

Bernie thought about the worst-case scenario she could imagine and said, "It was during your wedding, wasn't it?"

Kylie covered her face with her hands. "It was so horrible."

"Did you find them together?" Bernie asked.

"Yes. Right in the room that they keep for the wedding party. I'd forgotten my contact lens case and went back to get it. I saw them and ran out. Liam finally found me. He said it wasn't his fault. He said she came on to him and he'd never do it again. That he was so drunk he didn't know what he was doing and that he'd make it up to me."

Kylie put her hands down and touched her diamond studs. "He bought these for me the next day. They're perfect one carats. A matched set. I mean sometimes guys can't help themselves, right?"

"Right," Bernie said.

"And I promised him I'd forgive and forget. And that's what I've done. And as far as I know Liam has never gone near her again. And things have gone pretty well—up until now."

Libby reached over and gave Kylie a quick hug. "What did Duncan think about Liza's activities? If what you say is true—and I'm not doubting it is—how come he's still with her?"

"Oh, he doesn't know," Kylie confided. "She tells him she's going out with the girls and then she goes over to someone's apartment and does the dirty deed."

"Are you sure?"

"Absolutely."

"And no one is telling him what Liza is doing?" Bernie asked. Somehow she found that difficult to believe.

"No," Kylie said. "I think the guys are having too much fun putting one over on him."

"And you haven't said anything to him?" asked Libby.

Kylie shrugged. "It's none of my business, and anyway, Liam would have killed me." She looked at the clock on the wall. "I gotta go. I have to get to the gym." She pinched her roll. "I'm working on getting this off." She shook her head. "It's amazing what a bad marriage can do. I should have left when I caught Liam and Liza together. I mean if that's not a sign, I don't know what is."

"Luck," Bernie said.

"You too," Kylie replied as she turned and walked out of the store.

Libby and Bernie left too. They were quiet until they got back in the van.

Then Libby said, "Things are certainly getting curiouser and curiouser."

"And messier and messier. We seem to be muddying the waters."

"Well, we're certainly not injecting clarity into the situation."

"Or making Duncan look any better," Bernie observed.

"There is that. One thing is clear though," Libby said. "We really have to find Liza."

"The sooner the better," Bernie said as she started the van.

Libby consulted her watch. "But now we have to get those pies done."

Chapter 9

Sean lit his first cigarette of the day, inhaled and exhaled, sighing in pleasure. He'd been waiting for this for almost two hours.

"I wish you wouldn't smoke in the hearse," Marvin told Sean as they drove over to Pat Dwyer's office.

Sean had called Dwyer shortly after the girls had left to make sure he was going to be in his office and then he'd called Marvin and asked him to pick him up. This whole not being able to drive thing just sucked. But he'd used the time waiting for Marvin to call Orion. He hadn't picked up, so Sean had left a message on his voice mail. Truth be told, Sean didn't expect Orion to call him back, but at least he'd gotten the ball rolling. Sean was thinking about exactly what he was going to say to Orion when he did reach him when he realized that Marvin was still talking to him about his smoking.

"My dad complains," Marvin informed him.

"Why? The corpses aren't going to care," Sean told Marvin. "They're dead already."

"My dad thinks it's disrespectful."

"To whom?"

"Our clientele."

"Because the dead people are going to get throat cancer?" Sean scoffed, but he rolled down the window anyway so that the hearse would get aired out.

"You know that they know," Marvin told him.

"The bodies?" Sean asked, playing the innocent. "Now you're talking to the dead? Wow! You really do need to get into another line of work. Or maybe that's why you're so successful."

Marvin sat up straighter and gripped the wheel. He hated when Mr. Simmons did this. "I'm talking about your daughters, of course," he said stiffly.

"I know," Sean said.

"So you know that I was talking about them or you know that they know?" Marvin asked.

"Of course, I know that they know," Sean said. "I'd have to be a fool to think that they didn't know. They have noses, don't they? And I'm not a fool and neither are they. In fact, not only do they know, they also know that I know that they know."

"So why do you pretend that they don't know?" Marvin asked, genuinely puzzled by the conversation he was having with Libby's dad.

"Because then we'd all have to have a talk." Sean bracketed the word talk with his fingers. "And none of us wants to do that."

"I'm still not getting it," Marvin said as he realized too late that the light at the corner of Manes and Allen had turned red. Somehow he avoided slamming on his brakes and coasted to a stop instead.

Sean watched with approval. Marvin's driving was improving. Slowly. Very slowly. But at least it was going in the right direction. Which was something Sean gave himself a pat on the back for.

"It's simple," Sean told him when they were underway again. "If we had a discussion, my daughters would feel it was incumbent upon them to try and get me to stop smoking, which I'm not going to do. Heaven knows, I have few enough pleasures left to me at my advanced age."

"You're not that old. . . ."

"I'm old enough," Sean said.

"Not really," Marvin said.

"Fine. I feel old, okay?"

"Okay."

"Good." Sean didn't feel it necessary to refer to the disease that had plagued him for the last two years and now seemed to be in remission. He also didn't see the need to tell Marvin that the reason he thought his private hell had gone into remission was because he'd started smoking again. "As I was saying, I'm old enough, so I think that I should be able to take my pleasures where I find them. If my daughters don't know, we won't argue about it. Which seems to me to be a good thing."

"So you're advocating peace at any cost?" asked Marvin, who was still managing to keep his eyes on the road instead of looking at Sean. This was a difficult thing for Marvin to do since he was one of those people who always had to look someone in the eye when he talked to him or her. Doing this while maneuvering a heavy moving object upped the ante.

Sean cleared his throat before answering. "I wouldn't go that far," he told Marvin. "But I do believe that hypocrisy and/or willful blindness are wonderful tools when used correctly. In fact, I can honestly say that if more people engaged in those practices, life would be a great deal smoother."

"I'm not sure I agree," Marvin said. In the heat of the moment, he'd forgotten himself and turned to face Sean to see whether he was kidding or not. "In fact, I know that I don't."

"Eyes on the road," Sean barked. He sighed. Patience, he told himself. All things come to he who waits. Not that he believed that. Actually, the saying just irritated him. So why did he tell himself that? He wasn't sure, because it just made him even more annoyed.

"Sorry," Marvin muttered. He'd been doing so well too. He paused to let a truck go by him.

"Of course, you don't agree with me," Sean continued when Marvin was paying attention to the traffic again. "You're much too young. When I was your age I didn't believe what I just said to you either. I thought you could work everything out by discussing it. Now I know better. It takes being married for a long time to recognize the truth of what I'm telling you."

Marvin opened his mouth to speak, but Sean stopped him before he got any words out and said, "You'll thank me for this advice later on. I wish someone had told me what I'm telling you." And then Sean turned and looked out the window and thought about his wife Rose and about how much he missed her, and about all the things he would have liked to have said to her had he had the chance.

Marvin took the hint and remained quiet for the rest of the trip and concentrated on his driving. He'd made one slip-up already in that department and he didn't intend to make any more. He reflected that his driving goofs only happened when Libby's dad was in the car. The truth was that Mr. Simmons made him nervous, and when he got nervous he made mistakes. It wasn't that he didn't like Libby's dad. He did. He liked him a lot.

Better than his own dad, actually. But sometimes he didn't know what to make of him. He didn't know when he was kidding and when he was serious. Witness what Mr. Simmons had just said to him. Lying didn't seem to be the basis for a good relationship and yet he knew from Libby that her mom and dad had been happily married for thirty-five years, so maybe Sean had something there after all.

Marvin was still thinking about the conversation he and

Sean had had when he pulled into the small strip mall that housed Pat Dwyer's office. A former bar owner, Dwyer now owned several McDonald's franchises and was reputed to be raking in the money, not that you could tell from the location of his office, which was set between a take-out Chinese restaurant and a shoe repair place.

The strip was only six shops long. As Marvin parked the hearse he noticed that the tarmac was showing the after-effects of winter plowing, the sidewalk was beginning to show signs of wear and tear along the edges, and the lettering on some of the signs on the businesses had begun to fade.

Sean noticed it too as he tossed his cigarette out the window and got out of the hearse. Even though he was still walking with a cane, he didn't need help getting out of the vehicle and that fact alone cheered him up enormously. At least he could manage on his own now. He might be slow, but he was out of a wheelchair and moving under his own power and the tremors that had wracked his body were gone. His doctor couldn't explain it and his daughters said it was through his sheer bloody-mindedness. Sean smiled, suspecting that his daughters might be right.

"Nice ride," Dwyer commented when Sean and Marvin came inside. "Very funereal. It's good to see you're coming up in the world."

Sean grinned. "I can talk to Marvin's father. Maybe I can set something up for you as well."

Dwyer pointed to Sean's cane. "Fancy schmancy."

"Just got it," Sean said.

"I like the silver handle."

"Me too," Sean said.

Dwyer gave the cane a careful appraisal. "Kind of upscale for you, isn't it?"

"Everything is upscale to you, Pat," Sean said.

"I had a friend who had a cane like that once," Dwyer remarked. "He told me it was really useful."

"He must have gotten the model with the sword in it."

Dwyer laughed and gestured toward the seats in front of his desk. "I'll take that under advisement. Good to see you out and about," he said to Sean.

"Glad to be out and about," Sean replied.

Despite the amount of money Dwyer earned, Sean reflected that the guy did not believe in spending any of it on nonessentials. Which, Sean thought, may have been why Dwyer was so successful. And rich. He put his money where it counted. Into making more money.

Dwyer's office was as bare bones as you could get without doing business out of your car. He didn't have a secretary, let alone a personal assistant. In the event that he needed extra help, which was unlikely, he called a temp service. Otherwise he used a tax attorney and that was the extent of his payroll. He made his own phone calls and wrote down his own appointments and kept his own books. "That way I know what's going on and no one else does," he was frequently heard to tell his stepson, who wanted him to upgrade and move to a fancier place, just so he could brag about it, in Dwyer's opinion.

The only decorations in Dwyer's office were his wrestling trophies, his plaques from college—he'd been New York State champion back in the day—and the plaques commemorating the victories of the high school wrestling team he still coached. Other than that, Dwyer's office walls were bare. No point in wasting money on pictures, in his opinion. Or furniture either.

He'd gotten his desk at Walmart and his chair, file cabinets, and shelving at Sam's Club. The chairs that Sean and Marvin were now sitting on had come from a garage sale at Dwyer's church, as had the rug on the floor and the coffee maker on the small table in the corner. Dwyer could not see stopping and spending time and money buying coffee when he could make a perfectly respectable cup by himself.

Sean watched as Dwyer took a Cuban cigar out of the humidor on his desk—the cigars were the only luxury he allowed himself—clipped off the end with a small silver cutter and applied a match to it. When he'd gotten the cigar going, he said, "So I understand what you're doing and why, but I don't see how I can help."

Sean lit another cigarette and Dwyer pushed an ashtray across the desk for him. Watching both men, Marvin began to feel as if he was in a fifties movie. The only thing missing was the blond secretary.

"If I didn't think you could help me, I wouldn't be here," Sean replied.

Dwyer took another puff of his cigar and exhaled. "I'm listening."

"Nice to know. I already told you on the phone. I want to know anything you can tell me about Mulroney—"

"You think he's involved?" Dwyer asked before Sean could finish his sentence .

"Probably not," Sean conceded. "But the homicide did take place outside his establishment and it never hurts to be thorough."

"Lucy doesn't think so," Dwyer observed.

"No, he certainly doesn't," Sean agreed.

"Maybe if you'd been less thorough you'd still be chief of police and Lucy would be in a patrol car," Dwyer observed.

Sean thought about his answer for a minute. Then he said, "You're probably right, but I wouldn't go back and change the way I did things even if I could."

"I never thought you would want to," Dwyer replied, nodding at the truth of Sean's statement. Then he cursed as he flicked an ash off the front of his suit jacket. The jacket had small burn marks from his cigars all over it. "Anne is going to kill me," he said.

"How's she going to tell that this is a new one?" Sean asked. "You've got several already. I count eight."

"It's nine actually, and she can tell. Just like Rose could have told. Nothing gets by Anne."

"This is true," Sean said, thinking back to Rose and the accuracy of Dwyer's statement. He'd never been able to get anything by Rose. Ever. Although he'd tried really, really hard numerous times. Like with the fireworks. But Rose had always known when he'd bought them no matter how hard he tried to hide the fact. Amazing. He took another puff of his cigarette and refocused on the matter at hand.

"So did Mulroney have any ties to Sweeney?" Sean asked.

"You mean other than being Irish?"

"Yeah. Other than being Irish."

"And Sweeney being a four-star patron of said establishment."

"Yes. Other than that."

Dwyer tapped the remaining ash from his cigar into the ashtray and sat back in his seat. "You know I've been out of business with Mulroney for the last two years and we haven't exactly kept in touch."

Sean did the same with his cigarette. "Yeah. I heard from Clyde you guys weren't on the best of terms when you parted."

"You could say that," Dwyer said. "So I really don't know much about Sweeney. Two years ago I'd have told you that they weren't exactly tight."

"Do you know if Mulroney invested with him?" Sean asked.

Dwyer took a moment to relight his cigarette before answering. "Yeah. He always was a sucker for a quick buck."

"Well, he can't have been that badly hurt," Marvin said.

Both men stopped talking and looked at him.

"He bought a plane recently," Marvin stammered.

"A jet?" Sean asked.

"No. One of those little things, but even they're pretty expensive."

"And how do you know that?" Sean asked as he moved the ashtray a little closer to himself.

"Because my dad is thinking of buying one, so he was talking to him about it."

"Interesting," Sean said, turning back to Dwyer.

"Anything else?" Dwyer asked him. "Or can I get back to work?"

"As a matter of fact, there is one more thing. Your step-daughter."

"I was waiting for that," Dwyer said. He took another puff of his cigar and exhaled.

Marvin began to cough. "Do you mind?" he said, waving the smoke away with his hands.

"As a matter of fact, I do," Dwyer said. "No offense meant, but if it bothers you why don't you wait outside."

"And no offense taken," Marvin said as he shot up from his seat and started for the door. "I'll be in the hearse," he told Sean. And then he was gone.

Both men watched him go.

"Nice kid," Dwyer said after the door closed. "Nicer than his dad."

"That's for sure," Sean agreed. He leaned over and tapped the ash from the cigarette out in the ashtray.

"He's like my son. Sensitive." Dwyer took his cigar out of his mouth for a moment and regarded it before jamming it back in. "I'll tell you one thing. They sure don't make 'em like they used to."

"Cigars?"

"Guys."

"Agreed. They certainly don't," Sean concurred. "For that matter, they don't make anything like they used to. Look at cars. You used to be able to do an oil change by yourself. Now you have to take it to a mechanic."

"I hate sushi," Dwyer said suddenly. "But that's all my granddaughter wants to eat." He shuddered.

"Thank God Bernie and Libby don't like it," Sean replied. He made a face. "You'd have to stick a gun to my head to get me to eat raw fish."

"It costs a lot too. And for what? Nothing as far as I can see. What's wrong with meat loaf?"

"Or mac and cheese?" Sean asked.

"You know what I like about Libby's and Bernie's food?" Dwyer said.

"No. What?" Sean said.

"Besides the fact that it tastes good, you can tell what you're eating. It's not weird. Nothing like bacon ice cream or oxtails with lavender butter or that raw stuff one of my daughters-in-law is trying to push on me. Bah."

Sean couldn't think of anything to add, so he didn't.

The two men sat and smoked in companionable silence for a few moments, then Dwyer said to Sean, "You really expect me to tell you how to find Liza when she's obviously disappeared because she didn't want to be involved in this mess?"

"I'm not the police, remember?"

"So what I tell you is just going into a sealed box and no one is going to hear anything about it? Give me a break. You're working for the defense. Your guys are going to want her to testify."

"Isn't that the right thing to do in this case?"

Dwyer snorted. "Spare me. You're not talking to a sixteen-year-old kid now, you're talking to me. If Liza skipped, she must have had a reason."

"So you know where she is?"

"As a matter of fact, I don't," Dwyer said.

"But you have an idea."

Dwyer spread his hands apart. "Come on, Sean, give me a break. Let it alone."

"You said it wasn't a problem when I spoke to you on the phone earlier."

Dwyer looked away. "It wasn't then."

Sean's eyes widened in disbelief. "Oh my God, I don't believe it. You called Anne and told her."

"No. But I told you, it's like she's some kind of witch or something. She called just after I hung up on you."

"And you told her?"

"What do you think? Of course I didn't. All I said was that you were coming by. You know to, like, make conversation. But that was enough. She threw a fit."

Sean leaned forward and stared into Dwyer's eyes. "The kid is a jerk."

Dwyer shrugged apologetically. "You know it and I know it, and I even think in her heart Anne knows it, though she won't admit it to herself."

"That's what mothers do," Sean observed.

"So it would seem, but I still can't talk about her. It wouldn't be right. I have to live with the woman."

"It also wouldn't be right if Duncan Nottingham went to jail for Mike Sweeney's murder and Liza could get him off."

"If that were the case she wouldn't have run."

"So you're saying that Duncan is guilty and that he was putting pressure on Liza to lie for him? Is that what you're saying?"

Dwyer shrugged and leaned back in his seat. "Well, let me put it this way. It wouldn't surprise me if that were the case. Duncan always was a violent kind of guy. He was involved in that brawl down at Baker's Field. In fact, I was told he started it."

Sean snorted. "That's a hell of a lot different than holding someone's head under and drowning them and you know it, so don't give me that guff. Anyway, when it comes to brawls, you certainly didn't shy away from participating."

"Neither did you," Dwyer said.

Sean laughed. "In the bad old days."

"They were a lot of fun," Dwyer said.

"Yup," Sean said. "They certainly were. Not for the other guy though." He was silent for a moment, remembering the time Dwyer put a guy in the hospital with a fractured jaw and a broken arm. Then he said, "So what's Liza up to now?"

Dwyer shrugged. "A little of this. A little of that."

"I heard she dropped out of college."

"She said she thought the classes were a waste of time."

"I heard they were going to kick her out for drinking and drugging, so she decided to drop out first."

Dwyer raised an eyebrow. "Drugging? Is that a word?"

"I think you're trying to beg the question here."

"And not succeeding." Dwyer studied his fingernails. "Look, what can I say? The kid is a screwup. But that doesn't mean she isn't entitled to opt out if she doesn't want to deal with this Sweeney thing."

"I didn't say it did."

"I'm glad we agree on something."

"Look, all I want to do is talk to her. You can give her my number and tell her to call me."

"I can't," Dwyer said.

"Can't or won't?"

"Can't. She's not speaking to me."

"How come?" Sean asked.

Dwyer grimaced. "If you don't mind, I don't want to get into it right now."

"Not a problem," Sean said. He shifted his weight in the chair to get more comfortable. "I mean if we were talking about it, I'd be wondering if her not speaking to you had anything to do with the fact that she was supposed to buy into one of your franchises. That you were going to go fifty/ fifty with her."

Dwyer sat up a little straighter. "Where'd you hear that?"

Sean smiled and shrugged. "You're not the only one with sources, you know. People talk."

Dwyer straightened out his tie and patted it down. "I was doing it as a favor for her mom."

"And what happened?"

Dwyer sighed. "What happened was that when push came to shove, Liza didn't have the money. Wanted me to front it for her. Swore to me she'd pay me back. Hah. I had to tell Anne that wasn't going to happen. It was not, as you can guess, a very pleasant conversation."

"I can imagine," Sean said. "Where was she going to get the money from?"

"Her trust." Dwyer shook his head. "In my opinion, no one should give anyone control of their money until they're thirty-five. Forty would be even better. By that time they might develop some common sense."

"So what happened to the money?" Sean asked him.

"As far as I can tell, Liza lost it."

"How?" Sean asked. "What did she do? Misplace her piggy bank?"

Dwyer didn't say anything.

"Drugs? Bad investments?"

Dwyer remained silent.

"Both?"

Sean read the expression on Dwyer's face and knew that the answer was a yes. "I hear Sweeney and Duncan did a lot of coke."

"So do lots of other people," Dwyer pointed out, neither denying nor substantiating the charge as he took his cigar out of his mouth and knocked off the ash.

"And," Sean continued, "I hear they both lost a lot of people a lot of money."

"That's not so uncommon these days either," Dwyer

said. "I mean who gives thirty-year-old guys all this money and provides no oversight? That's like leaving an eighteen-year-old kid loose in a whorehouse. And on the other side, I think that all those people who lost their shirts—okay, not all but some —deserve what they got. Use some common sense, people. Perform due diligence. I mean you can't think that things are always going to go up. That's not the way the universe works."

Sean didn't reply to what Dwyer had just said even though he agreed with every word. He was too busy working out his next sally, so he just sat and studied the bare wall behind Sweeney's desk and thought. It was like playing chess. The trick was to keep two to three moves ahead.

When he'd figured out his approach, he stubbed out his cigarette in the ashtray and said, "If I recall correctly, Liza is a vindictive little thing."

"Like her mom," Dwyer said promptly.

No denial there, Sean thought as the men dropped back into silence. The only noises Sean could hear were the sounds of cars going by on the road. He briefly thought about adding to what he'd just said and decided against it. Either this approach would work or it wouldn't. He'd know in the next minute or so.

At the end of the minute Dwyer sighed. He picked a shred of tobacco off his lower lip and carefully deposited it in the ashtray. He's milking this for all it's worth, Sean thought as he watched Dwyer. Another minute went by.

Finally Dwyer said, "I heard Liza had a friend called Renee Conner she liked to hang out with over in Stuyvesant."

"You happen to have an address?" Sean asked, careful to keep his voice casual, careful to not give even the slightest indication that he'd won the game.

"Ostrom. Astrom. Something like that."

"Thanks," Sean said.

Dwyer waggled a finger at him. "Just remember you didn't hear this from me."

"What's to hear?" Sean said. "We're just two old guys shootin' the breeze."

"That we are," Dwyer said. "That we are."

"And if you're lying to me I'll come back and hurt you," Sean told him as he levered himself out of the chair and reached for his cane.

Dwyer nodded toward the cane. "With the sword you have in that?"

"Exactly." Sean winked at him. "Don't tell anyone."

"I'm reaching for the phone to call Anne right now."

"And while you're at it, don't forget to call the girls and tell them," Sean said.

"Yeah." Dwyer shifted his position. "They'd be real pleased."

Sean smiled. "They'd never believe it."

"You're right. They wouldn't," Dwyer agreed.

"Too quaint," Sean reflected.

"But very effective."

"Sometimes the old ways are the best ways," Sean said.

"Yes, they are," Dwyer agreed.

"For some reason I find that comforting," Sean said.

"Me too," Dwyer said.

And both men laughed at the thought.

Chapter 10

Marvin was daydreaming about what he and Libby were going to have for dinner—he was hoping she'd make roast chicken en cocotte with plenty of potatoes, carrots, and fennel strewn on the bottom of the pot—when he saw Sean come out of Dwyer's place. Marvin opened the door to get out and help him, but Sean waved him off, telling him he could manage by himself.

"I'm sorry about leaving like that," Marvin said to Sean once he was seated in the hearse. "All that smoke was getting to me."

Sean grunted. "Probably better that you weren't in there anyway. Dwyer might not have talked if you were."

"What did he say?"

"Once I threatened him with my sword cane he spilled the beans."

Marvin turned to stare at Sean.

"Jeez. I'm kidding," Sean said, taking in Marvin's expression. "Honestly." Sean hit the dashboard of the hearse with the flat of his hand. "Now power this thing up. We need to go to Stuyvesant."

"Stuyvesant?" Marvin repeated. "What's in Stuyvesant?"

Sean leaned over, grabbed the handle on the hearse's door, and slammed the door shut. "A possible lead, and I stress the word possible."

"But that's fifteen minutes away," Marvin objected.

"I know that," Sean said. He thought about smoking another cigarette and decided against it. Moderation in all things. Well, actually now that he had gotten old, he didn't have any choice. Before it used to take him a good night's sleep to bounce back from whatever. Now it took him four days—if he was lucky. "I have, after all, lived in this area most of my life."

"But, Mr. Simmons, I thought we were just coming here," Marvin complained, thinking of all the paperwork he had waiting for him back at the funeral home.

These days, dying was a bureaucratic nightmare. The days when you could just dig a hole and plant someone in the ground were long gone. Now there were endless forms to fill out. And cremations? He didn't even want to think about the paperwork for those.

"We were and we did and now we're going there. That's what police work is. Going from point A to point B to point C. And while you're at it," Sean said as he buckled up his seat belt, "see if you can find a listing for a Renee Connor on that new snazzy phone you just bought."

Marvin tried, but didn't come up with anything.

"That's okay," Sean told him. "I really didn't expect you to. No one lists in the phone book anymore. We'll do things the old-fashioned way."

"And what's that?" Marvin asked as he backed out of the parking space.

"By knocking on doors and asking people questions."

"Sounds like fun," Marvin told him.

Sean gave him a sharp look and realized he wasn't kidding. "It is," he told him. "It's one of the things I liked most about my old job."

* * *

Stuyvesant was a small town that numbered five thousand people. The town consisted of a seven-block main street full of nondescript shops, as well as a supermarket, a pharmacy, a small library, a liquor store, and three churches. Most of the houses were traditional wooden colonials with small lawns and slightly larger backyards. With one or two exceptions, none of the houses stood out. None were particularly grand or particularly inexpensive. They were all defiantly middle of the road. Even the plane trees and ginkgos along the side streets were unremarkable.

Stuyvesant's commercial area was a short walk from the Metro-North train station, which made sense since the town largely functioned as a bedroom community for New York City. Unlike Longely, however, the people who lived there tended to be lower and middle management types. Sean thought maybe that was why the town had fewer services and shops than Longely and the ones that the town did have were strictly utilitarian.

He figured that the people in Stuyvesant worked longer hours and came home later, which meant that by the time they got home all they had time to do was have a quick bite to eat, watch a little TV, and go to bed, before getting up the next day and doing it all over again. Recently, Stuyvesant had voted to combine its police department with Longely's as a money-saving initiative, and although the volunteer fire department was safe for the moment, Sean had heard that that too was on the table.

As he and Marvin drove through Stuyvesant Sean reflected that this was a perfect place to hide out. The place was large enough so new people wouldn't stick out and, more importantly, its population tended to come and go quickly, people moving up when they found better-paying jobs. Basically, unless you lived in Stuyvesant there was no reason to go to Stuyvesant. The place was like the Bronx. Everyone knew where it was, but no one wanted to visit.

Marvin found Ostrom Avenue quickly enough. Fortunately for Sean's and Marvin's purposes, the street was only three blocks long. Marvin parked the hearse carefully to avoid getting any dents in it—nothing worse than a banged up or dirty hearse, his father always said—and he and Sean started knocking on doors. Because it was early afternoon, most people weren't home yet and the people who were home hadn't heard of Renee Connor. Sean and Marvin had done almost a block and a half without any positive results and Sean was beginning to tire when they got lucky.

The man who answered the door at 249 was about thirty-five, with stubble on his chin and graying sideburns. He was wearing running pants, a T-shirt, and jogging shoes, and was holding a mug in his hand. The mug was clearly handmade and carried the inscription Best Dad in the World on it. Sean put him down as someone who had lost his job and was now a stay at home dad. That opinion was confirmed when a small boy and a fat yellow labrador came running out and joined the man at the door a moment later.

"Daddy, Daddy," the little boy said, pulling at the hem of the man's shirt. "Abby just ate the roast chicken off the counter."

Sean looked down at Abby. Abby wagged her tail. She did not seem at all repentant. In fact, she seemed rather happy.

"Abby, did you do that?" the man asked.

Abby wagged her tail even harder. Clearly the answer was yes. The man cursed under his breath.

"You said a bad word, Daddy," the little boy cried.

"Listen," the guy told Sean, "sorry, but I gotta go."

"One question," Sean said, not feeling it was necessary

to point out the obvious, which was that since the chicken was already gone, the damage had been done. "I'm looking for Renee Connor. Would you know if she lives around here?"

"She's away somewhere," the man replied. "But there's some lady house-sitting for her."

"Which house is Renee's?" Sean quickly asked.

"The blue and brown one down at the end of the next street. And now," the man told him, "I really have to go."

Sean could hear the man say to his son, "Your mother is going to kill me," as he was closing the door.

"It's all right, Daddy," Sean heard the little boy reply. "Don't worry. I'll tell her it was my fault." Then the door shut and Sean couldn't hear anymore.

"Let's drive down," Marvin suggested.

Which Sean thought was an excellent idea. So that's what they did.

"You think we're going to find Liza in there?" Marvin asked as he parked near the corner of the block the man in the house had indicated.

"We'll see," Sean said as he got out of the hearse.

The house they were looking for was the fourth house from the corner. It was blue and brown with a small lawn that was bordered by a chain-link fence. The house was in good repair, and as they approached the front walk Sean was cheered to see two cars parked in the driveway, one of which he feverently hoped was Liza's.

"What are we going to say to her?" Marvin asked Sean.

"How do you mean?" Sean asked absentmindedly. He noticed, or thought he noticed, that the front door was ever so slightly ajar. Well, sometimes people went into their houses and didn't close the door after themselves firmly enough so the lock didn't catch. Maybe this was one of those cases. Or maybe not.

"I mean," Marvin said, "what are we going to say? Are

we going to march up to her and introduce ourselves and tell her why we're here? It seems to me that if we do that, given the circumstances, she might just take off again."

"We'll see," Sean said as he noticed that the mailbox was full. He was beginning to get a bad feeling about things. "I haven't decided yet."

"I think we need a plan," Marvin countered while he and Sean mounted the porch steps.

"We might not need a plan," Sean said grimly.

Marvin turned to him. His eyes widened. "Why? I don't understand."

"Think about it, Marvin."

Marvin shook his head. "I don't get it."

Sean didn't reply. All of his attention was focused on the house. He slowly approached the door. When he got close enough he reached into the mailbox and took out a couple of pieces of mail and checked the addresses.

"Isn't what you're doing illegal?" Marvin asked nervously.

"Not unless I keep the letters," Sean told him. "Although most people would consider getting rid of junk mail doing them a favor."

"So does Renee Connor live here?" Marvin asked.

"According to Pizza Hut and GEICO she does," Sean said as he slipped the flyers he'd taken out back into the mailbox. "The question," Sean continued, "is whether or not Liza is staying here."

Marvin looked at his watch. "Okay. But if she's not, we can't look anymore today. I have to go back to work."

"I thought you liked doing this kind of thing," Sean said.

"I do," Marvin said with feeling. "It's just—" Then he stopped talking as he watched Sean put his hand up and ring the doorbell. No one answered. He could hear the bell echoing in the house. There was no TV or radio on. The place was silent.

Sean rang the bell again. Still nothing.

"I guess we should go," Marvin said, turning to leave.

Sean shook his head.

"But no one's home."

Sean put out his hand, grasped the doorknob, and pushed. The door opened. This, Sean decided, was not a good sign.

"I don't think we should go in there," Marvin said to him.

"Stay out here if you want," Sean told him as he took a step inside. Suddenly he wasn't tired anymore. His adrenaline had kicked in.

"This is really not a good idea," Marvin continued.

Sean ignored him and took another step inside.

"What if someone's here who's not supposed to be?" Marvin protested.

"Like the big bad wolf?" mocked Sean. He was now in the hallway. The first thing that hit him was how cold the place was. It was the same temperature inside and out. He wondered if the heat was off.

"I just think—" Marvin started to say, but Sean raised his hand and cut him off.

"Enough," he said to him. "I know what you think about what we're doing. You've already told me. At length. But I'm doing it anyway. So what I want to know is whether you're in or you're out. Because if you're out, that's fine. I won't hold it against you. But then wait outside. I can't think when you're going on the way you are. So what's it going to be?"

"In," Marvin said promptly. He recognized a losing battle when he saw one.

"Then let's go," said Sean, continuing on.

"I think I should be in front," Marvin said. "You know . . . because . . ."

"Because why?" Sean asked in a scarily pleasant voice. "Because I'm old? Because I'm senile?"

"That's not what I meant," Marvin protested.

"Then what did you mean?"

"Nothing," Marvin said, taking a step. "It's just that Libby . . ."

"Libby, what?"

"Nothing." Marvin bit his lip. He gave up. Clearly, anything that he said was wrong.

By now he and Sean were in the hallway. Sean noted that the floor plan was typically colonial. A central hall, which led to the stairs, separated the living room and the dining room.

"Anyone home?" Sean called as he stepped into the living room and took a quick look around.

Everything seemed in order. The TV was off. The sofa and the chairs seemed to be where they were supposed to be. The landscapes on the wall were still on their hooks. Sean stepped over and lifted the newspaper off the coffee table and checked the date. It was eight days old.

"Liza might not even be staying here," Marvin pointed out as Sean walked into the dining room.

"Maybe," Sean said, as he shuffled through the pile of mail on the dining room table. "But someone's been bringing in the mail. At least until recently." Sean gave the dining room another quick look before moving on to the kitchen.

"It could be one of the neighbors," Marvin said, forgetting his vow to himself to remain quiet.

Sean grunted as he opened the refrigerator. There was nothing in it except tofu, smoothies, and melon. One thing was for sure—the man in the house with the kid and the dog had been right about a woman staying here—no guy that he knew would be caught dead eating or drinking that stuff.

"Or maybe," Marvin went on, "Liza is here and she just went to the store or is off visiting a neighbor."

Sean sighed. Perhaps if he didn't answer Marvin, he'd get the idea and be quiet—although past experience told him that Marvin didn't pick up on cues very well.

Sean turned to him and in a fit of irritation said, "You're certainly not the strong silent type, are you?"

Marvin turned red. "I'm sorry," he mumbled. "It's just that when I'm nervous I tend to talk a lot."

Sean instantly felt bad. Being nasty to Marvin was like being nasty to a puppy. No matter which way he went, he couldn't win.

"Let's go upstairs, shall we?"

Marvin nodded.

As Sean climbed the stairs he got that feeling he always got in the pit of his stomach when something was about to go wrong. At the top step he looked around. From what he could see, three bedrooms and a bathroom ran off a central hallway. He decided to tackle the farthest bedroom first.

Walking down the hallway, Sean noticed that everything was in place, from the Oriental runner on the middle of the floor to the landscapes on the walls. He entered the first room. It obviously served as Renee's master bedroom. It had a canopy bed, a large chest of drawers, a couple of bamboo nightstands, and a large plasma TV hanging on the wall across from the bed. Everything looked nice and tidy. Marvin stood in the doorway and watched Sean take a linen handkerchief out of his breast pocket and use it to open first the closet and then the dresser drawers.

Marvin pointed to the handkerchief. "I didn't know people had those anymore."

"Got a big supply of them," Sean told him as he finished the second drawer and went on to the third.

"Can we go now?" Marvin asked.

"No," Sean replied, closing the bottom drawer. "We can't."

Marvin shifted his weight from one foot to the other. "May I ask why you're doing this?"

"Because I like to be thorough."

Sean left and walked into the second bedroom with Marvin trailing behind him. Again, nothing seemed to be disturbed. Sean observed that the furniture was a conglomeration of styles instead of a set, leading him to speculate that the pieces had been acquired over a long span of time and that this was the guest bedroom. The bed was made up. The blinds were down. A digital clock radio on the nightstand ticked off the minutes. The only thing out of place was a suitcase sitting on the carpet over by the closet.

Sean went over and opened it. It was empty. Then he walked over to the dresser and opened the drawers. The left side contained enough woman's belongings to tide someone over for a couple of weeks, while the other side was stuffed with more woman's clothing, leading Sean to surmise that Renee had made room for Liza's belongings.

"I bet this is where Liza's sleeping," he said to Marvin.

"If she's here," Marvin said.

"Oh, she's here," Sean replied as he moved on.

Marvin didn't say anything else. He just watched and thought, uncharitably, that Sean had been easier to deal with when he'd been less mobile. When Sean was done with the second bedroom, he and Marvin moved on to the third. That didn't yield any more information than the first two had. The third bedroom had been turned into a hobby room and contained a sewing machine, boxes of material, a table for cutting out fabric, an iron and an ironing board, along with a sofa and a coffee table that was covered with patterns.

"Can we go now?" Marvin asked again, when Sean was through poking around. "There's nothing here."

"After the bathroom," Sean told him.

"There isn't going to be anything in the bathroom," Marvin said.

"We'll see," Sean told him, although privately he thought that Marvin might be correct and that maybe his gut was beginning to fail him after all.

As it turned out, Marvin was wrong.

Chapter 11

Sean saw Liza the moment he walked into the bathroom. There was no missing her. She was lying stretched out, fully clothed in the bathtub. From the looks of the large dried splotch of blood on her white shirt, she'd been shot in the chest. Blood had pooled under her body as well. Marvin was right behind Sean. He looked at Liza's body and cursed silently.

"Okay. You were right," he told Sean. Now he was really sorry they'd come, instead of just a little bit sorry. This was going to mean nothing but trouble.

"Always am," Sean told him, grinning.

"You like this, don't you?" Marvin asked indignantly.

"The fact that she's dead? Hardly. What kind of man do you think I am?"

"That's not what I meant and you know it," Marvin protested.

Sean's grin grew. "Okay. You got me. Yeah. I got to admit that I do. Reminds me of old times. And who knows? We may even learn something. I saw some rubber gloves by the kitchen sink. Why don't you run down and get them for me?"

"What's wrong with your handkerchief?" Marvin asked.

"It's a bit awkward for what I need to do. Come on now. Time's a-wasting."

Marvin didn't move. "We have to call the cops," he told Sean.

Noting that Marvin already had his cell out of his pants pocket, Sean said, "Put that away."

"I can't."

"You can't or you won't?"

"I won't."

"Why is that?" Sean asked as he took in the crime scene.

"What do you mean, why is that? Are you kidding me?" The words just slipped out before Marvin could stop them, but that's what happened when Marvin got flustered. Unlike Sean or Brandon, he was the antithesis of cool. He'd fought that tendency his whole life but there didn't seem to be anything he could do about it. "Because what we're doing is illegal, that's why," Marvin cried.

Sean turned and gave Marvin his full attention. "You're wrong. What we're about to do isn't illegal. Exactly. We're operating in a gray area here," Sean said, which was pretty much true, although he had to admit there was a lot of room for interpretation here and that he was definitely pushing the envelope.

Marvin raised his phone. "I don't like gray."

"Who does?"

"You do."

"I used to uphold the law."

"Not anymore, as far as I can see."

Sean raised his hand. "Hold on a second before you make that call."

Marvin began tapping his toe on the floor. "I'm waiting," he said.

"Okay, most people don't like gray," Sean conceded.

"Unfortunately few things in life are black or white. Most are judgment calls."

"Is that what you wanted to tell me?" Marvin asked. "Because I don't think that's a very good argument. At all."

"No. What I want to tell you is this. If we don't look around now, we won't be able to after the police come. They're certainly not going to allow us access to the crime scene. This is our only shot. We have a responsibility to our client to find out as much as we can."

Marvin frowned. "But aren't the police supposed to tell Duncan's lawyers if they find something that will help with his defense?"

Sean snorted. If he'd been Bernie he would have rolled his eyes. "Yes, and the world could end tomorrow, but neither is very likely. *Supposed to* being the operative words here."

"They really won't tell us?" Marvin asked.

Sean laughed. "Welcome to the real world."

"Didn't you when you were on the force?" Marvin asked.

"I have to confess that most of the time I did, but there were times when I didn't."

"But why?"

Sean shrugged. "A variety of reasons. Because it was expedient. Because I thought it was going to let the bad guy get away. That's why I'm saying what I am." Sean pointed to Liza. "You know, she's not going to tell and I'm not going to tell, and if you don't tell no one is going to know."

"But someone might see us," Marvin said. "Like one of the neighbors."

"They might," Sean conceded. "However, if you noticed, there weren't any cars in any of the neighboring driveways, meaning that no one is home yet."

Marvin hung his head and lowered his phone. "No. I hadn't noticed."

"You should because things like that are important." Sean checked his watch. "Now my guess is that everyone is still at work or making their way to the train station right about now, which gives us a small window of opportunity to finish up here. So the faster you get me those gloves the faster I can do what I'm going to do so we can get out of here."

Marvin nodded at the body in the bathtub with his chin. "Maybe that's not even Liza."

"That," Sean replied, "is what I'm hoping to find out. And while I'm doing that you can look through the laptop on the dining room table and see if there's anything interesting in that."

"I just hope you know what you're doing," Marvin muttered.

"You're right," Sean snapped. "I've never done this before."

"Sorry," Marvin said.

"Apology accepted. So," Sean said after a moment had gone by, "do you want to tell me how long ago you think she died? Do you think you can do that?"

"Of course," Marvin said, affronted that his expertise was being questioned. He stepped forward and studied the body. "I'll tell you one thing. From the look of her, she's been dead for a while," Marvin said, his training taking over.

"How much is 'a while'?" Sean asked him.

Marvin shrugged. "One week at least. Maybe two, would be my best guess. I bet that's why the house is so cold. Keeps the deterioration down to a minimum."

"Kind of like a big cooler," Sean said.

"Something like that," Marvin told him.

"That's a long time for someone to be out of touch," Sean mused. "Especially these days with all the Facebooking and Twittering that's going on. You'd think someone would have sent out the alarm already." He thought back to the conversation he'd had with Dwyer, remembering what Dwyer had said about Liza being out of touch.

"Not if she was angry and had cut off communication with them," Marvin pointed out, echoing Sean's thoughts. "Or maybe she told them she was going away. Then they wouldn't expect to hear from her. Or maybe she didn't have any friends," he suggested. "That's another possibility."

"No. She had friends," Sean said.

"Why do you say that?" Marvin asked.

"Because these days you have friends even when you don't have friends. In any case, I'd be willing to bet that someone in the Corned Beef and Cabbage Club knew where she was because they were responsible for putting her here." And Sean pointed at the bathtub.

"You think?"

"Well, it sure wasn't an alien."

Marvin nodded and went to get the gloves. While he was doing that, Sean took a tissue out of the box on the top of the toilet tank and used it to open the medicine cabinet. There wasn't anything of interest in it. Judging from the contents, Renee was evidently subject to migraines and sinus infections and owned a large collection of perfumes and an even larger array of face creams. Looking at them made Sean glad he was a guy. Being a female seemed way too much work. Marvin came back up with the gloves just as Sean was closing the medicine cabinet door.

"Find anything?" he asked Sean.

Sean slipped the rubber gloves on. "Nope. Don't touch the laptop with your hands," he cautioned. "Use a paper towel."

"What am I looking for?" Marvin asked.

"Something of interest," Sean repeated, although he didn't have the vaguest idea what that could be.

"Like what?"

"Like you'll know it when you see it. Now get going. The faster we get this done, the faster we can get out of here."

"I'm on it," Marvin said, and hurried out of the bathroom and down the steps.

The moment Marvin left the room, Sean slowly and carefully lowered himself until he was kneeling next to the bathtub. He only hoped he'd be able to get up again as he leaned over and slipped his hand into the woman's pants pocket. He came out with a thin bright pink wallet, with a picture of Cinderella on it. A kid's wallet, he thought as he flipped through it.

He pulled out her driver's license. Well, one thing was for sure. The woman was definitely Liza. Not that he had really thought the body lying in the bathtub would be anyone else. That would have been too much of a coincidence and Sean didn't believe in coincidences.

According to the information listed on the license Liza was twenty-seven, one hundred twenty-five pounds, and five feet six inches tall. She'd listed her permanent address as her mother's house. Sad. The wallet also contained two credit cards and a bunch of business and appointment cards.

Sean glanced at them before putting them back in Liza's wallet. She'd had an appointment with the dentist to get her teeth cleaned next week and an appointment to get her hair cut the week after that.

She evidently got her morning coffee at Bruegger's because she was carrying one of their punch cards, and she rode the subway because she was carrying a Metro card, which told Sean that she got down to the city on a fairly regular basis. She didn't have too much cash on her—but she did have two hundred dollars, which told Sean that robbery hadn't been the motive. She was also still wearing her watch and her jewelry, which consisted of a diamond tennis bracelet and two smallish diamond ear studs. Another indication that this hadn't been a burglary gone bad. He put everything back in Liza's wallet the way he found it and replaced it in her pants pocket.

He found Liza's cell in her other pocket and took that out. It was a smart phone, which meant it had a lot of stuff stored on it, and for the first time Sean was grateful to his daughters for making him get one, because now he would know how this one worked. He wished he could keep it and go through the information at his leisure, but his conscience wouldn't let him do that. He was pushing things as it was. Taking evidence from a crime scene was a felony and he wasn't prepared to go that far.

And then he thought of the next best thing. He got out his phone and used the camera on it to photograph Liza's contact list, texts, and most recent calls. He'd never used the camera on his phone before, but he figured that that should work. Hopefully. When he was done, he put his phone away and replaced Liza's phone in her pocket, after which he stood looking at the crime scene until he'd memorized every detail. Then he went downstairs.

"Did you find anything?" he asked Marvin when he got back into the study.

Marvin beamed. "I most certainly did," he said.

He was about to tell Sean exactly what it was that he had found when there was a loud noise. The front door swung open and the Longely police poured in with the chief of police at the helm. Well, three policemen poured in, to be exact, but given the circumstances, Sean reflected that it was enough.

Chapter 12

Marvin looked at the police and then he looked at Sean. "You told me we'd be fine," he said reproachfully.

Sean shrugged his shoulders. "Trust me. We will be."

"I'm not so sure about that," said Lucy, aka Lucas Broadbent, head of the Longely police force and Sean's mortal enemy. He leered at Sean. "No. I'm not sure at all."

"A pleasure to see you, Lucas," Sean said. "As always."

"A pleasure to see you too, Sean," Lucas replied.

"I have to say I'm impressed with the speed you got here," Sean told him.

Lucas gave a modest smile. "We strive to be the best."

"And the fastest."

Lucas's smile grew. "Especially in this case."

"I find it interesting that you got here with such rapidity. May I ask how that happened?"

Lucas patted his belly, which Sean noticed had grown considerably larger since the last time he'd seen its owner. "Good police work."

Sean almost said *What are you, delusional?* but bit the words back in time. "Meaning?" he said instead.

Now Lucas was out-and-out grinning. "Not that I have

to tell you, but I will because that's the kind of guy I am. We got a tip."

"A tip?" Sean repeated.

"That's what I just said. A tip. Getting deaf in your old age?"

"Only to fiddle-faddle."

Lucas flushed. "What's that supposed to mean?"

"Nothing," Sean said. "Go on."

"We got a tip that there was a body in the house and we came to investigate. And here we are and here you are. Now it's your turn to explain why you're here."

"Simple," Sean said. "We were following up a lead on the Duncan case. As I'm sure you are aware, we've been hired by Bree Nottingham to help in the investigation."

"Why, I'll never know," Lucy said. "I told her not to waste her money. But that's another issue."

Sean ignored the jibe and went on. "We knocked, but there was no answer and then I noticed that the door was ajar. . . ."

"And you had nothing to do with that?"

"Absolutely not," Sean replied with as much indignation as he could manage, although he had been fairly good at jimmying locks open in the past. "Check the latch if you want. . . ."

"Don't worry. We will," Lucy assured him.

"Anyway, as I was saying," Sean said, raising his voice, "I pushed the door open and we went inside."

"And then?" Lucas said.

"And then nothing. We called but no one answered."

Lucas raised an eyebrow. "At which point most people would have left," he said. "Or called the police."

"I was going to," Sean lied. "But I was afraid Liza had come to harm so we continued on."

"How noble," Lucy said sarcastically.

"I think so." Sean smiled complacently and smoothed out the front of the V-necked beige cardigan he was wearing. "Risking life and limb and all of that. I was thinking that Marvin and I might deserve a departmental medal. Anyway," Sean hurried along before Lucy could reply, "Marvin and I had just gone upstairs and discovered Liza's body. We were about to call you when you came through the door, saving us the trouble."

"Imagine that," Lucy snapped.

Sean kept smiling. "Yes. Just imagine. I must say that was very thoughtful of you."

Lucy's jaw muscles expanded. He stared at Sean. Sean stared at Lucy. Marvin looked at both of them and wished he were someplace else. Anyplace else.

"I could have you arrested," Lucy told Sean.

"For what? Trespassing?"

"For interfering with a criminal investigation."

"Oh, please." Sean made an impolite noise. "You need to calm down. I told you we just got here," he said.

"I don't believe you."

Sean put his hand over his heart. "I'm crushed."

"Good. You're also arrested." Lucy nodded in the direction of one of the uniforms standing in the hallway. "Cuff these two," he said, pointing to Sean and Marvin. "And take them to the station house and book them."

Sean held up his hand. "You don't want to do anything hasty now," he told Lucy as the uniform moved toward Marvin, who at this moment was sporting a deer caught in the headlights look.

Lucy smirked. "Oh. But I think I do."

"You have to prove your charges," Sean told him. "If you don't it's not going to look good."

"For who?"

"For you."

"Explain that to me," Lucy asked, clearly enjoying himself.

"With pleasure. Considering Bree hired us, she might be upset about what she will undoubtedly see as gratuitous interference with our investigation," Sean replied. "And if Bree gets upset, then the mayor and the council board will also get upset, and if they get upset . . .Well, these days they're cutting municipal services everywhere. Look at what happened in Stuyvesant. After all, you don't want to look like a twit."

"Pardon me?" Lucy said. "Am I hearing correctly? Did you just insult me?"

"Not at all. I didn't say that you were a twit," Sean replied. "I just said you would look like one."

Lucy flushed and took a step forward.

"Not that you are," Sean said quickly. "I never meant to imply that. But you know what people are like. Always thinking the worst."

By now Lucy was practically nose to nose with Sean. "We'll just see what's what," Lucy said. "I want to know what you took out of here."

Sean did a fairly good imitation of wide-eyed innocence. "What's there to take?" he asked.

Marvin's head swiveled back and forth watching first one man and then the other. He felt as if he was at a tennis match.

"Empty your pockets," Lucy commanded.

Sean shrugged and did as told. "Satisfied?" he asked Lucy as Lucy looked down at the contents of Sean's pockets, which were now sitting on the dining room table.

"No. I'm not," Lucy said as he picked up each item, scrutinized it, and put it down.

Sean knew this was all for show; the only thing Lucy was good at was looking as if he knew what he was doing. But there was always a possibility that Sean could be wrong. He forced himself to breathe normally when Lucy picked up his cell phone by reminding himself that Lucy was even less technologically adept than he was and therefore could not have possibly figured out what Sean had done with his camera.

Lucy turned to Marvin. "Now you," he ordered.

Marvin hastily complied.

"Can we go now?" Sean asked as he took his stuff back.

Lucy pushed Marvin's belongings back to him. "Yeah. Get out of here. But if I find anything missing . . ."

"I know," Sean said, finishing the sentence for him. "You'll come and have me arrested."

"That's one hundred percent correct," Lucy said. Then he told the policeman to let them go and turned and went up the stairs.

"The question," Sean said to Marvin once they were out the door, "is who supplied the tip."

"No," Marvin countered. "The question is why I let you talk me into these things in the first place."

Sean clapped him on the back. "Simple. Because it provides a degree of excitement your life lacks. Plus I'm your girlfriend's dad, so you need to be nice to me."

"Yeah. But then I catch hell from Libby for allowing you to get into these situations."

"Just don't tell her," Sean suggested. "I know that I won't."

"You may have a point," Marvin conceded.

"Too bad I didn't get to see what you found on the laptop," Sean said, switching topics. "All we needed was five minutes more."

Now it was Marvin's turn to grin. "You can see it. I copied the files."

"With what?"

Marvin dug out his thumb drive. "With this."

"It's so tiny," Sean marveled.

Marvin's grin got bigger. "It's large enough to store what we need to."

They started walking to Marvin's hearse.

"See," Sean said, leaning on his cane. "I told you things would work out."

"They nearly didn't," Marvin objected.

"Piffle."

"Piffle?"

"Yes, piffle. It's an old word that means nonsense."

"How old are we talking here?"

"Before you were born old. Now tell me about the files," Sean urged.

"I think I'd rather you see them. I have a laptop in the car," Marvin said, anticipating Sean's next comment.

Sean didn't say anything, but he was beginning to gain respect for Marvin's technological prowess.

A moment later, both men were sitting in the hearse. Sean rolled down the window and lit a cigarette. He figured he'd earned it. He watched curiously as Marvin reached under the seat, pulled out his laptop, opened it, and inserted the flash drive in it. A few seconds later the Flash 'n' Go icon came up on the screen. Marvin hit the file called Watch This and turned the screen toward Sean.

"Have a look," he said quietly.

Sean did. He was looking at pictures of Liza and Liam having sex. Marvin hit the mouse again. There was a picture of Connor and Liza. Next came a picture of Patrick and Liza. As Sean looked at them he was grateful to Marvin for showing him the photos in private. He would have found it embarrassing to see them with his daughters.

"Busy girl," was Sean's only comment.

"The pics could be Photoshopped," Marvin suggested.

"Meaning?" Sean asked.

"They might not be real, Mr. Simmons."

"Wouldn't that be hard to do?" asked Sean.

"Not really." And Sean listened while Marvin explained how it could be done. "Just a thought," he continued. Then he said, "I wonder if Duncan knows," as he logged out and shut down the computer.

"Only one way to find out," Sean said as he focused on the ambulance pulling up next to Renee Connor's house. "Ask him."

A moment later, two men got out and pulled out a gurney. Sean told Marvin to go. They didn't need to be there to see Liza's body carried out.

"This isn't good for Duncan, is it?" Marvin asked as he put the hearse in gear.

"Probably not," Sean allowed. "Probably not."

Chapter 13

Bernie, Libby, and Clyde were waiting for Sean and Marvin when they walked through the door into the flat. When they did, everyone stood up and clapped.

"Good going," Clyde told Sean and Marvin.

"You heard?" Sean asked Clyde.

"Everyone at the station heard," Clyde said as he, Bernie, and Libby sat back down.

"I thought we were going to get arrested," Marvin said.

Sean pointed to Marvin. "He's exaggerating."

"Somehow, I don't think so," Libby said.

"The fact that you didn't must have made Lucy very sad," Clyde reflected. "I don't think I've seen Lucy more excited since the time when he caught the Hernandez brothers stealing steaks out of the Elks Lodge."

Sean leaned his cane against his armchair and lowered himself into it while Marvin plonked himself down on the sofa next to Libby.

"You should have warned us," Sean told Clyde.

"I couldn't. I left my cell at home." Clyde pushed his glasses back up the bridge of his nose. "Besides, I knew you'd be all right. You always are."

Libby got up and poured some coffee for her dad and for Marvin.

"So who called in the tip?" Sean asked Clyde after he'd put cream and three teaspoons of sugar in his cup and stirred everything around.

Clyde took a bite of his linzer cookie. "Not a clue." He chewed and swallowed. He loved Libby and Bernie's linzer cookies, but then he loved their lemon bars and brownies too. When it came down to it, he couldn't think of a cookie that they made that he didn't like. "Lucy was in his office when he got a call on his cell and the next thing I know he's running around, yelling for everyone to follow him, and heading out the door."

Sean leaned forward and took a sip of his coffee. Perfect. Libby and Bernie's coffee had spoiled him for anyone else's. "What was Lucy saying?"

"Just that there was something important and he needed three men."

"And you don't have an idea of who made the call?" Sean asked.

Clyde took another bite of his linzer cookie and flicked a crumb off the leg of his pants. "None. Could have been a baboon from Barbados for all I know. Like I said, Lucy took the call in his office. I'll see what I can find out, but I'm not very hopeful. Maybe he mentioned something to one of the guys on the way over."

"Will any of them talk to you?"

Clyde shrugged. "Minor might. He owes me for covering his ass when I caught him downing a shot at the Dome when he was on duty."

Sean put his mug down and ran his finger over its rim. "It would be interesting to know," he mused. "Very interesting indeed."

Libby took Marvin's hand and gave it a quick squeeze. "Are you okay?" she asked him. "Because you look a little bit upset."

Sean made a noise somewhere between a snort and a sneeze. "Of course, he's fine. Give him a little credit. He's not a baby."

Marvin squeezed Libby's hand in return. "No. I'm okay. Really."

Sean raised his hand up. "See. I told you." He pointed to himself. "What about me? Why don't you ask whether or not I'm fine?"

Bernie rolled her eyes. "Come on, Dad. We can see that you're okay." She got up and poured her dad some more coffee.

"Maybe not. Maybe someone is trying to set me up," Sean said as he took another gulp of coffee and put his cup down.

"Dad, don't you think you may be overstating?" Bernie asked.

"Maybe. Probably. But you have to admit that Lucy showing up there and then is suggestive."

Bernie folded her legs into a lotus position. "Of something."

"It could be coincidence," Libby suggested.

Sean just turned and looked at her.

"Right," Libby said. "I forgot to whom I was talking."

At which point Clyde cleared his throat and said, "It might be more profitable if we thought about this logically. We should ask ourselves who would do that and why. I mean, with all due respect, I don't see what this scenario was meant to accomplish."

Sean stretched his right leg out and massaged his knee. It was starting to ache. "I have to admit I don't either. But I have a hard time believing the timing was a coincidence. I mean the body is lying there for a week, possibly two, and Lucy gets the call now?"

Marvin put in his two cents. "Maybe someone was watching the house and decided to take advantage of our presence."

"Marvin, we didn't see anyone."

"That doesn't mean no one was there, Mr. Simmons."

Clyde nodded. "It is a better explanation, Sean."

Bernie unfolded her legs and stretched them out. For some reason her new heels were killing her hamstrings. "All I know," she said, "is that I was afraid I was going to have to bail you two out."

"For what?" Sean scoffed. "Trespassing? Don't be silly."

"I'm sure Lucy could come up with something better than that," Clyde observed. "Like interfering with an investigation. That's a felony."

"A Class E felony, Clyde."

"It's still a felony, Sean."

"He wanted to," Sean said, laughing at the memory. "But he couldn't make it stick."

Marvin reached over for a cookie. "I think it was because he was scared of Bree."

"Everyone is scared of Bree around here," Libby said. "She has more power than God."

Clyde chuckled. "Or at least the mayor. Lucy must have been furious."

Sean started massaging his other knee. He was going to have to build his quads up again. "Well, he wasn't a happy camper. I will say that."

Clyde took a final bite of his linzer cookie and wiped his hand on the napkin in front of him. "I wish I could have been there to see that." Then he changed topics. "So, Sean, Marvin, tell us what you found."

And they did. Marvin told them about the files he'd found on Liza's computer and Sean described Liza's body and passed around his cell phone with the photos he'd taken of Liza's texts and the last three calls she'd made. It turned out that none were particularly notable. One was to her friend Renee Connor, one was to her stepdad, and one was to Duncan. The two voice mails on Liza's phone were similarly unhelpful. One message was from her hair salon and the other was from her Avon representative.

"Probably calling to tell her to pick up her order," Libby said.

"Or place one," Bernie added. "We should call and check these numbers out." It turned out they were as represented. Liza had wanted to change her haircut appointment and she'd ordered some moisturizer from Avon that had to be picked up.

"She didn't seem to have much of a social life," Bernie observed, after she'd hung up. "What did she do for a living anyway?"

"Nothing, as far as I know," Sean replied. He ran his hand over his face. The day had tired him out more than he thought. "She lived off her trust fund. Or at least she had been before everything went south."

Clyde took a quick glance at his watch. He had to get going soon, so he could pick up Mrs. Clyde at the mall. They had a big sale on kitchen equipment, although why his wife continued to buy that kind of stuff was beyond him. If she wasn't the worst cook in the world, she was certainly one of the top contenders. Not that he'd ever say that to her.

Sean noticed Clyde glancing at his watch. "Do you have to get going?"

"Got to pick up the missus at the mall. She's buying one of those fancy new coffee makers, the kind that grinds the coffee and brews it and probably drinks it for you as well."

"Do you think it will help?" Libby asked him. Mrs. Clyde was well known for her ability to burn coffee.

"Nope," Clyde said. "Not in the least. But if it'll make her feel better, who am I to stand in the way? She has many fine attributes. Unfortunately, cooking isn't one of them." Clyde reached over and grabbed another cookie. Talking about his wife's cooking ability or lack thereof had made him hungry. He turned to Sean when he was done. "You think Liza's and Sweeney's deaths are related?" Clyde asked.

"Hard to think they wouldn't be," Sean answered.

"That's what I'm thinking too," Clyde agreed. "Too much of a coincidence otherwise."

Libby leaned over and poured Marvin a little more coffee. She knew he liked it and she wanted to make sure he had all he needed. "But it could be."

"Yes, it could be," her dad said. "But it probably isn't."

"So we're assuming that the same person who killed Sweeney also killed Liza?" Bernie asked.

Sean and Clyde both nodded.

"I think that's a good supposition to work with," Clyde said.

Sean leaned back in his armchair. "Both murders happened in the same time frame. In addition, both are similar in nature," he said.

"I don't see how," Bernie replied.

"Think about it," Sean urged.

"I still don't see it," Bernie said after a minute had gone by and she'd given up.

"Neither do I," Libby added. "So what do you think it all means?" she asked her dad a minute later.

Sean nodded to Bernie and Libby. "Why don't you two tell me?"

"Dad, it would be faster if you told us," Bernie said.

"I know it would," Sean answered. "But I really want you girls to try. It's good practice. And besides, it's more fun."

"For who?" Libby asked.

"For me," Sean said.

Bernie and Libby both grinned. They had played the evidence game with their dad as long as they could remember, much to their mother's dismay. She thought that crime scenes were not things one discussed with young girls. But

Bernie and Libby had always loved the idea of figuring things out—especially when their dad gave them a nickel for each correct conclusion they reached—and the habits of thought they'd learned had stood them in good stead ever since.

Libby closed her eyes for a minute as she marshaled everything she'd heard from Marvin, Sean, and Clyde. A moment later she was ready.

"You said the door was open," Libby began.

"Very slightly ajar," Sean said.

"And it wasn't forced open?" Bernie asked.

"Nope," Sean said. "No sign of forced entry."

"So that means that Liza opened the door to whoever killed her," Libby said.

"That is correct," Sean said.

"It could have been a salesman," Libby said, thinking out loud.

"Or someone who was asking directions," Sean said. "Or a neighbor."

"But that won't get us anywhere," Libby continued. "So let's say she opened the door to someone she knew."

"Someone who knew she was staying there," Bernie corrected. "Since it wasn't her house. Has anyone gotten in touch with Renee Connor, by the way?"

Clyde answered. "She's on a cruise in the Hawaiian Islands. She's flying home tonight."

Marvin looked down at his hands, then looked back up. "Not a nice homecoming," he observed. "That's for sure."

"Not at all," Bernie agreed. "I think I'd want to sell the house if that had happened in mine. But then, who would want to buy it?"

"You'd be surprised," Clyde responded.

"Would you?" Libby asked him.

"Yeah," Clyde replied after he'd thought about it for a minute. "If I could get it for a better price."

Bernie laughed and brushed a lock of hair off her face.

"Well, I guess we can count Renee out," she said, getting back to the matter at hand. "Being as she was on a cruise and all. Therefore we're talking about a friend or a relative or a coworker who Liza invited into the house."

Sean leaned back. "Well, she didn't work so she didn't have coworkers, and according to Dwyer and you, she didn't have lots of friends."

Bernie snagged a cookie and ate half. "Maybe she didn't have friends, maybe she had customers," she said, thinking about the pics on Liza's laptop.

"Bernie, we don't know that," Libby protested.

"You're right, Libby, we don't. But Brandon might." And Bernie dug out her phone and called him. "Nope," she said when she hung up. "I was wrong. No customers. Not too many friends either, as far as Brandon knows."

"So we're all agreed she wasn't a social butterfly," Sean said.

Marvin stifled a yawn. Being with Libby's dad always wore him out. "Maybe she was blackmailing the guys from the Corned Beef and Cabbage Club," he suggested. "Has anyone considered that she might have been using the pics on her laptop for that. It could be a, 'give me money or I'll post them on the Web' kind of deal."

Libby beamed at Marvin as if he'd discovered the laws of the universe. "Now that's a definite possibility."

Marvin beamed back.

"Let's stick to the agenda," Sean said.

"There's an agenda?" Bernie asked her dad.

"Yes, Bernie. There is." Sometimes Sean felt as if he were herding cats. "There's a lot to go over and we need to do it in a systematic way. And right now we need to talk about how Liza was killed. Then we can go on to other stuff. Agreed?"

"Agreed," Libby said.

There was a brief pause, then Bernie said, "You said she

was shot in the bathtub in the second floor bathroom, right, Dad?"

"Yes, I did," Sean said.

"Were there any signs of a struggle?" Bernie asked.

"None," Marvin said. "At least none that I could see, right, Mr. Simmons?"

"Right, Marvin." Sean leaned forward a little. "Everything was where it was supposed to be. There were no signs of a fight in the house. And it didn't look as if anything had been searched. Or if it had been, whoever did it was certainly very careful about it."

"And Liza was fully dressed?" Bernie asked.

"Down to her shoes," Sean said. "And none of her items of apparel look as if they'd been touched in any way. Her hair was combed. Her makeup was on."

Libby chewed on her cuticle for a moment, then said, "To state the obvious, people don't usually get in the bathtub with their clothes on."

Sean smiled. He could see that his daughters were getting it. "No, they don't. So what would make her do that?"

Bernie grinned. "Besides a photo shoot."

Sean laughed. "Yes, Bernie, besides a photo shoot."

"Well, the obvious possibility is that someone had a gun, pulled it out, marched her upstairs, and shot her."

"That's one possibility," Sean said.

"There's another?" Libby asked.

"I think so," Sean answered.

"What?" Bernie asked. "That Liza took Ambien and sleepwalked herself into the tub?"

"Something like that," Sean said.

"How something like that?" Clyde asked.

"Well, I can see a scenario where Liza and her visitor sat down and had some coffee or tea or soda and that the visitor doped it up and led her upstairs, put her in the tub, and then shot her."

"Why do something like that?" Bernie said.

Sean shrugged. "I'm guessing to make her more compliant. So she would do whatever anyone told her to."

"Kind of karmic with her putting the stuff in Duncan's beer and all," Libby said.

"Isn't it, though?" Sean said. "When I looked at Liza's body the thing that really struck me was that she was so neat. She was just lying there and the angle of the wounds suggests that someone shot her looking down at her."

"Whoever killed her could have made her lie down," Libby suggested.

"That's a possibility too," Sean admitted. "Although my gut tells me to go with the second scenario. People always freak out at the end. It's human nature."

"The killer could have shot her and then neatened her up," Marvin said, thinking of what they did in the funeral home.

Sean stopped massaging his hands and took another sip of coffee. By now it was lukewarm, but he liked it that way. "I guess we'll know after the ME gets through, right, Clyde?"

Clyde put on a long face. "Hey," he groused. "It's not as if this is my case. I have to poke around to get to see the report. I could get in trouble."

"You want brownies?" Libby said.

"You think I can be bribed?" Clyde asked in a tone of mock horror.

"Most definitely," Bernie answered.

Clyde smiled. "Mocha brownies with cashews and you're on."

Sean shook his head. "You always were a cheap date, Clyde."

Clyde put his hand on his heart. "You mean I could

have held out for brownies and ginger snaps? I want to renegotiate."

"Too late, Clyde," Libby said. "A deal is a deal. Now, to get back to where we were . . ."

"Which is where?" Marvin asked. "I think I lost track."

Libby patted Marvin on the knee. "We're at the place where someone one way or another got Liza into the bathtub and shot her. Why the bathtub?"

"Less chance of leaving DNA around," Clyde said promptly.

"And," Marvin added, "if you lower the house temperature the bathtub stays colder and that helps preserve the body."

"Also," Sean said, "the bathroom helps muffle the sound of the shots. And you've got water right there to wash up. Very convenient."

Bernie got up and started walking around. "And nothing was taken."

"Nothing that we know about," Sean told her. "Of course, we don't know what wasn't there so it's hard to say."

Libby dug into the pocket of her shirt, got out two chocolate kisses, offered one to Marvin and took the other. Then she unwrapped it and popped it in her mouth. After she was done savoring it, she said, "Here's what I don't understand. Liza had those pictures on her laptop and the laptop was in plain sight. But no one took it. Doesn't that prove it wasn't one of the Corned Beef and Cabbage guys?" Libby asked.

"Not necessarily," Bernie said. "Maybe they didn't know. Or"—Bernie raised a finger—"maybe they didn't care."

"I would think they'd care," Clyde said.

Bernie rebuttoned the top button of her blouse. "Given the tenor of the times, maybe, maybe not. Maybe Liza wasn't trying to blackmail the guys. Maybe the pics were just a hobby for her."

"Some hobby," Clyde muttered.

"Well, some people hunt animals and mount their heads on the wall. And others . . . well, others do what Liza did."

At that moment Clyde's cell phone rang. He took it out of his pocket and answered it. Sean could tell from the expression on Clyde's face that it wasn't Mrs. Clyde. He kept on saying "yup." Then he said "thanks" and hung up.

"That was one of the ADAs," he said. "He called to tell me they're thinking of charging Duncan with Liza's murder."

"I was afraid of that," Sean murmured. "What's their basis?"

"The photos on Liza's laptop. Lucy is claiming Duncan killed her out of jealousy."

Sean gave a sigh of relief. "That's not going to hold."

"Have they arrested Duncan yet?" Bernie asked Clyde.

Clyde shook his head. "Lucy is in there debating it with the ADA even as we speak."

Sean steepled his fingers together. "I'll bet anything it's a ploy to get Duncan and his lawyer to the table."

"You think?" Bernie said.

"I know," Sean replied.

"All I know," Libby said, "is that Bree will not be pleased."

Bernie chimed in with, "That's putting it mildly. I think she's going to want answers."

"We all want answers," Sean said.

"Especially Duncan," Marvin said.

"Assuming he didn't do it," Clyde said.

Marvin looked around the room. "Well, we are, aren't we?"

"What?" Sean asked him.

"Assuming he didn't kill anyone."

"I guess we are," Libby said, thinking back to her talk with Duncan. She thought he was an arrogant SOB, but he wasn't a murderer.

"We're hoping he didn't kill anyone," Bernie said.

Sean nodded toward Bernie and Libby. "You should go talk to Duncan now. He'll be upset and it's always easier to get someone to talk when they're in that state."

"I guess you're right," Libby conceded as she saw her carefully constructed workday vanishing.

Sean raised an eyebrow, but didn't say anything. He didn't have to. Bernie stood up.

"We're on it, Dad. Come on, Libby. Let's go." And without even looking to see if her sister was following her, she got up and walked out the door.

"We have two chocolate cakes and seven pies to make," Libby called after her, feeling a momentary stab of resentment. Sometimes she thought she was the only one who remembered they had a business to run.

Bernie's voice floated back up. "The crusts are made. I'll get Amber to make the filling and put the pies in the oven. She can't possibly mess them up."

Libby thought that was an optimistic statement if she'd ever heard one, but she got up and followed Bernie out. This was the last thing she wanted to do, but she really didn't want to fight with her dad either. And anyway, if they hurried, she might be back in time to take the pies out of the oven.

Chapter 14

Bernie kicked the van up to forty miles an hour, making it to Bree's place in fifteen minutes flat, which was definitely some kind of record. She'd just finished parking the van in front of the guest house and she and Libby had exited the van and were walking up the path to the front door when Duncan came out.

"I don't have time to talk to you now," he said to both of them. "I have to be at my lawyer's office stat."

"To talk about Liza?" Bernie asked.

"That's right. Now if you'll excuse me . . ."

"My dad found the body," Libby told him.

Duncan snorted. "That's what my lawyer said. I thought you guys were supposed to be on my side."

"We are," Libby told him.

"It's not working out that way. Your dad goes in, finds the body and now I may be charged with a second homicide. Good work. If I were my aunt I'd make you give back the money."

"Hah," Bernie said. "That's one of the stupidest things I've ever heard anyone say. It wasn't as if Dad did it on purpose," Bernie said indignantly. "He wanted to talk to Liza. Believe me, the last thing he wanted to find was her body. It just made trouble for him," she said as she scrutinized Duncan.

He looked as if he was going to work. Freshly shaven, Duncan was impeccably turned out in an expensive charcoal gray pin-striped suit, pale pink shirt, and a pink and gray paisley patterned tie. If Duncan hadn't told her, Bernie never would have guessed he was going to see his lawyer.

"What are you looking at?" he demanded.

"You," Bernie replied.

Duncan put his hands on his hips. "Meaning?"

"Well, it occurs to me that you don't seem very sad about Liza," Bernie noted. "Or upset."

"I'm not," Duncan growled. "Not now. She made me the laughingstock of my friends."

"So you knew what she was doing?" Libby asked.

Duncan shook his head. "No. Not until my lawyer told me."

Libby unbuttoned her parka. It had gotten warmer as the day wore on. "And none of your friends let on?"

Duncan looked incredulous. "Of course they didn't. Do you think I would have stayed with her if they had?"

Bernie shrugged. "Maybe. Some guys get off on that kind of thing."

Duncan pointed at himself. "Well, I am most definitely not one of them."

"So you really didn't know?" Libby said, watching him carefully.

Duncan took two steps. By now he was almost nose to nose. "What are you, deaf?"

Libby held her ground. "No. Just making sure."

Duncan's eyes narrowed. He took a step back. "And do you believe me?"

"As a matter of fact, I do," Libby said.

Duncan laid his hand on his chest. "Be still my heart. I am so relieved."

Bernie kicked a small rock off the path. "Wow, Duncan. You really don't play well with others, do you?"

Duncan smiled despite himself and turned toward her. "I take it you believe me too, Bernie?"

Bernie shrugged her shoulders. "I'm a harder sell than my sister. I'm still trying to decide. So when was the last time you saw Liza?" she asked.

"I already told you—we went home together, and I passed out, and when I woke up she was gone."

"So you say, Duncan."

Duncan shot his cuffs. "Yes, Bernie. I do."

"And you didn't try and call her?"

"No, Bernie. I didn't."

"Why not?"

Duncan looked down for a moment, then looked back up. "Frankly, Bernie?"

"Yes, Duncan. Frankly."

Duncan sighed, then said, "Because, if you really want to know, I was relieved I didn't have to deal with her anymore. She was becoming a pain in the ass."

Libby leaned forward slightly. "How so?" she asked.

Duncan scratched his chin. "How can I say this nicely?"

"Just say it, Duncan," Bernie ordered.

He straightened his tie. "Fine, then. It's simple. Liza saw us as having a future together and I didn't. And I think that made her nuts."

"Did she take pictures of you too?" Bernie asked.

"Pictures?" Duncan acted surprised. "What pictures?"

"The kind of pictures that are on her laptop," Libby said.

Duncan's eyes widened. He looked genuinely puzzled. "I don't know what you're talking about," he said.

Libby looked at Bernie and Bernie looked at Libby. Bernie looked at Duncan again. He was looking at his watch.

"Listen," he said. "If you're not going to tell me, I really have to go. I have to be in Westerly in half an hour."

"What did you think we were talking about back there when you said that Liza had made a fool of you?" Bernie asked Duncan.

Two red dots appeared on Duncan's cheeks. His eyes narrowed. "I thought you were talking about the fact that Liza slept around with everyone, including my friends, and that evidently I was the last to know."

"No," Bernie said. "We were talking about the sex pictures Liza had on her laptop."

"Of who?"

"Of whom," Bernie corrected.

Duncan waved his hand impatiently. "Who cares? Who are you talking about?"

Libby stepped in before the situation degenerated to a grammatical free-for-all. "We're talking about your friends," she said. "Liza had pictures of her and your friends on her laptop. They were all engaged in . . . inappropriate behavior."

"As in having sex," Bernie added helpfully.

Duncan wrinkled his forehead. "You're saying the Corned Beef and Cabbage Club had group sex?" he asked incredulously.

"No," Libby cried. "Individually."

Duncan shook his head. "By themselves? That's even worse."

"No, no, no," Libby said, stamping her foot in frustration. "Connor, Patrick, and Liam all had sex with Liza at different times and she photographed them doing it. I can't believe you didn't know that," Libby finished.

"And I can't believe it either," Bernie said.

"How could I have known, Bernie?" Duncan asked.

"Simple. You looked on her laptop. The pics were on her desktop."

"I didn't look."

"Never?" Bernie asked.

"No. Never."

"I find that difficult to believe," Bernie said, thinking of the times she had casually glanced at Brandon's laptop when he wasn't around. It wasn't anything she was proud of, but it was hard to resist, in the same way that checking out people's medicine cabinets was.

Duncan frowned. "Believe what you want, but I never did. Liza never brought it with her when she came over to my place. I mean she wasn't the kind of person who carried her laptop around."

"And you never went to her place?" Bernie asked.

"What? Are you kidding me?" Duncan asked in disbelief. "Give me a break. She lived in the basement of her parents' house. I mean it had a separate entrance and all, but there was no way I was going over there. And you know what? I bet none of the guys knew they were having their pictures taken, because that's the kind of person Liza was. A sneaky bitch." He grinned. "Serves them right."

"Who?" asked Libby.

"My so-called friends." Duncan bracketed the word friends with his fingers. Then he checked the time on his cell phone again. "Now I really have to go. This has not been a pleasure."

And before Bernie and Libby could say anything else, Duncan hopped in his car and whizzed out of the driveway, turned right on the road, and lost himself in the oncoming traffic.

Chapter 15

"Do you believe him?" Libby asked Bernie once Duncan's taillight had vanished into the traffic.

"About the pictures?"

"Yes, Bernie. About the pictures."

Bernie folded her arms across her chest. "You know, Libby, I almost think that I do. It'll be interesting to talk to the remaining members of the crew and hear what they have to say."

"But not now," Libby said, more forcefully than she intended. "We have to get back to the shop."

"We will," Bernie said as she turned and studied the guest house.

Watching Bernie study the cottage, Libby knew exactly what her sister was thinking. "Absolutely not," she said.

"Absolutely not, what?" Bernie said, playing the innocence card.

Libby pointed to the ADT sign that was on the lawn in front of the main house. "That's why not."

"We don't know Bree actually has a security system installed in the guest house," Bernie told her. "She could have just put the sign up."

"You're right. She could have," Libby said. "But knowing Bree, I find that highly unlikely."

"I don't. I think that's exactly the kind of thing she'd do," Bernie opined. Bree was one of those odd people who'd buy a Mercedes, but keep her house at fifty-five degrees because she didn't want to spend money on the utility bill.

Libby bent down and retied her sneaker before she slipped and fell, something it would be just her luck to do. "I don't want to find out if you're wrong," she told her sister after she stood up. "As far as I'm concerned one family brush with the law is enough for the time being. And anyway, Duncan is our client. You don't do things like that to your client."

"Is that written somewhere in the Detective Rule Handbook?" Bernie asked her.

Libby ignored her. "Now, do you want to drive or shall I?"

"I will," Bernie grumped. "But we're missing a good opportunity."

"To get arrested," Libby said, unable to resist the temptation to have the last word.

Bernie muttered something and stomped toward the van, with Libby following. They hit traffic on the way, so it took them a half hour to get back to A Little Taste of Heaven.

"Jeez," Libby said when she walked through the door and saw how packed the shop was.

The moment she and Bernie had threaded their way through the crowd and stepped to the other side of the counter, Amber pulled them aside and told them they were running low on cookies. Someone Amber didn't know had come in and almost cleaned them out.

"I guess it's good we came back when we did," Bernie said grudgingly as she and Libby headed into the kitchen and got straight to work.

An hour later, working as fast as they could, Libby and Bernie had finished making two batches of chocolate-chip peanut-butter cookies, a batch of snickerdoodles, a batch of pecan shortbreads, and two batches of mint-chocolate brownies with chocolate icing.

Libby was taking a short break and sampling one of the brownies that she'd just finished icing, while she admired the pies Amber had made. She was complimenting her on a job well done when the kitchen door slammed open and Bree came storming in with Googie, one of the counter boys, right behind her.

"I tried to stop her," he told Libby. She noted Googie was practically wringing his hands in dismay.

"It's okay," Libby replied. She nodded to the front. "Go back and wait on the customers."

"Are you sure?"

"I'm positive," Libby said firmly. Then she turned to Bree. "So," she said. "To what do we owe the pleasure of this visit?" Not that she didn't have a pretty good idea already about what Bree wanted.

As it turned out, Libby was one hundred percent correct.

Bree put her hands on her hips. Her face was flushed. "I don't believe it," she said.

Bernie put down the pan she was washing and came over. "What don't you believe?" she asked Bree, noting as she did that today Bree was in head-to-toe hot pink Chanel.

Bree clutched at her pocketbook. "That you're standing here doing nothing when they're charging Duncan for Liza's murder. I told him that girl was no good. I told him she was going to get him into trouble, and she has. But has he ever listened to me? No. And now that he's gotten himself in trouble, I'm the one who has to bail him out," Bree ranted. "My sister is positively useless. I have to take care of everything. Absolutely everything. My back is killing me and I had to miss my appointment with my massage therapist today because of this. It'll be another week before I can get to see him!"

"Yes," Bernie said dryly. "I've always found murder to be inconvenient in the extreme."

"What do you mean by that?" Bree snapped. "Are you being sarcastic?"

"Not at all," Bernie murmured, having decided that maybe her mother had been right and there was nothing to be gained by being a smart-ass. "I'm sorry I misspoke."

Mollified, Bree opened her bag, took out a Xanax, and popped it in her mouth. "I'm just so upset. So upset. I can't believe this is happening to us." She closed the bag with a loud snap.

Given the emotional tenor, Libby decided not to point out that whatever was happening was happening to Duncan, not to Bree. "So where are they holding Duncan?" she asked instead.

"At the cottage. He's under house arrest. House arrest." Bree's voice rose at the indignation of it all. "He has to wear an ankle bracelet. It's horrible. He shouldn't be charged with any of this. The whole thing is ridiculous and it just keeps getting worse and worse."

A sentiment Bernie was inclined to agree with. At least the getting worse part. "Well, I guess that's better than being in jail," Bernie said, trying for optimism.

Bree sighed and patted her chest. "I have to hire guards around the clock. Do you have any idea how much that costs?"

"A lot?" Libby said tentatively.

Bree's nostrils flared. "That's putting it mildly. I could take a three-month cruise around the world for what I'm shelling out for this." Bree frowned. Talking about it had put her back in a terrible mood. She shook a finger at

Libby. "I want you to do something about this. I want you to do something about this now. Not stand around and bake things, for heaven's sake. This is an emergency."

"What would you like us to do?" Libby asked.

Bree took a step toward Libby and poked her in her shoulder with her finger. "What do you mean, what do I want you to do? What kind of stupid question is that? Obviously, I want you to find the killer and I want you to find him now, so we—meaning my family—can get on with our lives."

"It could be a woman," Bernie said, just to have something to say.

As Bree whirled around and faced Bernie, Bernie told herself that she never knew when to leave well enough alone. Then it occurred to Bernie, as she noted Bree's complexion getting redder by the minute and the slight slur in Bree's speech, that Bree might have stopped off for a cocktail or two or three along the way. After all, even though Bernie couldn't smell the alcohol on Bree's breath, that didn't mean anything. Bree could be drinking vodka. Which made sense to her because if she was in Bree's position, Bernie thought she might be inclined to hit the bottle right about now.

Bree waved her hands in the air. "Listen," she told Bernie. "I don't care if the killer is a man or a woman. I don't care if the killer is a pink baboon. I paid you a large sum of money and I expect you to do your job, not make things worse."

"But," Bernie said, "we told you that—"

"I don't want excuses. I want results," Bree snarled. "Otherwise . . ." She stopped. Then she whirled around and stalked out of the kitchen.

"Wow," said Amber. "That was pretty intense. Was she drunk?"

Bernie clicked her tongue against her teeth. "Maybe so."

"I've never seen Bree that out of control before," Libby observed.

"Yeah," Bernie said. "She was a tad upset."

"A tad?" Amber said. "A tad? What do you think she meant by 'otherwise'?"

Libby shook her head. "I don't know, but I'm sure it's nothing good."

"Could she do something bad to us?"

"Like what?"

Amber shrugged. "I don't know. Close us down."

Bernie laughed. "No. But on the other hand, it's never good to have an influential member of the community mad at you if you're a business owner."

"See," Libby said, "I knew this would happen if we took this case."

"Whine, whine, whine," Bernie shot back.

"So what are you going to do?" Amber cried.

Libby patted Amber on the back and said, "We're going to try to get to the bottom of this. Just the way we were doing before."

"Only faster," Bernie added. "Here, have a snicker-doodle." And she took one off the tray and handed it to Amber, then took one for herself.

The recipe was her mother's and Bernie had never meddled with it because it was perfect. As she ate it she thought about the interplay between the cinnamon and sugar against one another. The clash of the sweet and the spicy really couldn't be beat, she decided. But then salty and sweet weren't too bad either. Witness the combo of milk chocolate and salt or caramels and salt.

Amber rubbed her hands together. "But what if Duncan is guilty? What if you can't find proof that he didn't murder those two people?"

"Simple. We'll make some up," Bernie told her.

"My sister's kidding," Libby said, catching the expression on Amber's face. Then she tried to reassure her. "Don't worry. If anything is there, we'll find it."

Amber looked dubious.

"What?" Bernie asked Amber. "You don't think we will?"

"It's not that," Amber told her as she nervously wound one of her pink pigtails around her finger. Last week her hair had been bright orange.

"Then what is it?" Libby asked.

Amber fidgeted some more.

"Well," Bernie said.

"I think you will . . ." Amber replied.

"But?" Libby said.

"But not everyone does," Amber said.

"And who would everyone be?" Bernie asked.

Amber let go of her braid. "Okay. You know how I delivered that big tray of cookies to the school fund-raiser?"

Bernie and Libby both nodded.

"Well," Amber went on, "there were two cops there and they were talking. The big one, the one with the short hair and the kinda funny nose who always buys two cranberry-orange muffins and a light coffee to go with two sugars . . ."

"Don Rhodes," Bernie said promptly. "What about him?"

"I think I heard them betting on finding evidence, and Rhodes said you were going to lose. The other cop said you were going to win."

"Who was the other cop?" Libby asked.

Amber bit her lip while she thought. After a moment she said, "He was kind of a short guy." Amber touched underneath her eye. "Has some kind of scar there. Comes in occasionally for ginger chicken and potato and leek soup."

"Cole," Bernie said promptly. "I always liked him. I wonder how big the betting pool is."

"Bernie," Libby warned.

"I was just thinking, Libby."

"Well, don't," Libby told her sister. "I think we have enough drama around here as it is."

Chapter 16

As Sean hung up the phone, he thought about what Orion had just told him. It was certainly interesting, but he wasn't prepared to share the information with Libby and Bernie yet. He wanted to check some things out first. Orion could be lying. Although he really had no reason to. But then, Sean mused, sometimes people did anyway. Heaven knows he'd seen enough of that.

On the other hand, Orion had called him back and he didn't have to. There was that. Oh well. Eventually everything would sort itself out. It always did, given enough time. And on that thought Sean clicked on the television and settled in to watch the six o'clock news while he wondered what was for dinner.

Despite Bree's outburst, progress on the Duncan case came to a halt over the next two days. Even though Bernie and Libby needed to talk to the remaining members of the Corned Beef and Cabbage Club ASAP, that wasn't possible. They were going to have to wait until Monday morning since Liam, Patrick, and Connor and their significant others had gone to Vegas for a long weekend and weren't scheduled to return to Longely until late Sunday night.

This left the Simmonses with little to do regarding the investigation.

By Sunday morning Bernie was suffering from a severe bout of impatience. She felt she had to do something. In addition, the bet between Rhodes and Cole gnawed at her. She couldn't seem to let it go. Especially because she kept seeing the smirk Don Rhodes had given her when she and Libby ran into him at the supermarket on Saturday afternoon. Libby told her she was imagining things, but Bernie knew she wasn't.

When Bernie broached the subject of their lack of progress in the case to her dad, he waved her off, telling her that he was working another angle and that he'd fill her in when he knew more. That annoyed her. Then he told her to calm down, and that annoyed her even more. But truth be told, at that moment everything annoyed her.

Bernie went into the kitchen downstairs to whine to Libby about how their dad was acting, but Libby, who was knee-deep in making a terrine, didn't want to hear about it.

"Dad's correct," Libby told her. "Everyone will be back in less than twenty-four hours. We can do what we need to do then." She pointed to the office. "On the other hand, we are really behind on our book work. We have papers that need to be filed and forms that need to be filled out. Now might be a good time to do that."

"You're right," Bernie admitted reluctantly, not being able to think of an alternative answer quickly enough. This, of course, was the last thing she wanted to do. She hated paperwork and there was a lot of it when you owned a business. Way too much, if you asked her.

Bernie went in and started in on the filing, but she kept on thinking of Mike Sweeney and what they knew and what they didn't know about him and about how she could ask better questions of Liam, Patrick, and Connor if she knew what to ask. And what better way to do that than taking a peek inside Mike Sweeney's house? After all, if you want to know about a crime, start with the victim. At least that's what her dad always said. After about twenty minutes of staring at the invoices from Chocolates Inc., invoices that she was sure she'd already paid, she stood up and went into the kitchen.

"What are you doing?" Libby asked as she watched Bernie fill a large thermos with coffee and grab four muffins.

"I'm going out," Bernie told her, heading for the door.

"I can see that. Where? To do what?" Libby asked.

But Bernie didn't answer her.

Maybe she didn't hear me, Libby thought as she turned back to consider the salmon and spinach terrine en croute that she was making. It was one of those complicated fussy productions that she made every once in a while only to rediscover that she really didn't like doing things like this, which was why she didn't make them very often. They tasted good, but not good enough to justify all the time and effort it took constructing them.

Bernie had heard her sister, however. She had just chosen not to answer her. Was it so wrong not to have a discussion with her sister or by extension with her dad on what she was about to do? What was the big deal? She was just going to walk into Mike Sweeney's apartment and take a quick look around, for heaven's sake. And with Brandon's help that should be a piece of cake. After all, what good was a set of lock picks if you never used them? It was like having a pair of Manolos that you never wore.

Which is why Bernie had arrived at Brandon's house at eight-thirty in the morning armed with a large thermos of French roast coffee, light on the sugar and heavy on the cream, and four muffins, two banana-chocolate-chip, one corn, and one blueberry, woke him up, dragged him out of bed, and into his Jeep. Half an hour later she was having second thoughts about the wisdom of her course of action.

"I changed my mind. You don't have to do this," Bernie told Brandon as they sat in his Jeep in the Rite Aid parking lot, which was kitty-corner to the house Mike Sweeney had lived in. It was almost nine o'clock on Sunday morning and the lot was deserted. It was gray and raw out, the kind of day where people woke up, looked out the window, and rolled over and went back to sleep. Which was one of the reasons Bernie had decided to do this.

Brandon turned off the engine, took another sip of his coffee, and polished off the second banana-chocolate-chip muffin before saying, "Let me get this straight. You woke me up to ask me to do this, dragged me out of bed under protest, and now you've changed your mind? What are you, nuts?"

Bernie sniffed. "There's no need to be so insulting."

"Insulting?"

"Yes. Insulting. I changed my mind because you're being so grumpy."

"Because I've had four hours of sleep." Brandon thought for a moment. "No. Make that three and a half."

"Whose fault is that?" Bernie demanded. "Yours obviously. Anyway, as I was saying, since you're being so grumpy and after I brought you coffee and muffins too—"

"I'm not being grumpy," Brandon protested. "I'm tired."

Bernie tossed her head and threw her hair back. "Well, whatever you are, I'm changing my mind about having you help me." She poured herself another half cup of coffee and took a sip. It was excellent if she had to say so herself. And the Demerara sugar she was using added just the right caramel undertone. "I'll do this by myself."

"How are you going to get in?" Brandon asked her. "Break a window?"

Bernie straightened up and put her coffee cup in the holder. "I can pick a lock if I have to," she told him.

"Not with my picks you can't."

"I can do it without them," Bernie told him. Which was entirely untrue, but she was not going to admit the converse.

"If you had three hours, maybe," Brandon scoffed. "And even then I doubt it."

Bernie shook a finger at him. "There you go insulting me again."

"I'm not insulting you." Brandon eyed the blueberry muffin. "I'm speaking the truth."

"Your truth, which is vastly different from everyone else's truth." Bernie put her hand on the door handle. "I don't care what you think. I'm doing it."

"Really?" Brandon said as he gulped down the remaining coffee in his cup.

"Yes. Really."

Brandon raised an eyebrow. This he felt was not a good idea. For several reasons. The most obvious one being that Bernie would get caught and then he would have to try to explain to Bernie's father how this had happened. It would not be a nice conversation.

"Does your father know what you're doing?"

Bernie smiled. "Of course he does."

"You're lying. Your father would absolutely not approve of your doing this."

Bernie flushed. "I'm not lying," she told him even though she was.

"Right. I can always tell when you are."

Bernie opened her eyes as wide as possible. "Why would I lie?" she asked.

Brandon snorted. "Don't do your Miss Innocent look with me. I'm immune to it. Your dad would pitch a fit."

"So what if he does?"

"So he would blame me."

Bernie sniffed. "Excuse me. I'm not chattel, you know. I'm an adult."

"Sometimes you don't act like one," Brandon observed.

"I really resent that," Bernie said. "Furthermore, I think my reasons for doing this make sense."

"You never told me your reasons."

"Yes I did. You weren't listening."

"I was asleep."

"That's no excuse."

Brandon sighed. "Okay. Tell me them again."

So Bernie explained. Mostly. Leaving out the part about the bet, which might not even be true because Amber could be somewhat fuzzy from time to time.

"At this moment," she told Brandon, who was finishing up the last of his coffee while he listened, "the only evidence the police have are the pics we found on Liza's laptop."

"So you've said." Brandon stifled a yawn. He was so tired even the coffee wasn't helping. "To my mind those point to Liam, Connor, or Patrick. Which is a good thing," he added.

Bernie brushed a lock of hair out of her eye. "One would think. But if that were the case the DA wouldn't have charged Duncan."

Brandon frowned. "I know."

"Which is why I want to look in Sweeney's house and see if we can find some evidence pointing to someone else."

"I'll tell you one thing," Brandon said, sitting back in his seat and turning the heater in the Jeep up a little to combat the chill. "From what I've seen at the bar, Duncan never struck me as the type of guy who would kill a woman over something like that. He'd just walk away and bad-mouth her on Facebook." He shrugged. "But then you never really know what someone will do, do you?"

"No, you don't," Bernie said, thinking back to some of her less fortunate past encounters with the opposite sex.

Brandon was silent for a moment, then said, "There were no pictures of Sweeney on the laptop, right?"

Bernie nodded. "That is correct."

"And the two murders are supposed to be related."

Bernie nodded again. "That's what the police are saying."

Brandon took a sip of his coffee. "But you don't think so?"

"No. I do." Bernie ate the last bit of her corn-bread muffin.

"So then why did Duncan kill Sweeney? The police say it had to do with the photos. But Sweeney didn't have anything to do with the photos. Unless he's on another site. Or unless the police know something we don't."

"Exactly," Bernie said. "Which I don't believe is the case. At least, according to Clyde it isn't. Which leaves us going back to the scenario of Duncan being set up."

"And how will looking through Mike Sweeney's house help to prove that?" Brandon asked.

Bernie bit her lip. "Honestly, I don't know. I guess I can't think of anything else to do."

Brandon crumpled up the paper cup he'd been drinking coffee out of and threw it in the garbage bag on the floor of his Jeep. "What makes you think you'll find something at Sweeney's house that the police haven't?" he asked.

Bernie turned and faced him. "But that's the point," she cried. "The police haven't been there yet."

Brandon blinked. "I don't believe it."

"That's what Clyde said and there's no reason for him to lie."

"That's just too . . ."

"Irresponsible?" Bernie asked.

"Why would they do that?" Brandon said.

Bernie shrugged. "I'm guessing because they think they have the culprit, so they don't have to investigate further. That's why I want to get in there now."

Brandon sighed. Bernie smiled. She knew she had him.

"I should be shot," he said.

Bernie leaned over and hugged him. "All you have to do is open the back door for me. Then wait in the car."

"I don't think so," Brandon said.

"I don't want to get you in trouble," Bernie told Brandon in her most pious tone as she pulled her hoodie up and zipped up her jacket.

"It's a little late for that," Brandon observed as he did likewise. "My dad always told me that women lead you astray."

Bernie laughed and punched Brandon in the arm. Then he and Bernie got out of the Jeep and climbed over the metal guardrail that separated the pharmacy from the house that Mike Sweeney had been living in. It was showtime.

Chapter 17

Mike Sweeney's house wasn't a very prepossessing structure as far as houses in Longely went. It was a plain, two-thousand foot, two-story colonial with a picture window that fronted the street, a brown double-shingle roof, a long driveway, and an unattached garage out in the back. The house had been painted all white and the back-yard was half grass, half blacktop. From where Brandon was standing, he couldn't see any shrubs or flower beds, which surprised him. Somehow he'd expected something a little jazzier from a man who had spent five hundred dollars on a pair of shoes for himself.

This was also bad news because there were no trees or shrubs to hide what he was planning to do. On the other hand, the house was bordered by two vacant lots on either side, which was good news because that meant that there was less chance of being seen by the neighbors.

"They changed the zoning regs after they tore down the houses," Bernie explained before Brandon could ask. "And now those lots are too small to build on."

"Weird."

"I know."

Brandon held out his hand. It had started to drizzle.

Great. Now he was going to be cold, wet, and tired. The perfect trifecta. He crossed his arms over his chest and went back to studying the rear of Mike Sweeney's house. "So they just left them like that?"

Bernie shrugged. "Sometimes I don't get the planning board at all."

"Why'd they tear them down?"

"They weren't up to code. At least that's what they said."

Brandon waited for Bernie to continue. After a moment she did. "But I heard that Pat Dwyer . . ."

". . . Your dad's friend?"

"More of an acquaintance really . . . I heard that he was the person who was instrumental in getting the buildings torn down, that he had a thing going with the owners of the houses."

"Lovely," Brandon said. "Real estate as a blood sport."

"It might not be true," Bernie said. "It's just a story I heard."

"It probably isn't," Brandon agreed, although he wouldn't be surprised if it were. What Bernie had described sounded like a small town kind of thing and Longely was nothing if not a small town.

Bernie shivered. The cold was cutting right through her. She should have worn her leather bomber jacket instead of the EMS nylon shell she had on. "So, Brandon, how do you want to do this?" she asked, changing the subject.

But Brandon didn't answer her. He was busy looking at the Jeep. He bit his lip as something occurred to him.

"What?" Bernie asked.

"I was just thinking that I don't like leaving the Jeep in the lot," Brandon told her. "We're the only vehicle here."

Bernie hugged herself tighter. "So?"

"So if the cops come by they might wonder what the Jeep is doing there. I'm going to move it somewhere where it will be less noticeable. I'll be back in a sec."

"I'm going with you," Bernie told him. It was too cold to stand around and wait.

Brandon shrugged and headed for the Jeep, with Bernie in tow. A couple of minutes later Brandon had parked the Jeep around the block from Sweeney's house.

"I'm not sure this is better," Bernie said before they got out of the Jeep.

"Neither am I," Brandon confessed. "But at least we don't stick out like a sore thumb."

"On the other hand, anyone who's looking out the window can see us going by."

"Unlikely," Brandon told her. "You said it yourself. No one is going to see us because everyone is still asleep."

"I hope so," Bernie murmured as she got out of the Jeep and gently closed the door.

Now that they were going to do this, she was having second thoughts. She crossed to the sidewalk and began to walk toward Mike Sweeney's house. Her head was down and her hoodie hid her face. She decided she looked like someone who had been out too late the night before and was doing the walk of shame. Brandon joined her.

"Ready?" he asked.

Bernie nodded, glad for the fact that she was wearing leather gloves and a scarf. When they reached Mike Sweeney's house, they followed the driveway, which curved around to the back of the house. No vehicles were parked in the driveway or in the garage. Brandon went over to the door, climbed the two steps, and knocked.

No one answered.

Brandon knocked again. "It's the Fuller Brush Man," he called out.

Again no one answered. Bernie noticed that the blinds on the upstairs windows didn't move, which meant no one was peeking out of them. Okay. Maybe she'd watched a few too many late night movies.

"The Fuller Brush Man?" Bernie echoed.

"Yeah. The Fuller Brush Man."

"You're kidding, right? The Fuller Brush Man hasn't come around for thirty years. Maybe more."

"Oops. I guess I should tell everyone I'm a Jehovah's Witness, then."

Bernie rolled her eyes. "Yeah. You definitely look like one," she told Brandon as he moved closer to the door. She sniffed. "Do you smell something?"

"Nope," Brandon said, while he scrutinized the lock.

Bernie wrinkled her nose and sniffed again. "Well, I do. I could swear I smell gas."

Brandon stopped, lifted his head, and took a sniff. "I don't."

Bernie shrugged. Maybe she was imagining it, although she did have an excellent sense of smell. Unlike Brandon, who had been known to eat deli meat that was way past its expiration date. Or maybe the smell was coming from somewhere else. That happened sometimes. Yes, she told herself. That's probably what it was, she decided as she watched Brandon take the set of lock picks out of his pocket. She'd been there the night he'd won them from a guy called Mark the Thief in an all night poker game down on the Lower East Side.

Brandon studied the lock. It was an older model, which was good. Fortunately, it wasn't one of those double-cylinder dead-bolt jobbies, the kind people put in when they wanted an extra layer of security. Now everyone used them, but back in the day they were fairly uncommon.

One of those would demand more skill than he had. But the one in front of him was definitely pickable. Brandon knew this because when he'd won the picks, he'd spent weeks practicing with them on locks like these. But that had been a while ago. And like any other skill, picking locks demanded constant practice. It was a use it or lose it kind of thing.

Brandon stretched his fingers out several times and then

rubbed his palms together to warm up his hands and lim-
ber up his fingers as he studied the lock. He chose the second pick from the left and inserted it into the opening. It
was too loose. He went up to the next size. This one fit.

Brandon closed his eyes and wiggled the pick. He felt it
catch. He leaned forward and applied a little pressure and
turned. He could feel the cylinders moving. He applied a
little more pressure. Then he turned the doorknob and
opened the door.

"After you, my lady," he said, bowing low.

Bernie scanned the driveway and the side lots. No one
was visible. She just hoped it stayed that way and that no
one had caught sight of them. Hesitating at the open door,
she questioned what she and Brandon were about to do.
Because if anyone came over and asked, she didn't know
what she was going to say. For once she was at a loss for
words.

Oh well. She'd deal with that if it happened. Bernie took
a deep breath and stepped inside. As she studied the interior, she realized that the smell of gas was even stronger in
the small room they were standing in than it had been outside.

"Don't you smell it?" she asked Brandon.

Brandon shook his head.

"You have to," Bernie insisted.

"Well, I don't. I have a cold and I can't smell anything."

"Well, I do," Bernie told him.

"Fine," Brandon said as he looked around.

The room he and Bernie were standing in had four jackets hanging on pegs, five pairs of boots neatly lined up on
a rubber mat, and three garbage recycling cans, all of
which looked full.

"It looks as if no one has been here since Sweeney
died," Brandon commented. "I wonder where his parents
are." But as soon as Brandon said that he remembered
that Sweeney had no family. He was an only child and his

dad had died when he was ten and his mom had died three years ago.

Bernie didn't comment. She was too busy sniffing the air. Although the gas wasn't making her gag, it definitely was pervading everything.

"I think we should get out of here and call the utility company," Bernie said.

"I think you're overreacting, but if you want to we will."

"Overreacting?" Bernie repeated indignantly. "A gas leak is really dangerous."

"It can be," Brandon said. He nodded toward the door in front of them. "I bet that's the kitchen. Maybe Mike left the oven on."

"Maybe," Bernie said. "Though I can't imagine Sweeney cooking anything."

"Neither can I," Brandon agreed. "But he must have. He had his kitchen done. It cost him a lot too."

Bernie thought of Bree's kitchen. "That doesn't mean he was going to use it. Libby and I have cooked in some one-hundred-thousand-dollar kitchens and the only thing that's been used in them is the microwave to heat up coffee."

Brandon turned to face her. "So are we going in or not?"

Bernie was torn. On the one hand, she desperately wanted to go in and check out Mike Sweeney's house and this could be her last chance. On the other hand, she wasn't looking forward to stepping into a room full of gas. "Maybe, if we aired the place out and came back later," she suggested.

Brandon shook his head. "Probably not. By that time everyone will be up and about."

Bernie ran her hand through her hair. "I know, I know," she said. "Give me another minute to think." As she was trying to decide what she should do she spotted a button on the wall about three inches off the floor. "What's that?" she asked Brandon as she pointed to it.

Brandon laughed. "That's Sweeney's doggie doorbell."

Bernie shook her head. "His what?"

"His doggie doorbell. I remember him telling the guys about it. It's a joke. Here. Let me show you." And Brandon used the point of his shoe to press the buzzer. Nothing happened. "That's odd," Brandon said. "It's supposed to go woof, woof, woof."

"But what's the point?" Bernie asked.

Brandon shrugged. "What can I say? Sweeney had an odd sense of humor."

And Brandon pressed the buzzer with his toe again.

Again nothing happened.

Then Bernie felt, rather than heard a whoosh. It was like all the air was being sucked out of the room.

The next thing she knew she was lying flat on her back on the tarmac of the driveway outside Mike Sweeney's house.

Or what was left of it.

She turned her head and caught a glimpse of Brandon. He was lying a short ways away. His mouth was moving but she couldn't hear what he was saying.

Chapter 18

Sean Simmons and Marvin were a little over a block away when they heard the explosion. They'd been on their way to Sam's Club to pick up some supplies for the shop and had just passed what looked like Brandon's vehicle. Sean pointed to it.

"Is that Brandon's Jeep?" he asked Marvin as they drove by it.

Identifying people through their cars was not Marvin's strong suit. "I don't know. It looks like it."

"It does, doesn't it?"

"I suppose so, Mr. Simmons." Marvin had other thoughts on his mind, like what to get Libby for her upcoming birthday.

Sean clicked his tongue against the roof of his mouth. "Back up a minute," he ordered Marvin.

"Why?" Marvin asked, doing as he was told.

"So I can see if that is Brandon's Jeep." They'd gone by so quickly, he hadn't had a chance to catch the license plate number.

"It is," Sean said after he'd read it.

Marvin looked at his watch. "Libby wanted us back right away," he reminded Sean.

Sean grunted. "Five minutes one way or another isn't going to make any difference."

"It will to Libby," Marvin pointed out.

Sean ignored him and rubbed his chin. "I wonder what Brandon is doing here."

"Visiting someone?" Marvin said.

Sean didn't say anything.

"Can we go now, Mr. Simmons?" Marvin asked. Aside from wanting to get to Sam's Club and back, he was blocking traffic.

"In a minute . . . Mike Sweeney lives around here, doesn't he?" Sean asked.

"Around the corner," Marvin replied. "Why?"

"Well," Sean said. "Brandon is here and Bernie isn't at home and Mike Sweeney's house is on the next block, so what do you think? What conclusions do you draw from that?"

"That I think we should go to Sam's Club," Marvin said.

"And I think we should drive around the block and check out Mike Sweeney's house and see if Bernie and Brandon are up to something."

"And if they are?" Marvin asked.

Sean had just been about to answer when he heard the blast.

"What was that?" Marvin cried.

"An explosion." Sean pointed to a plume of smoke coming from around the corner. "Isn't that where you said Sweeney's house was?"

"Yes," Marvin whispered.

He and Sean looked at each other.

"Move," Sean said.

Marvin put his foot on the accelerator and raced around the corner. As they rounded the bend both men could see flames shooting up out of the back of Sweeney's house. Marvin screeched to a stop, threw his door open, and ran out of the car. It took Sean a little longer. As he was getting out of the car, another vehicle pulled up next to Marvin's.

Pat Dwyer rolled down the window on his vehicle. "What happened?" he asked Sean.

"Some sort of explosion," Sean said. "Bernie and Brandon may be in there. I'm going to check."

Dwyer's complexion got a shade paler. "That's terrible. What can I do?"

"Call nine-one-one," Sean told him.

As he hurried toward Sweeney's house Sean was dimly aware that people on either side of the street were emerging from their houses. They were wearing pajamas, raincoats, slippers, and looks of shock on their faces. Sean's heart was beating rapidly as he hurried toward the backyard. He was going as fast as he could, but nevertheless the walk to the backyard seemed to be taking forever. And all the time he was walking he was praying that Bernie and Brandon hadn't been inside the house when it had gone up.

When he rounded the driveway he saw his daughter and Brandon on the grass. Marvin was with them. They both looked dazed and covered with soot, but they were standing and that was the important thing. Thank you, God, he said silently as he rushed toward them.

He hugged Bernie. "Thank heavens you're not hurt," he cried.

Bernie was cheered to realize that even though her ears were ringing, she could hear what her dad was saying. Then Sean held Bernie at arm's length and asked her what the hell she was doing there.

"I might say the same to you and Marvin," Bernie replied.

"We were on our way over to Sam's Club to get some stuff for your sister," Marvin told her.

"And we were investigating," Bernie said.

Brandon limped over to Sean. He'd done something to his ankle, which hurt every time he put weight on it. "It was my idea, Mr. Simmons."

Sean snorted. "Very noble, but very unlikely. Now what happened?"

Bernie explained. As she did, the four of them watched the fire. It was shooting through the second floor of the house. A plume of black smoke hovered in the air. Sean couldn't help thinking that whatever was in that house—if there was anything in the house that pertained to the murder—was now gone. This case had been nothing but a series of dead ends since he and the girls had started on it.

"Didn't a gas line blow up somewhere in California a couple of months ago and take out a whole block?" Marvin said.

Sean nodded.

Bernie looked at his face and read the expression on it. "You don't think that's the case here, do you?" she asked.

"I think it could be," Sean said slowly. "It probably is. But I think it's awfully convenient given what's been going on, and you know I'm not a big one for coincidence."

"So you think the house may have been booby-trapped?" Brandon asked him.

"Let's say it wouldn't surprise me." Sean regarded him. "Tell me exactly what happened," he instructed.

"We smelled gas . . ." Brandon began.

"I smelled gas," Bernie corrected.

"Fine. Bernie smelled gas and I rang the bell and"— Brandon gestured toward the fire—"and then there was that."

"You were lucky, Brandon," Sean said.

"Tell me something I don't know, Mr. Simmons."

Sean was just about to answer him when Dwyer rounded the bend. "I called nine-one-one and the firemen are on their way," he announced. He stopped when he saw Bernie and Brandon. "Jeez," he said.

"I know," Brandon said.

Bernie nodded. She reached over and took Brandon's hand. "Let's go," she said.

In the distance she could hear the fire engines approaching. The last thing she felt like doing now was staying and answering questions. What she wanted was a bath and a drink, in that order.

"If they want us they know where to find us," she told her dad.

"So much for Mike Sweeney's house," Brandon said as he fished his car keys out of his pocket. "You gotta figure by the time they put the fire out there's not going to be much left to look at."

"I still don't understand what happened," Bernie said. "You pressed the buzzer and then whoosh. There was the blast."

Brandon dodged a man and a woman going toward Sweeney's house. By now Brandon figured that most of the people on the block were either there or on their way. "I think what happened," Brandon told her, "was that the house was filled with gas fumes and the bell sent out a charge that set the gas off."

"So what do you think?" Bernie asked him. "Do you think my dad is right about this being on purpose?"

"I'm not sure," Brandon answered. "There could have been a gas leak. On the other hand, wouldn't someone have smelled it?"

"I would think so," Bernie said. "People smelled the gas in California. They even reported it, but no one from the utility company came out."

"At least the house is far away from the other ones." Brandon took a deep breath. The adrenaline that had kicked in after the explosion was beginning to fade and he knew from prior experience that he and Bernie were going to crash soon.

"Sweeney could have left the oven on," Bernie postulated.

"He could have," Brandon replied. "If Mike ever cooked at home. Which he didn't. He didn't even make coffee for himself. He used to buy it on his way to the train station."

"You said that Sweeney had had his kitchen remodeled. Maybe there was a leak in the gas pipe."

"He got his kitchen remodeled six months ago," Brandon said.

"Maybe there was a crack in the gas line."

Brandon raised an eyebrow. "Remember, you smelled gas coming from inside the house, not outside."

Brandon unlocked his Jeep and Bernie got in. She leaned her head against the headrest and closed her eyes. Suddenly she was exhausted.

"It makes no sense," she said when Brandon got in the Jeep. Her lips felt so heavy it was an effort to move them. "Why would anyone go to all that trouble?"

Brandon shrugged. "I'm not sure. Maybe because there was something in there that whoever did it didn't want anyone to find."

"But then why not break in and steal it? This seems way over the top. No. I think it was an unfortunate accident. Nothing else makes any sense."

Brandon didn't reply. Suddenly he was too tired to talk. He knew it would take every last ounce of his energy to drive over to Bernie's place.

Chapter 19

"Nice shot," Libby said, pointing to the picture on the news of Mike Sweeney's house burning.

Bernie reached across the table for the pepper mill. "It's their lead story," she noted.

"Understandable," said Sean. His fork hovered above his plate as he tried to decide what he wanted to eat next. "After all, it's not every day that a building explodes here," he said, spearing a slice of bacon.

It was nine o'clock on Monday morning and Libby and Bernie were upstairs eating a second breakfast with their dad.

"Well, they seem to think it was an accident," Libby noted as she took a bite of her toast. "At least that's what the reporter is saying."

Bernie took a bite of her feta and spinach omelet, followed by a bite of French peasant bread slathered with butter. She was still a little shaky from yesterday, but the act of eating was calming her down, as it always did.

"What does Clyde say?" she asked her dad.

Her dad ate another strip of bacon and a forkful of his home fries before answering. "He says that the fire chief thinks it's an accident too. That there was a crack in the gas line and the gas built up over time. Of course, that's just a hypothesis. They'll never be able to prove it because there's nothing left to examine. You were really lucky, Bernie," Sean said as he wiped his hands on his napkin.

"I know, Dad," Bernie said quietly, not wanting to think about what could have happened because it gave her the heebie-jeebies.

Libby turned to Bernie. "And you think it was an accident too, right?"

"Yeah, I do. But Brandon doesn't."

Libby turned to her Dad. "What about you?"

Sean held up his cup and Libby filled it for him and then stirred in cream and sugar. Sean nodded his thanks and took a sip. Perfect. As always. "I think," he said slowly, "that I'm inclined to side with Brandon on this one."

"How so?" Bernie asked.

"Let me count the ways." And Sean raised his hand and ticked them off on his fingers. "First Sweeney is murdered, then one of the people he hangs out with is killed, and then his house blows up. I'd say that goes beyond having a bad week."

"Okay," Bernie told him. "But remember if we hadn't pressed the buzzer the place wouldn't have exploded."

"Maybe not then, but it would have eventually," Sean countered. "And there's this. If there was a crack in the gas line and the leak had been going on for a while, why didn't anyone in the neighborhood smell it?"

"Maybe they did, Dad," Bernie said.

"Not from what I heard yesterday." Sean popped another slice of bacon in his mouth. God, he loved this stuff.

"All I can say, Bernie," Libby told her sister as she reached over for another slice of toast, then opened the jar of strawberry jam she'd made last summer and put some on the bread, "is thank heavens you and Brandon weren't hurt."

"And that there were empty lots on either side of

Sweeney's house," Sean added. "Otherwise there could have been a really bad outcome."

Everyone fell silent as they drank their coffee, contemplated the possibilities, and listened to the murmur of business being conducted below as the sounds floated up through the floorboards. The nine-fifteen Metro-North bound for Grand Central whistled in the distance.

Sean looked at the clock on the wall. "The train's three minutes late."

"The train's been three minutes late for the last six weeks," Bernie said. "It's because they're fixing the track outside Rhinebeck."

Everyone fell silent again.

"Bree was in this morning," Libby said suddenly.

Sean and Bernie groaned simultaneously.

"Where was I?" Bernie asked.

"You'd run out to pick up more paper goods at Sam's," Libby answered.

"Lucky me. What did she want?"

"Coffee and a chocolate croissant."

"That's it?" Bernie asked.

"She apologized," Libby replied. "Kind of."

"Define kind of," Bernie ordered.

"She said she was feeling out of sorts these days because of the enormous pressure she was under and she hoped we'd understand that, but that we really had to push the investigation along."

"Those were her words? Push the investigation along?" Sean asked.

"Pretty much."

And with that comment Libby downed the rest of her coffee and the three of them started discussing the best way to talk to Mike Sweeney's friends, considering that their last conversational attempts at RJ's hadn't gone that well.

"We could always show up at their doorsteps," Bernie said.

"You could and they could refuse to speak to you," Sean said.

"We'll just have to make them want to, that's all," Bernie replied.

"Simpler said than done," Sean noted. He sighed, thinking of the days when he was chief of police in Longely and had the power to compel someone to talk to him. But those days were long gone and they weren't coming back.

"It'll work," Libby said. "We'll just nag them to death. We'll call it the 'mom approach' to investigating."

Sean laughed. "It always worked for Rose."

"Exactly," Bernie said. Her mother had made a fine art of extracting information by repeatedly asking the same question.

"Speaking of investigating," Libby said. "I think we should revisit Duncan and see if he has anything new to say."

"Sounds like a good idea to me," Sean said. "The sooner we get this mess cleaned up the happier everyone will be."

Chapter 20

It was ten that evening when Brandon called Bernie. "Yahoo," he trilled when Bernie picked up her cell.

"Yahoo, yourself," Bernie replied. She could hear the sound of people talking in the background. "It sounds busy there."

"It is busy here."

"It's Monday night." Traditionally RJ's was busy Thursday, Friday, and Saturday nights and dead on Mondays and Tuesdays.

Brandon snugged his phone between his shoulder and his ear and started making a Singapore Sling. "What can I say, Bernie? Times are bad and everyone evidently needs a drink. Or two. In any case, I'm calling to tell you that one of the gruesome threesome is here. Patrick just walked through the door."

"Thanks. We'll be right over," Bernie said, and hung up. She tossed her phone down on the coffee table and nudged Libby, who was asleep on the sofa, with her elbow. "Let's go," she said. "Patrick is at RJ's now."

Libby groaned. Bernie nudged harder.

Libby opened her eyes. "Ouch, Bernie. That hurt."

"It was supposed to. Seriously, Libby. We have to go."

Libby yawned and sat up. "Why?"

"I just told you."

"I didn't hear you. I was dreaming about a chocolate wishing well."

Bernie rolled her eyes. "Leave it to you to come up with something like that. Brandon called. Patrick is at RJ's. We've got to get down there so we can talk to him."

Libby started to lie back down. "Can't we do this tomorrow? I want to go back to sleep."

"No. We can't." Bernie took her sister's arm and pulled her upright.

"Fine." Libby held up her hands in a gesture of peace. "You're right. You're right." She yawned again and ran her fingers through her hair. "All I can say is that I hope he'll talk to us."

"He'll talk to us," Bernie said.

"Why should he? Even Dad said that."

Bernie scowled. "Of course he'll talk to us. He'll want to convince us of his innocence."

"Of course he will," Libby parroted. "Because we did so well with him at RJ's the last time."

"You're always so negative," Bernie shot back.

"I'm not negative, Bernie. I'm just realistic. Which is more than I can say for some people."

"You mean me?" Bernie demanded.

"No. I mean the man in the moon." And Libby got up and put on her jacket.

"Aren't you going to comb your hair and put on some makeup?" Bernie asked her.

Libby didn't even bother turning around when she answered her. "No, Bernie. I'm not. I'm going exactly like this. If you don't like it I can always stay home."

Given the way things were going, Bernie thought it was probably better not to argue the point. Instead, she dashed into the bathroom, brushed and fluffed out her hair, and quickly redid her makeup. When she came out Libby was already in the van waiting for her.

RJ's parking lot was full and Libby had to park in the lot next door.

"I wonder what's going on here," Libby asked as they walked across the lot.

Bernie shook her head. She didn't know. Then she remembered. "Basketball."

But she didn't remember who was playing. Neither she nor her sister read the sports pages. It wasn't something that was on their radar.

When Bernie pulled open the heavy wooden door and walked in, a wall of noise hit her. All the tables were filled, people were lined up four deep at the bar, and others were leaning against the wall and talking in small groups, while they watched the TV that was mounted above the bar.

Brandon was in the weeds, as they liked to say in the restaurant biz, and it took Bernie a couple of minutes before she could catch his eye. When she did, he paused for a moment to nod in Patrick's direction before he went back to serving.

Bernie had to stand on tiptoe to look around. These were the times when she wished she was six foot. Five-foot-three just didn't cut it in situations like these. At first all she saw was a sea of bobbing and weaving heads, but after a moment she spotted Patrick. He was leaning against the bar watching the dart game in progress and drinking a beer.

"This is like the subway during rush hour," she muttered to herself as she and Libby elbowed their way through the hordes of imbibing commuters.

"Boy, it's crowded," Bernie said to Patrick as soon as she and Libby were within speaking distance of him. She had to yell to be heard over the din. To say that these were not ideal circumstances in which to talk to someone was to put it mildly. She began to wonder if Libby hadn't been right after all.

Patrick glanced at her briefly and turned back to the game.

Bernie tried again. "Nice tan," she observed.

Patrick finally turned to her. "Refresh my memory. Tell me why I should care about what you think."

Bernie did her best imitation smile. "How about because my sister and I are charming and funny and we make great-tasting food."

"Give me a break," Patrick said.

"I take it you disagree," Bernie asked Patrick as he went back to watching the game.

Libby decided it was her turn to try. "So how'd you do in Vegas?" she asked him.

Patrick took a sip of his beer. "How about you girls go somewhere else and leave me alone? Do you think you can do that?"

Libby turned to Bernie. "Did you hear what he said?" she asked her sister.

"I did indeed," Bernie replied. "Do you think we should?"

"Leave him alone?"

"Exactly."

"I'll let you know in a minute." And Libby turned back to Patrick and said, "Bernie said you'd want to talk to us so you could convince us of your innocence, but I said you wouldn't. I said that you were innocent so why would you want to talk to us? That Sweeney's and Liza's deaths were painful subjects and you wouldn't want to revisit them."

Patrick nodded. "Exactly," he said.

Libby pressed on. "We have one hundred dollars riding on the bet, so I guess I have to thank you for my winning."

"I guess so," Patrick conceded.

He was still keeping his eyes fixed on the dart game in progress, but his body wasn't as stiff as it had been. I'm winning him over, Libby thought. "I am a little surprised though," she continued. "Or maybe confused would be a better word. Duncan is a really good friend of yours, correct?"

"We've already been through this. What's your point?" Patrick asked impatiently.

"My point," Libby said, "is that I don't understand why you don't want to talk to us, painful as the topic might be. I'd think that you'd want to do whatever you could to clear your pal Duncan's name."

Patrick took his eyes off the game to look at Libby. "I don't have to do anything because they won't convict him. The whole thing is ridiculous. They have nothing to go on."

"They have physical evidence," Libby observed.

"It's circumstantial. It can be challenged in court," Patrick replied.

"Yes, it can," Libby agreed. "However, the prosecutor thinks they have a strong enough case to bring to trial. Otherwise the powers that be wouldn't have charged Duncan in the first place. Now, we believe he was set up, and unless we can prove that to be the case, your friend is going away for life."

Patrick didn't say anything.

"Glad you're not a friend of mine, that's all I can say," Bernie said.

"Duncan can take care of himself," Patrick answered.

"Let's suppose what you say is right. That Duncan can take care of himself. There's something else you should be concerned about," Bernie told him.

"Like what?"

"Think about it," Bernie said.

Patrick made an impatient gesture with his hand. "Frankly, the only thing I want to think about is you two leaving me alone."

Bernie raised a finger. "Give me one more minute," she

said, and then continued on without waiting for Patrick's answer. "You had a group of friends and two of them are dead and one of them is being held for their murder."

"So?" Patrick said. "Your point is?"

"So do you believe that Duncan killed Liza and Sweeney?" Bernie asked.

"No. I don't. Of course I don't," Patrick replied emphatically. "That's ridiculous. I already told you that."

"Then," Bernie said, "that means that someone else set up Duncan to take the fall for the two murders. Now, how do you know that that someone isn't interested in killing you and everyone else in your group as well?"

Patrick blinked. He put his beer down. "Why would anyone do that?" he asked.

Bernie smiled inwardly as she reflected that he was beginning to sound worried. "I don't know," she said. "Why would someone blow up Mike Sweeney's house?"

"But that was an accident," Patrick protested.

"Was it?" Bernie said. "I'm not so sure. Maybe your place will be next."

Patrick brought his face down until it was inches from Bernie's. "You're pulling this stuff out of your ass."

"First of all, that's rude," Bernie told him. "Second of all, judging by your reaction, I'd say you believe me. And thirdly, you have a blackhead on your nose you should take care of."

Patrick put his hand up to his nose, realized what he'd done and took it off. "Listen," he said to Bernie and Libby, "I don't know anything. I don't know why Mike Sweeney was killed. I don't know why Liza was killed. And that's the truth."

"I don't believe you," Libby said.

"Then don't," Patrick said. "I couldn't care less."

"I'll tell you what I think," Libby told him. "I think that Mike Sweeney lost a lot of people a lot of money and that maybe Liza helped him do it. So maybe they just screwed over the wrong person. Or maybe Liza helped kill Sweeney and whoever she helped decided to shut her up. Maybe you'll be next."

Patrick threw up his hands. "I'll say one thing for you. You definitely have a great imagination."

"Nevertheless," Libby said, "they're both dead. That is a fact that can't be argued with."

Patrick reached over, grabbed his beer, and took a healthy slug. "Let me repeat this for the nine-hundredth time. I can't help you. I can't help you because I don't know anything."

"Maybe you do and you don't know it," Bernie said.

"I don't. I don't. I don't," Patrick said, raising his voice. "What do I have to do to get you to believe me?"

Bernie turned to Libby. "What do you think Patrick has to do?" she asked.

"He could give us some of the names of the people who lost money because of Mike," Libby answered.

Patrick cackled. "What, are you two kidding me? Everyone lost money for everyone in the last two years. That's the nature of our business."

"Yeah," Bernie said. "I know. We live in this world too. But I understand that Sweeney's losses were higher than most and that he wasn't called Churn Em and Burn Em Mike for nothing. I have it on good authority that his losses were especially steep. Sometimes as much as fifty percent. Especially for his chums—a group you belong to."

Patrick was silent for a moment. Then he said, "His brokerage firm has a list of his clients. You'd have to get it from them."

"So you guys never talked about business?" Libby asked Patrick.

"No, we didn't," Patrick said.

"Somehow I find that difficult to believe given the circumstances," Libby responded. "I mean I always talk business with my friends."

Patrick shrugged. "Good for you. But we don't. We leave the office in the office."

Libby snapped her fingers. "Which leaves us with another possibility."

Patrick groaned. "Spare me, please."

"I will," Libby said. "But the killer might not. Because maybe the person who killed Sweeney and Liza isn't some random pissed off investor, maybe it's one of the other people in the Corned Beef and Cabbage Club. How does the old saying go, Bernie, the one about how we always kill our nearest and dearest?"

"It's we always kill the things we love, Libby."

Libby nodded. "That's so true, Bernie." She turned to Patrick. "You should think about that," she told him. "Who knows, you may be next on the list. Don't you agree, Bernie?"

"Without a doubt, Libby," Bernie said.

Libby unzipped her hoodie. It was definitely warm in the place with all the people crowding around. "If I were Patrick, I'd be really worried right now."

"Well, so would I, Libby. But I guess Patrick figures he can take care of himself."

"That's because he's a tough guy, Bernie, and tough guys never ask for help."

"I wish I was like that, Bernie."

"Me too, Libby."

Patrick looked from Libby to Bernie and back again. "Are you two through with the dog and pony show?" he asked.

Bernie looked around. "I'm confused. I don't see a dog or a pony. Do you, Libby?"

"Definitely not, Bernie."

Patrick's jaw muscles tightened. "I'm tired of listening

to you two. I am done," he said, enunciating each word. "Finished. Are we clear?"

Bernie smiled. "No need to get offensive. I think we're done too. Just let me ask my sister to make sure. Libby. What do you think? Do you have anything else to add to what's already been said?"

Libby shook her head. "Nope. I think we've said everything we have to say."

Bernie reached over and clapped Patrick on the shoulder. "Good luck. You know where we are. If you ever want to tell us anything, don't hesitate to give us a call. Hopefully, it wouldn't be too late. And if it is, we'll be at your funeral."

And with that Libby and Bernie strolled out of the bar.

Chapter 21

The silence hit Bernie and Libby as soon as they stepped outside of RJ's.

"I must be getting old," Bernie said to Libby. "I mean I never thought I'd say this, but the quiet is nice."

"I always thought so," Libby said. She reflected that whereas Bernie had loved going to rock concerts and sitting in the front row so she could feel the bass pulse through her body, she had always preferred folk music with an acoustic guitar accompaniment. Libby paused to zip her hoodie back up. Then she popped a chocolate kiss in her mouth, while Bernie took a deep breath of fresh air.

"That was fun in a weird kind of way," Libby said after the chocolate had dissolved in her mouth.

Bernie stuck her hands in her jacket pocket and started toward the van. "Kind of like bear baiting."

"I'm surprised Patrick didn't slug us," Libby told Bernie as she fell in step with her sister. "We were incredibly annoying."

They skirted the cars and climbed the grass incline to the neighboring parking lot.

Bernie chuckled. "If we were guys he would have, that's for sure. I mean if I were him I would have wanted to kill me in there. But that's the advantage of being female. We can be as annoying as we want and all Patrick can do is be rude or leave. He can't even yell that loudly at us. At least not in public. It makes him look bad to treat a female that way."

By now Libby and Bernie were at the van.

"That's so unPC, Bernie," Libby said as she walked around to the passenger side and hopped in.

"I know. And I don't care. After all, we all have to work with what we have," Bernie replied once she was inside their vehicle.

Bernie inserted the key in the ignition, then left it there. It was chilly in the van, but she didn't want to turn it on, thereby possibly attracting attention to it. She was thinking she should have worn warmer socks and brought some gloves along, as well as a flask of hot chocolate—not cocoa—chocolate with cinnamon and maybe a pinch of red pepper—when Libby spoke.

"Speaking of work," Libby was saying, "do you think this will?"

Bernie shrugged. "Well, I think what we did in there is definitely going to stir things up a bit," she replied. "At least I hope it will."

"So what do we do now?" Libby asked.

"We sit and we wait," Bernie said, rubbing her hands together.

"For how long?" Libby asked. "Because I'm freezing. Can't we turn on the van?"

"No. We can't," Bernie said. "Patrick might see the exhaust when he comes out and change his mind about what he's going to do."

"That's *if* he comes out, Bernie."

"*When* he comes out, Libby."

"He could just call. That's what I would do."

"Not if he's paranoid."

Libby crossed her arms over her chest and sank down in

her seat. "Fine. All I know is that if I get pneumonia it's going to be your fault."

"Stop whining. I'm cold too."

"I'm not whining," Libby said.

"Then what would you call it?" Bernie demanded.

"Being cold and uncomfortable and communicating that fact to you."

"Jeez," Bernie muttered. "What a crybaby."

Libby turned toward her. "What did you just say?"

"Nothing. I didn't say anything."

"Good." Libby took two more chocolate kisses out of the pocket of her hoodie and offered one to Bernie.

Bernie shook her head. "No thanks. Do you have an inexhaustible supply of those things?"

"Pretty much. Some people have Xanax, I have chocolate. Personally, I think chocolate is better." Libby was quiet for a moment while she unwrapped the kisses and popped them into her mouth. "I don't see how people do stakeouts," Libby said after she'd savored the taste. She knew lots of foodies disdained milk chocolate as inferior, but Hershey's Kisses were her comfort food and she was sticking with them. They'd seen her through her mom's death, her breakup with Orion, and holidays at the store and she wasn't about to abandon them now. "And anyway," Libby continued, "we're going to have to go soon because I have to pee."

"Tell me you're kidding," Bernie said.

"Nope. I'm not," Libby said, even though she really didn't have to go that badly. She was just tired and bored and wanted to go home.

"Why didn't you do it when we were in RJ's?" Bernie demanded.

"Duh. Obviously because I didn't have to go then. I think it's the cold."

Bernie shook her head. "Can you wait a little while, at least?" Sometimes she just wanted to murder her sister.

"I guess," Libby said. "What's your definition of a little while?" she asked.

"Fifteen minutes."

"Fine," Libby said, trying not to smirk. "I'll try for fifteen minutes, but I'm not promising anything."

Three minutes later the door to RJ's opened and a group of people came walking out. As they stopped to button up their coats, Bernie pointed to the man at the far right. "Look," she said to Bernie. "There's Patrick."

Libby leaned forward and squinted slightly. Bernie was right. It was Patrick. She and Bernie watched as he hurried across the parking lot and jumped into an Infiniti.

"Expensive car," Bernie observed.

"Would you expect anything less?" Libby asked.

"No. Not really," Bernie replied as she started the van.

"We're not going to be able to keep up," Libby commented as Bernie put the van in gear.

"There is that problem," Bernie allowed, since the van didn't go over forty miles an hour on a good day and the Infiniti probably did ninety without even thinking about it. "But hopefully—fingers crossed—Patrick will take the town streets and then that won't be a problem."

"And if he doesn't?" Libby demanded.

"Then," Bernie said, "we're going to be out of luck."

But as it turned out, the sisters weren't. Patrick's car took a right on Ash and a left onto New Castle. Then it traveled five blocks and made a sharp left onto Kramer and another sharp left onto Mountainview.

"Where is he going?" Libby asked.

"I guess we'll find out," Bernie said.

She dropped back so Patrick wouldn't spot her, which would be easy enough to do because the van was nothing if not visible. When she made the turn onto Fellows, she thought she'd lost him, but then she spotted the Infiniti turning into the drive of a brown ranch house in the middle of the block.

"Isn't that Connor's parents' house?" Libby asked Bernie. They'd catered a surprise birthday party for Mrs. Connor last year.

Bernie nodded. "Now that I think of it, I overheard Mrs. Dorchester telling Mrs. Stein that they were down in Florida until mid-April."

"Maybe they came back early," Libby said, indicating the lights in the house.

Bernie shook her head. "That's not their car in the driveway. They had a Honda Civic. I remember because I had to move it." She indicated the Jeep Cherokee parked in front of Patrick's Infiniti. "I think that's Connor's car."

Libby watched Patrick get out of his car, slam the door shut, and stride up the driveway. He looked furious. "I guess we'll know soon enough."

"I guess we will," Bernie said.

"Can't you get any closer?" Libby asked her. "It's hard to see from here. Or hear anything for that matter."

Bernie moved the van another three feet. "Yeah. We need to get one of those miracle ear things that let you eavesdrop on conversations five hundred yards away." She put the van in park. "How's that?" she asked Libby.

"Better but not great."

"Well, I can't get any closer. I mean we do have *A Little Taste of Heaven* airbrushed on both sides of the van."

"I know," Libby said. "It's certainly not the ideal vehicle to do detective work in."

"That's for sure." Bernie watched Patrick ring the doorbell. "The only saving grace is that I think Patrick is too upset to notice us."

"And if he does we can always drive off," Libby said.

Bernie made a noise of agreement. She wasn't answering Libby because all of her attention was focused on the door. A moment later, Connor answered.

"Now, that's interesting," Libby said. "What's he doing

here? He owns a co-op down in the Pines and I heard he and his wife were closing on a McMansion in Liberty."

"Maybe he's house sitting for his parents," Bernie said.

"Maybe he is, but knowing Connor, I don't think so. He's not a helpful kind of guy."

Bernie rubbed her hands together. The chill was beginning to get to her. "Speaking of his wife, I wonder where the good Priscilla is? Such a charming creature."

Libby laughed. "You're just jealous of her sense of style."

Bernie smiled. "Yes. That must be it."

A moment later Bernie's question was answered when Priscilla joined Connor at the door.

"God, she's like a refugee from the cover of a bad pulp fiction novel," Bernie said, looking at her. Priscilla was wearing skintight leopard pants, a slinky low-cut black top that her boobs were falling out of, and platform shoes. Bernie shook her head. "She amazes me no matter how many times I see her—and I don't mean that in a good way."

"I figured," Libby said.

"You," Priscilla screeched. "What are you doing here?"

For a moment Bernie thought Priscilla was talking to her. Then she realized that she was screaming at Patrick.

"I told you never to come here," she yelled at him.

"Listen," Patrick began, but Priscilla cut him off. "No, you listen. You and your friends are responsible for this. We wouldn't be here if it wasn't for you. Now get out of here and don't come back." And she slammed the door in Patrick's face.

Patrick rang the bell again. No one answered. He gave the door a kick, then he turned around and headed back to his car.

"What do you think that's about?" Libby asked.

"I'd say bad investments," Bernie said as she watched

Patrick take out his cell and make a call. Then he backed out of the driveway and zoomed off.

A moment later the door to Connor's parents house opened again and Connor came out. Bernie and Libby could hear Priscilla screaming "don't you dare leave" in the background, but Connor slammed the door and headed for his SUV.

"Well, one thing's for sure," Bernie said to Libby as she watched Connor pull out into the street and make a left, the same left that Patrick had made. "We did stir things up." When Connor was about a quarter of a block away she started the van and pulled out into the road, but by the time she got to the end of the block Connor was nowhere in sight. "Drats," she said to Libby. "Should we go left or right?"

Libby looked down the block in either direction. She couldn't see any cars moving. "I don't know," she said. "I think we may have lost them."

Bernie sat in the middle of the street with the van's engine idling. "They could be heading back to RJ's," she said.

"Or the park or movies or the library or to get a slice of pizza," Libby said. "We really don't know."

"Maybe we should drive around and see if we can spot them," Bernie said.

"I have a better idea," Libby told her sister. "Let's go back to the house and talk to Priscilla."

Bernie nodded as she turned the idea over in her head. "I like it. I like it a lot. Except there is one tiny flaw with that plan, Libby. She hates me."

"Everyone hates you. Maybe she's forgotten what you said by now."

"I so doubt it. Priscilla is the kind of person who still remembers who sat in front of her in second grade."

"You could be right," Libby said. "But even if you are,

204 Isis Crawford

what do we have to lose? After all, the worst she can do is slam the door in our faces."

"And you do have to pee," Bernie said.

"Yes, I do," Libby agreed even though she didn't. But she wasn't going to go back on her lie now. That would have been bad form.

"Okey-dokey," Bernie said as she turned the van around and parked it in Connor's parents' driveway.

"It really wasn't very nice what you said about Priscilla's eyelashes," Libby said to Bernie as Bernie put the emergency brake on, because the driveway was on a slant and the van had a tendency to roll.

"I didn't mean for her to hear it," Bernie replied. "I didn't think she would repeat it."

"You can't say everything that pops into your head," Libby told her sister.

"Can I help it if her eyelashes did look like caterpillars? My God. They were awful."

And with that she and Libby got out of their vehicle, walked up the path lined with fairy lights and dotted with little wooden cows, and climbed up the five slate stairs that led to the entrance way. The sisters could hear the sound of the television coming from inside the house.

"Go on and ring," Bernie said to Libby. "It was your idea."

Libby hesitated for a moment. Then she put her hand up and pressed the bell.

Chapter 22

Sean looked up at Orion standing in front of him. To say Sean was surprised to see Orion standing there like that was putting it mildly. Especially since he'd just gotten off the phone with him less than twenty minutes ago.

Orion unzipped his jacket. "You look surprised," he said.

Sean put his coffee mug down on the side table. "That's because I am."

"But you said you wanted to talk to me when I spoke to you on the phone just now, that you wanted to hear what it was I had to say."

"And I do." Sean sat up straighter in his chair. "I just never figured you for popping up here. I figured you'd want to talk somewhere else. Somewhere . . .ah . . . a little more neutral."

Orion shifted his weight from one foot to the other. "Hey, if you don't want me here I understand. I'll be happy to leave."

"No. No. It's fine with me. But let's just say that Libby would most definitely not like seeing you here," Sean told him, indicating the flat with a nod of his chin. He was surprised at how much he still disliked the guy. Even after all this time. But business was business and in this case that came first. After all, over the years he'd talked to lots of people he didn't like in order to get the information that he needed.

"Don't you think I know that?" Orion said. "Give me some credit. Why do you think I don't come in the shop anymore?"

"Because you're afraid of being poisoned?" Sean asked, breaking the tension between the two men.

Orion laughed. "She would, wouldn't she?"

Sean grinned despite himself. "Let's just say I wouldn't be eating anything Libby offered me if I were you—although to be fair she's not as rabid as she once was—so maybe she'd just make you really sick instead of dead."

"Whew." Orion passed the back of his hand across his brow in a mock gesture of relief. "That makes me feel so much better."

"Figured it would," Sean replied.

Orion scratched behind his ear, then put his hand down by his side. "The only reason I'm here is that I was passing by right after I spoke to you and I saw Libby and Bernie going out, so I figured why not come up and save you the bother of meeting with me."

"Very thoughtful of you." Sean looked Orion up and down. "You seem to be doing well for yourself."

"I'm not doing badly," Orion allowed.

Sean pointed to Orion's shoes. They were brown and cream-colored saddle shoes. "Aren't they like the ones Mike Sweeney was wearing when he was killed?"

Orion glanced down at his feet. "I don't know, but it wouldn't surprise me if they were. Lots of the guys are wearing things like that now."

"So what does a pair of those cost?" Sean asked.

"Five hundred dollars a pair, give or take a couple of bucks. What can I say, Mr. Simmons?" Orion continued, catching the expression on Sean's face. "The market has treated me well."

"Evidently." It amazed Sean that those shoes would go for that much. He remembered his mom trying to get him to wear saddle shoes when he was in high school, but he'd absolutely refused. Too preppy. "I'll say this," Sean continued. "You're certainly doing a lot better than you were doing when you were with Libby. You didn't even have a job half the time. No. Scratch that. You almost never had a job. Most of the time you didn't have enough money to put gas in your car and here you are buying five hundred dollar shoes. Nice to know that the American dream is still alive and well."

"It has been for me." Orion looked down at the floor, then back up at Sean. "The time I was with Libby was a bad patch in my life." He spread his arms apart. "I treated a lot of people very badly, Mr. Simmons. I acted in ways I'm not proud of."

"Like stealing Libby's car and picking up Suzy and going down to New York City for the weekend?" Sean said.

"Yeah. Like that," Orion said. "But then I got off the pills and got my mind back. You know I *did* try and talk to Libby. I *did* try to apologize to her, but she wouldn't talk to me. Maybe I should have written her a note, Mr. Simmons."

"She probably would have torn it up," Sean said. And if she hadn't I would have, he added silently.

"That's what I figured. Do you think she'll ever forgive me?" Orion asked.

"Doubtful," Sean said, thinking back to the way Libby had reacted to the mention of his name not that long ago.

Orion hung his head. "I really did treat her horribly, Mr. Simmons."

"Words are cheap," Sean told him. "Especially coming from you."

"I mean it," Orion protested.

Sean wasn't sure whether Orion did or didn't, but did it really matter? Not really. The trick was not to allow himself to get sidetracked by the past and to focus on what he needed to know. And he fully intended to do that. After he said one more thing.

Sean folded the newspaper he'd been reading and laid it on the side table next to him. "You know," he informed Orion after he'd taken a sip of his coffee, "for about a year or so I wanted to hurt you really, really badly for what you did to my daughter. And if I were younger and in better shape, I might have done that, but I'm not." There he'd said it.

"I can understand," Orion said.

"No," Sean said, contradicting him. "I don't think you can. And I don't think you will either until you have a daughter of your own some day. But she's doing all right now, no thanks to you."

"Marvin's a good guy," Orion observed.

"Yes, he is," Sean agreed.

Orion looked around. Then he said, "It feels funny being here after all this time."

"I would imagine," Sean said dryly.

"And Libby is happy?"

"Yes. I think she is."

"That's good."

The conversation came to a standstill. "Like I said when you called me," Orion offered after a moment had gone by, "anything I can do to help, I will. It's the least I can do."

"I appreciate the sentiment," Sean said. "But you'll understand if I don't ask you to sit down."

Orion nodded. "Totally."

"I guess," Sean said, "even though I know what happened wasn't all your fault, that Libby had something to do with it as well, the bottom line is that I don't like you very much, so why don't you tell me what you have to say and then leave."

Orion nodded his head again. "I totally value your honesty."

"This isn't a sales call," Sean told him. "You're not selling me financial instruments. So do you have something to tell me or not?"

"I do," Orion replied. "But the whole thing is very technical."

"Simplify it for me."

"Okay." Orion rubbed his hands together. "To begin, the whole group—"

"The Corned Beef and Cabbage Club?"

"Yeah. Those guys have been running a kind of a Ponzi scheme."

"Was Duncan involved?"

"You betcha, along with the other chowderheads. See, everyone was getting along fine and then everyone started losing money and then suddenly they weren't getting along so fine, and Sweeney was the person that lost the money for them.

"Rumor has it that not only did all of them lose a lot of money, but that the feds were coming in and Sweeney was about to hand his friends over to them in return for minimal jail time. But that's just a rumor and there are plenty of rumors floating around and most of them aren't true."

"Do you think this one is?" Sean asked Orion.

"I don't know," Orion told him. "I really don't."

"So what were these guys doing?"

"This is where it gets technical. . . ."

"I'm sure a bright guy like you can translate it into English," Sean said.

"I'll try," Orion told him as he rocked back and forth on his heels.

"You do that," Sean said.

Orion thought for a moment and then began. "Okay," he said. "The bottom line is this. People were trading back and forth with one another, kiting up the prices of financial instruments, financial instruments that mostly consisted of insurance packets. Insurance policies that were taken out on people and then sold to other people."

"They can do that?" Sean asked.

"Oh yeah. People have been doing it for years. It's perfectly legal."

"So I can take out a policy on Libby and sell it to someone else?" Sean asked.

"Or," Orion replied, "even better. You can take a policy out on someone and not tell them."

"And if they die, I'm the beneficiary?" Sean asked.

Orion nodded.

"Sounds like a recipe for disaster to me," Sean said. "Could someone have written a policy on Sweeney?"

"They could have," Orion told him. "But since he was murdered it wouldn't pay off. I mean if they'd wanted to do that, they'd have to find some less obvious way to kill him. As in, he'd have to be a heroin addict and OD."

"Someone did that?" Sean asked.

"Last year in DC."

"Someone actually sold a life insurance policy on an addict?"

Orion shrugged. "It's a strange, strange world out there, Mr. Simmons."

"Is there any way to check and make sure about Sweeney?"

"I can't," Orion said. "Aside from it being extremely difficult, I'd have to get into the system and check and I'm not authorized to do that. Besides, these policies are written in one place, then sold to someone else, then rebundled with other policies and sold to yet another person and so on down the line. It would take weeks to untangle all the strands, months if the person who did it didn't want to be found."

"And you can't do it?" Sean asked.

"Absolutely not, Mr. Simmons."

"Is it that you don't have the ability or the desire?" Sean asked him.

"Both, Mr. Simmons. I don't have that kind of technical know-how and I don't want to lose my job and land up in jail."

"Do you know anyone who could?"

Orion shook his head again. "You're talking about a real geek here and I don't know many of those."

"So you'd need a subpoena to get to the bottom of this," Sean said, a subpoena he was positive the DA wouldn't issue.

"I'm guessing that you would."

Sean didn't reply immediately. He was distracted by the sound of the rain on the windows. The weather channel had warned that a nor'easter was on the way. It looked as if it had arrived.

"And anyway," Orion continued, "I don't think it's true. It's just too far-fetched. I can't imagine any of those guys doing something like that. Kicking someone in the head, yes. Doing this, no."

"You may be right," Sean said. Sweeney's death had seemed to him to be a crime of impulse brought on by anger and alcohol, not a carefully planned, bloodless, staged scenario. He shifted his weight around in his chair. He'd been sitting too long and would have to get up soon. "So how does Liza tie in with all of this?" Sean asked Orion.

Orion shrugged. "As far as I know, she doesn't."

"No word about her at all?" Sean insisted.

"No. She was a trader groupie."

"Trader groupie?" Sean repeated.

"Yeah. Like the cop groupies. She was one of those girls who liked trader action instead of cop action—it turned her on—so she hung around with the traders. She made the rounds, although I understand she was with Duncan before she died. Maybe he got fed up and did her."

"Maybe," Sean said. "Did you hang around with her?"

"No, Mr. Simmons. I didn't," Orion said.

Sean thought he might be lying, but he wasn't sure. "And who was Liza with before Duncan?" Sean asked.

"I think she was with Patrick. Or maybe Connor. I don't know. I have trouble keeping those guys straight. They all look alike to me."

"What do you hear about Duncan?" Sean asked, changing the subject.

"In what sense?"

"In any sense."

"Not much really. He hung with the other guys. He trades in derivatives. He likes to gamble—does a lot of options and puts—and lost lots and lots of money with Sweeney. Way more than he can afford. He's about an inch shy of declaring bankruptcy, but then so are the other guys for that matter. Do you want me to ask around?"

Sean nodded. "That would be helpful. Anything else to tell me?"

"That's about it." Orion glanced at his watch. "Well, if that's the case . . ."

"Go on," Sean said. "Get out of here before Libby and Bernie come back."

"Thanks." And Orion turned and went down the stairs.

Sean could hear Orion closing the bottom door behind him. He sat for a while and watched the raindrops beating on the windowpane and tried to make sense out of what Orion had said, but it really didn't seem to go very far in explaining what had happened. He had the distinct feeling that he was missing something, something big.

But he was confident that the answer would come to him in time. It usually did. A cigarette would help the process. He always thought better when he smoked. Sad but true. Unfortunately, he couldn't do that now. Well, he could. He could go downstairs and huddle in the doorway and light up. But he wasn't that desperate yet. And besides, there was a chance that someone would see him and tell Bernie and Libby, or even worse, his daughters would catch him when they came back, and he wasn't in the mood to listen to the lecture that was sure to follow.

Chapter 23

"Someone around here definitely has a cow fetish," Bernie noted as she took in the mailbox designed to look like a cow, the mat on the porch that said, *udderly glad to see you*, and the wreath decorated with milkmaids and milk pails.

Libby was just telling Bernie that she thought that that was a safe thing to say when the door flew open.

"It's the Simmons sisters. How charming," Priscilla said, looking at them. Her tone was not hospitable. Neither was her glance.

"I know you don't like us very much," Bernie began. Talk about stating the obvious, she thought. "I know we've had issues in the past."

Priscilla scowled. "Why? Just because you're a snot and you think you're better than anyone else? Just because you told Suzy that my false eyelashes reminded you of caterpillars and gave you the creeps? My good, expensive eyelashes that I got in Saks," Priscilla added.

So much for forgetting, Libby thought. This was going to be interesting.

"I never really said that," Bernie lied.

"You most certainly did," Priscilla shot back.

"She really didn't," Libby said, feeling as if she should contribute to the conversation. Sisterly solidarity and all that stuff.

Priscilla and Bernie both ignored her. Fine, Libby thought, feeling miffed. So much for sisterly solidarity. Be that way. See if she cared.

"No, Priscilla," Bernie told her. "What I said was that I admired you for wearing eyelashes like that and that I wished I could have, but that on me they would have looked like caterpillars crawling over my face." Bernie held up her hand. "May God strike me dead if I'm lying."

Libby waited for the thunderclap and the hand to descend from the heavens. Nothing happened. And it hadn't ever since Bernie had started to say that at age twelve. As always, she was both amazed and appalled by her sister's ability to lie.

"I don't believe you," Priscilla said. But Bernie thought she sounded less sure of herself than she had before.

Bernie put her hand down. She didn't believe in the whole "may God strike me dead" thing, but on the other hand there was no sense in pushing her luck either. "It's true," she told Priscilla. "I think Suzy just misheard me . . . maybe on purpose." Lie number two.

Priscilla nibbled on her lower lip while she thought. "Well," she finally said. "It's true that she never liked you very much."

"No. She didn't," Bernie agreed. And that was true. "I didn't even know that she had said that to you." But that statement wasn't.

Priscilla folded her arms over her chest while she considered what Bernie had said. Bernie could see that Priscilla was wavering. Bernie was trying to think of what else she could say to convince Priscilla of her truthfulness when Priscilla's eyes narrowed. Damn, Bernie thought. It was too late. As someone who'd been involved in retail for a long time, she recognized that she'd lost the moment.

"I still don't believe you," Priscilla told Bernie. "You almost had me, *almost* being the key word, but I'm not buying what you're putting out."

Bernie shrugged. She could but try. "Fine," she said. "Don't believe me. But could you let us in anyway? My sister really has to pee. . . ."

Libby leaned forward and put on what she hoped was a sincere smile. "I do," she said.

"And," Bernie said, "no matter what you think of me, we really do need to talk."

Priscilla tapped the crystal of her diamond-encrusted Rolex watch with a long carmine fingernail. "Why now? Are you nuts? Do you know what time it is?"

"Yes. I realize it's late," Bernie said.

"And I really do have to pee," Libby said.

Priscilla raised an eyebrow. "And you came all the way to Connor's parents' house to use their bathroom?" she asked her. "It must be very special for you to make the trip out here."

"Actually we were following Patrick from RJ's," Libby replied, having decided that in this case honesty was the best policy. "And he ended up here. And now I have to pee."

"I know where the scumbag ended up," Priscilla said. "I threw him out."

"We saw," Libby said. "And we saw Connor going after him."

Priscilla's eyes narrowed. "He's a scumbag too," she said. "They're all alike. Guys that is."

"Not really," Bernie said.

Priscilla ignored the comment. "Why were you following Patrick?" she asked Libby.

Bernie could see that Priscilla's interest was piqued. This is a good thing, she thought. Maybe they'd end up talking after all. "That's why we have to have a chat," Bernie told her. Watching Priscilla's face, she could see her features softening ever so slightly. Yes, Bernie thought. She's going to invite us in.

A moment later, Priscilla gave it up. "Okay," she said as she fingered her earrings. "Yeah. Come in. What the hell. The bathroom is down the hall, the third door on the right," she said to Libby.

"I appreciate this," Bernie said to Priscilla once they were inside and Libby had disappeared down the hall.

Priscilla put her hands on her hips. "So what's going on? How come you're following Patrick?"

"We've been hired to help with Duncan's defense. . . ."

Priscilla's eyes lit up. "And you think Patrick might have something to do with Sweeney's murder?" she asked.

"Possibly," Bernie replied in as noncommittal a voice as she could manage. She didn't feel it necessary to mention that the same could be true of Connor or Liam.

"See," Priscilla said, shaking her head. "I told Connor those guys were no good. I told him to stay away from them. But did he listen? No. He did not."

Bernie shook her head sympathetically. "My mother always said you were known by the company you keep," she added in a pious tone. It was a phrase that used to absolutely infuriate Bernie, so she was amazed to hear it coming out of her mouth now.

"That is so true," Priscilla said. "And now look where we're living." She gestured at the living room. "I think I'd rather be shot."

"It is very white," Bernie allowed, peering inside.

"Very white?" Priscilla shrieked. "It's all white! Everything in this house is white! I feel as if I'm in some simultaneous deprivation tank. . . ."

"I think you mean stimulus deprivation tank," Bernie said.

Priscilla waved her hand in the air. "Whatever." She leaned in toward Bernie. "And you know the worst thing about this?"

"That you're living with your mother-in-law?"

"Even worse?" Priscilla said.

"What?" Bernie asked.

"On top of everything else, Connor's mother is a neat freak. I mean totally. I'm afraid to walk across the floor here. I might get footprints on the white shag carpet. I mean who has white shag carpet? That's so seventies. And this is the original one." Priscilla pointed down. "If that doesn't say it all I don't know what does."

"I can't believe that," Bernie said, because she couldn't.

"It's true," Priscilla said. Then she nodded toward the outside with her chin. "And what about the cows? How do you like them? That's what I think too," Priscilla said when Bernie remained diplomatically silent.

"So how come you're here?" Bernie asked her. "I thought you guys were buying a new house?"

Priscilla gave a bitter laugh. "That was pre Mike Sweeney. Him and Liam and Patrick and Duncan talked Connor into this stupid investment, and not only did he use his money, he used mine as well."

"Oops," Bernie said, thinking of what the other guys' wives had told her.

"You can say that again," Priscilla agreed. "One thing I can tell you. I will never, ever share a checking account with anyone, ever again."

"I could see that," Bernie said, remembering when Orion had taken money out of Libby's checking account, money that they'd needed to pay their sales tax.

Thank heavens her mother had been dead when that had happened. She couldn't imagine what Rose would have done. Well, that wasn't true. She could imagine. Rose would have run straight to her dad and her dad would have gone out and hurt Orion really, really badly. As it was, she and Libby had kept it to themselves.

"You have no idea what that's like," Priscilla said to Bernie.

"Actually," Bernie said, "I think I do."

Priscilla gave her an appraising glance but didn't ask Bernie who she was talking about. Instead Priscilla said, "I'd like to kill him."

"Who?" Bernie asked just to hear Priscilla say it.

"Mike Sweeney, of course. Only he's already dead."

"Then that could be a problem. I don't think you can do it twice."

Priscilla didn't smile at Bernie's crack. Instead she took a deep breath and let it out. "I told Connor and told him not to do this. I begged and I pleaded, but you know what he told me?" Priscilla paused.

She obviously wanted to have Bernie ask her what Connor had said to her, so Bernie did.

"No. What did Connor tell you?" Bernie asked.

"Connor told me that Sweeney knew what he was talking about and I was just this dumb nothing."

"He actually said that?" Bernie asked.

"Those were his exact words." And Priscilla crossed herself. "I swear to God. But I went to see Sweeney anyway and he told me to stop yammering."

"Someone saying something like that to me would have bothered me," Bernie observed. "A lot."

Priscilla glared at Bernie. "What? You think it didn't bother me?"

"It couldn't have bothered you that much because you're still with Connor."

"Believe me, Bernie. It bothered me plenty."

"Then why are you still with him?" Bernie asked.

Priscilla shrugged. "I don't know."

"You still love him?" Bernie said softly. She remembered that even after Orion had robbed Libby's bank account, she had still stuck up for him. It had taken walking in on him with another woman to finally persuade her that Orion was a no good kind of guy.

Priscilla turned her head away. "I guess maybe I still do," she said in a very soft voice. "Is that stupid, or what?"

Before Bernie could think of anything to say, Libby came out of the bathroom and walked down the hall. The moment was past, Bernie reflected. And maybe that was a good thing, because she really didn't have any words of wisdom to convey.

"That's the first time I've ever sat on a soft toilet seat," Libby said to Priscilla, effectively changing the tone of the conversation.

"Weird, isn't it?" Priscilla said.

"Very," Libby said.

"Priscilla and I have just been talking about Mike Sweeney and the rest of the gang," Bernie said, filling Libby in.

"Really?" Libby said. "Anything interesting?"

"Everyone is broke," Bernie said.

"Thanks to Mike Sweeney," Priscilla added.

"Besides that?" Libby asked.

"We haven't gotten any farther yet," Bernie said.

Priscilla leaned forward. "I'll tell you this—Duncan hated Mike Sweeney. Absolutely hated him."

"Why?" Bernie asked.

Priscilla nodded knowingly. "Because Sweeney got him fired." Then she leaned back against the wall, crossed her arms over her chest, and smiled a satisfied smile.

Bernie frowned. That wasn't the impression she had. "Are you sure?" she asked Priscilla. "I thought Duncan was still working."

Priscilla fingered one of her gold hoops. "That's what he wants everyone to think so he pretends he is, but he isn't. Not really."

"And you know this for a fact?" Libby asked.

Priscilla nodded.

"How did you find out?" Bernie asked. "Did Connor tell you?"

Priscilla snorted. "Don't be stupid. Connor never tells me anything. Like ever. He thinks I'm too dumb to talk to. He only wants to do . . . other stuff."

"So how do you know?" Libby asked.

"I know because Liza gets . . . got her nails done at my manicurist and when I was there Liza happened to come in and Sylvia told me that Liza was having a fit because Duncan got canned and now she couldn't . . . wouldn't be getting the plastic surgery that Duncan was going to pay for." And Priscilla looked down and inspected her nails. They were three inches long, bright red, with little gold stars painted on them.

Obviously not real, Bernie thought, following Priscilla's gaze. "What was Liza going to get?" Bernie asked Priscilla.

"A boob job, of course." And Priscilla looked down and contemplated hers. "I'm lucky I'm naturally endowed."

"Yes, you are," Bernie agreed, although she had her doubts about whether or not Priscilla's were real.

"So did your manicurist tell you what happened?" Bernie asked Priscilla.

"No. Not really," Priscilla replied. "All she said was that they let him leave. Or rather that's what they gave out publicly. Something about downsizing. But the truth is they fired him. And told him if he didn't leave they were going to have him arrested."

Bernie and Libby exchanged a quick glance. This was definitely new.

"Interesting," Bernie said. "Usually firms do that when someone has done something and they don't want anyone else to know," she mused, thinking out loud.

"Like what?" Priscilla said.

"Like something to do with money," Libby replied promptly. "Like people stealing money from clients and firms replacing the money they took so that their clients don't know and thereby go somewhere else. Do you think your manicurist would speak with us?" she asked Priscilla.

Priscilla wrinkled her nose. "I guess she might have, but she's gone. She got married and took off for some weird place like North or South Dakota. Or maybe Idaho. I dunno. Anyway, some place that no one would like to go to."

"Do you happen to know her married name?" Bernie asked.

Priscilla clicked her tongue against the roof of her mouth while she thought. "Longview? Longbranch? Or maybe it's Lowengard? I wasn't listening that closely. In any event I know it starts with a *lo*. Sorry I can't be more help."

"Not a problem," Bernie said. "Let's try another question."

Priscilla giggled. "Gee. I feel as if I'm on the *The Price Is Right* or something. Give me another question."

"Okey-dokey. So how long ago did this thing with Duncan happen?" Bernie asked Priscilla.

"Him getting fired?" Priscilla asked.

"Yes," Libby said.

But Priscilla didn't answer Bernie's question. "Do you hear that?" she said instead.

"What?" Bernie asked because she didn't hear anything.

Chapter 24

"What am I listening for?" Bernie asked.

Priscilla didn't answer. She had her head cocked and was listening intently.

"I don't hear anything either," Libby said.

"He's about two blocks away," Priscilla informed them.

A moment later, Bernie and Libby both heard the sound of a car coming closer.

"Who?" Bernie asked.

"Connor," Priscilla answered.

"He should get his muffler fixed," Libby noted. "It sounds as if it's on its last legs."

Priscilla swallowed. She put her hand over her lips. "You two have to go. You have to go now. Please."

Bernie looked at her. Priscilla looked nervous. No. Not nervous, she decided. Scared.

"Why?" she asked Priscilla. "What's the rush?"

"Connor just . . . he doesn't want anyone to know that we're living with his parents. That's all." Priscilla rubbed her hands together. She was speaking so quickly now, running her words together, that Bernie and Libby had to concentrate on what she was saying. "He's embarrassed so he'll be really, really pissed if he sees you here. Then he'll know I've been talking to you and he'll be upset. He's funny about things like that."

"You talking to other people?" Libby asked.

"Well, talking about work stuff and our finances and things like that. He's a very private person, that's all."

"You seem scared," Libby told her, stating the obvious.

Priscilla smiled wanly. "It'll be fine. I'll be fine. He just yells a lot. I'm used to it." She listened some more. "He's almost here."

Libby was about to tell her she had to be kidding, but Bernie caught her eye and shook her head imperceptibly.

"How about," Bernie said to Priscilla, "if we just tell him we dropped in to talk to you about an order you placed?"

"At this time of night?" Priscilla asked. "And for what?"

"His birthday cake," Libby said.

"Connor's birthday is in June," Priscilla replied.

"Fine. Then for a special dinner you were making for him. And you wanted to surprise him and we were passing by and decided to take a chance and see if you were home," Libby said as Connor's car roared into the driveway.

"I don't know," Priscilla said.

"I think it's going to have to do," Bernie told her. She had to admit that the story wasn't the greatest. She wished she could think of something more plausible, but at the moment her mind was a blank.

"It'll be fine," Libby added with uncharacteristic optimism.

The three women heard Connor's car door slam shut. Then they heard him coming up the stairs. As one they all turned toward the door. A moment later the door flew open and Connor came in. His hair and jacket were wet from the rain. Libby and Bernie noted that he didn't look like a happy camper. Bernie wondered whether that was because he'd gotten wet or whether he'd caught up with Patrick, and if that was the case, she wondered what Patrick had said to him. Probably nothing good, judging by Connor's expression.

Bernie plastered a big smile on her face and said, "Hi, Connor. Don't mind us. We were just leaving."

Connor looked startled to see them. And then he looked angry. "What the hell are they doing here?" he demanded of Priscilla, ignoring Bernie and Libby.

This did not sit well with Bernie. "Hey," she said to Connor before Priscilla could reply. "There's no need to be rude."

Connor turned toward her. "What are you? The manners police? For your information, I'm not being rude. I'm merely inquiring of my wife why we have visitors so late in the evening, which I have a perfect right to do since you are in my home after all. Is that all right with you?"

"It's fine," Bernie told him. She turned to Priscilla. "Should I tell him?"

Priscilla didn't reply and Bernie was afraid Priscilla was about to drop the ball when she rallied and said, "I guess you're going to have to."

"Tell me about what?" Connor demanded.

"We just dropped by to discuss the dinner we were catering for you. Your wife wanted to surprise you."

"At this time of night?" Connor asked incredulously.

"Well, we were just passing by and happened to see you going out of the house so we decided to take advantage of the situation," Bernie told him. Even as she was saying it she decided it sounded pretty lame.

Connor looked at Priscilla. "Is that true?"

Priscilla nodded. But she averted her eyes and studied a patch of carpet on the living room floor. Dead giveaways that she's lying, Bernie thought.

"Well, I don't believe you," Connor said to Priscilla.

Before Priscilla could say anything, Connor turned to

Bernie and Libby. "You two followed Patrick here, didn't you?"

"That's ridiculous," Bernie replied.

"Is it?" Connor replied.

"Yes, it is. Are you saying my sister lied?" Libby said, trying to sound indignant, but sounding squawky instead.

"Yes. I'm saying your sister lied," Connor replied, mimicking Libby's tone of voice.

Libby raised her chin. "I resent that," she said.

"Wow. That makes me feel really bad," Connor sneered. "Patrick told me he thought he saw your van in the rearview mirror and here you are. Amazing coincidence, wouldn't you say?"

"It's called synchronicity," Bernie said. Then she decided to play it straight, because the approach she and Libby were using obviously wasn't getting her anywhere. "Is that what Patrick said?" she asked Connor, changing the subject.

"As a matter of fact, Patrick did," Connor replied.

"Is that why you went after him?" Libby asked.

"Why I went after him is none of your business," Connor snapped.

"So you're not going to tell us what you think about what we said to him?" Libby continued.

Connor smiled. The smile reminded Libby of a shark's. All teeth. Nothing else on Connor's face moved. "I'll be happy to tell you what I think. I think you two are just trying to rattle him."

"It looks as if we succeeded," Bernie noted. "Maybe because we're correct."

"You are so wrong on so many different levels," Connor scoffed. "You just got Patrick in an off moment. But he and I had a chat and now he realizes that what you said is all lies. You just want to get Duncan off the hook and get one of us on it."

"I do want to get Duncan off the hook," Bernie told

Connor. "You're right about that. But I am telling the truth."

Connor stuck his face in Bernie's. "It's been a long day and my patience is exhausted. You and your sister are nothing but a couple of troublemakers," he snarled. "Now I want you to get out of here before you get hurt."

"And who is going to hurt us?" Bernie asked, standing her ground. She was damned if she was going to let herself get run off by this bozo. *Bozo.* It was a nice word. She liked it.

Connor pointed to himself. "I am."

"I'd like to see you try," Bernie flung back at him, although looking at Connor's face, she regretted the words. What am I doing? she thought. Why can't I ever learn to keep my mouth shut? This guy was a rugby player. He outweighed her by eighty pounds, easy. He could put her in the hospital with one swat of his hand.

"You should go," Priscilla said to Bernie and Libby over Connor's shoulder.

Connor whirled around. "Was I talking to you?"

Priscilla cringed. "N-no," she stammered.

"Then stay out of this," Connor told her. "You've done enough damage already."

"But, Connor, I really didn't say anything," Priscilla wailed.

"She didn't," Libby said.

"Did you?" Connor asked Priscilla.

"No," Priscilla said. She raised her hand. "I swear."

Bernie noted that Priscilla's voice was quivering. "We're going," Bernie said hastily. She realized she didn't want to get Connor any angrier than he already was for Priscilla's sake. "We're going right now."

And she and Libby turned to leave. As soon as they were out the front door, Connor slammed it behind them.

"He has quite the temper," Libby observed as they walked down the path to the sidewalk. Bernie and Libby both put up the hoods of the jackets they were wearing to shield their faces from the rain. "Maybe we should have stayed."

"No. I think we would have made it worse if we did that," Bernie said as she stopped and turned and listened for any sounds coming out of the house.

Libby disagreed. "I'm not so sure about that."

Bernie didn't say anything.

"Why are we standing here?" Libby asked.

"To make sure that Priscilla is all right," Bernie replied. "To make sure we don't have to call the cops."

Libby suddenly felt embarrassed that she hadn't thought of that too. She and Bernie stood there motionless for a couple of minutes. They were listening to what was going on inside the house. But all they heard was the television, just like before they'd gone inside. They didn't hear anything breaking, they didn't hear Connor yelling, they didn't hear Priscilla screaming. There was nothing except the sounds of raindrops pattering on the steps and the path, the occasional car going by on Liberty Avenue, and a dog barking down the street.

"I think I found something significant in the bathroom," Libby said once she and her sister had gotten in the van. "Maybe."

"What?" Bernie asked.

"A plastic bottle full of Oxi," Libby said.

"Judging from what we've seen here, I can understand why Priscilla would want to have something like that, although if it were me I'd have taken a sledgehammer to her husband's head by now," Bernie said.

"So violent," Libby said.

"Sometimes that's the only way you can get your point across," Bernie replied.

"Anyway," Libby continued, "the bottle didn't have Priscilla's name on it."

"Connor's?"

"No one's," Libby said.

"So what did the label say?"

"There was no label."

Bernie put the key in the ignition and turned on the van. "So how do you know the pills are Oxis? They could be vitamins."

"I recognize them from when Marvin broke his foot. And since they didn't have a label, I'm betting they're not prescription."

"I wonder if Connor's hooked on them," Bernie mused as she turned on the windshield wipers.

"Maybe we should drive over and ask Duncan," Libby said. "He might know."

"And as long as we're there, we could ask him about getting fired too."

Bernie pinned her hair back up. "Being efficient. I like it."

"Of course, he may be asleep," Libby said.

"Then I guess we'll just have to wake him up," Bernie replied as she pulled onto the road.

"At least we know that he's home," Libby noted as she leaned over and turned on the radio. "He's not going anywhere with that ankle bracelet on, that's for sure."

"I'll say one thing for Connor," Bernie observed after a few minutes had gone by. "He sure is a good fit."

"For killing Sweeney?"

"Yeah. He has the strength and the temper."

"That he does," Libby agreed.

Chapter 25

It had started to rain hard now, the drops pelting the windshield, and as Bernie drove toward the guest house where Duncan was staying she was struck by the lack of security. Bree had said she'd had to hire round the clock guards, but if they were there, Bernie sure didn't see them. But then Bree tended to exaggerate. Not that Bernie was complaining.

"Ready?" Bernie said to Libby after she'd parked the van as close to the guest house as she could get.

Libby nodded and they got out of the van.

The light was on in the guest house and as Libby and Bernie drew nearer they could hear a TV pitchman nattering on about the wonders of Viagra.

Bernie pulled up her hood. "Then let's do it."

Libby did likewise and she and Bernie ran to the door and banged on it. Duncan answered it a moment later.

"What?" he said.

Clumps of his hair were sticking up in the back of his head and Libby decided that he obviously hadn't shaved for at least a week, maybe more. He was holding a bottle of beer in his hand and was wearing pajama bottoms that came down to the tops of his feet thereby hiding the ankle bracelet, a T-shirt that said *Rock or Die* on it, and no shoes.

"What do you want?" he asked, waving the bottle of beer around.

Bernie noted that his speech was slightly slurred. He's probably drunk, she thought. "We want to talk to you," she said, pushing her way inside before Duncan could say no. It was too nasty to stay outside arguing.

Libby followed. As she and Bernie looked around the inside of the cottage, it was obvious to Libby that the place looked a lot worse than the last time she and Bernie had been there. All visible surfaces were covered with garbage. Apparently Duncan wasn't doing well with captivity, even captivity-lite.

There were pizza boxes and KFC buckets and empty bags of take-out food on the dining room table, and open Styrofoam containers half full of old, uneaten, greasy Chinese food strewn over the coffee table. The floor was littered with empty beer and soda bottles, Starbucks coffee cups, and energy drink cans. Piles of socks, pants, and shirts lay crumpled around the perimeter of the living room floor. A faint smell of garbage and must pervaded the air.

"What's the matter?" Bernie asked after she'd looked around. "The maid hasn't been in here recently?"

Duncan shrugged. "What can I say? I've been sick."

Libby studied Duncan for a moment, then said, "You don't look as if you've got anything that a shower and a shave won't cure."

"Ha. Ha. Ha," Duncan said. "Very funny. I'm depressed. Okay? You would be too if you were under house arrest."

"I probably would be," Libby agreed. "But that doesn't mean I wouldn't be picking up after myself."

"Aren't you going to invite us to sit down?" Bernie asked, trying for a friendlier tone.

Duncan shrugged. "Sure. Go ahead if you can find the space."

"Not a problem," Libby said. She went over to the sofa, gathered up the junk mail, newspapers, and magazines that were strewn all over the cushions and dumped everything on the floor. "There we go. Now it's clean. Well, clear."

"Hey," Duncan protested as Libby sat down. "There was no call to do that. Be more respectful of my stuff, if you don't mind. I knew where everything was. I had a filing system going on there and now everything is on the floor."

"Filing and piling. I like it. I never realized that the two words are just a letter apart," Bernie said as she joined her sister on the sofa. "Kind of like lying and dying."

Duncan frowned. "What's that supposed to mean?" he asked.

"Nothing," Bernie told him. "It's just a random observation."

"You're nuts," Duncan told her. "This is what you came to my house to tell me?"

"Nope. But I can tell you that I think I know what you have," Bernie replied.

"And what's that?" Duncan replied.

Bernie smiled and brushed a strand of hair off her forehead. "I think you have a bad case of the self-pities. That's what I think you have."

"Thank you, doctor," Duncan told her. He took a long gulp from his beer bottle. "Now that I have a diagnosis I feel so much better. So again I ask. Why are you here? There must be some reason other than to break my balls."

"Tch-tch," Bernie said. "So rude."

"But so true," Duncan replied.

Bernie pointed to the beer in his hand. "Get me and my sister one of those and I'll tell you."

"Fine," Duncan grumped, and he half walked, half stumbled into the kitchen.

"Hey, be careful you don't trip over anything," Libby called after him.

Duncan didn't reply. Libby and Bernie heard the sound of the refrigerator opening and closing and then the sound of a cabinet drawer doing the same thing. A moment later Duncan was back juggling two open India Pale Ales in one hand and his in the other.

"I hope you like this because it's all I have," he said as he concentrated on walking slowly and carefully across the room, which was not an easy task considering everything strewn all over the floor.

"Not bad," Bernie said after she'd taken a sip of the IPA. She looked at the label. "Not bad at all. Do you think India Pale Ale was developed in India?"

"I don't know and I don't care. All I do know," Duncan said, "is that Sweeney liked them. He turned me on to them. Before that I was strictly a Blue Label kind of guy." Duncan lifted his beer bottle. "A toast to Sweeney."

Libby and Bernie followed suit. "To Sweeney," they both said in unison.

Duncan perched himself on the edge of the armchair that faced the sofa. As Libby studied him, she reflected that not only had his hygiene gone south, but that he'd lost at least ten pounds since she'd last seen him. The perfect prep look that he'd sported was gone and Libby decided that she liked him way better scruffy. This time Libby was the one who started the conversation.

"So," she said, getting straight to the point, "how come you got fired?"

Duncan belched. "I didn't get fired," he said. "I quit."

"That's not what Priscilla said," Libby told him.

Duncan belched again.

"Is that your answer?" Libby asked.

Duncan stared at her for a moment as if he were collecting his thoughts. Then he said, "Priscilla is a stupid cow and I have no idea what the hell Connor sees—or has ever seen—in her."

"One of Priscilla's friends said Mike Sweeney got you fired," Libby told him, seeing no reason to get into the manicurist thing.

Duncan took another slug from his bottle, realized it was empty, and got up to get another one. "She's a lying cow too," he threw over his shoulder as he stumbled toward the kitchen. "Whoever she is." A moment later he was back in the living room with another opened bottle of beer. "You're all lying cows."

"You mean all women?" Bernie said, asking for clarification.

"Absolutely. Every single one of you is a cow. It's a well-known fact."

"Does that classification include Liza?" Bernie asked Duncan.

"Especially Liza." Duncan flung the two pairs of jeans that were on the armchair onto the floor with his free hand and plopped himself down. "She was the biggest cow of all. Only she wasn't a cow, because she milked everyone else. Get it? Ha. Ha. Ha." And he slapped his knee. "Well, I think it's funny," he told Bernie and Libby when they didn't laugh, "even if you don't."

Libby took a sip of her beer and put it down. "Are you saying that Liza blackmailed people?" she asked, thinking of the photos they'd found on Liza's laptop.

"What I'm saying," Duncan told her, "is that Liza was real good at getting things out of people and not giving anything back. With her it was all me, me, me."

"So if that was the case, why were you with her?" Libby asked.

"Because she had a nice ass," Duncan said. "And she wasn't half bad in bed either."

"So high minded," Bernie said.

"Hey," Duncan retorted. "It is what it is."

"Whatever that means," Bernie said.

"You want me to lie?" Duncan demanded of Bernie.

"Not at all," Libby said, jumping into the conversation. "But, Duncan, didn't it bother you when she was with your friends?"

Duncan glared at her. "I don't want to talk about that. That topic is off limits."

"Okay." Bernie held up her hands. "We can talk about something else then."

Duncan took another drink. "Like what?"

"Like what we were talking about before."

Duncan belched. "And what was that?"

"We were talking about why you were fired," Libby reminded him helpfully.

Duncan scowled. "I already told you I wasn't fired." He took another gulp of beer. "I was asked to quit. There's a difference."

"You care to elucidate on that topic?" Bernie asked.

Duncan frowned. "Elucidate? Is that like educate or something?"

"Elucidate as in explain," Bernie said.

"I already did," Duncan told her.

Bernie turned to Libby. "Do you think he did?"

"I didn't hear it, Bernie. Did you?"

"Absolutely not, Libby."

Duncan's scowl deepened. "Then you two should have been listening more carefully."

Bernie leaned slightly forward and looked Duncan in the eye. "Let's try this again, shall we?"

"Let's not," Duncan said.

Bernie continued anyway. "Did Mike Sweeney have anything to do with your getting let go?"

Instead of answering, Duncan took another gulp of his beer.

"I'm right, aren't I?" Bernie asked.

"So what if you are," Duncan said sullenly.

"How much did he have to do with it?" Libby asked.

Duncan turned to her. "He had everything to do with it, the low-life son-of-a-bitch."

"How so?" Bernie asked.

Duncan raised the hand that wasn't holding the beer. "I am sworn to secrecy." He gave her a big, sloppy grin.

"Meaning you signed a confidentiality agreement?" Bernie asked.

"Meaning bad things will happen if I talk."

"Rubbish," Bernie said. "Bad things have already happened."

Duncan shrugged his shoulders and sat back in the chair. "The fates will decide," he said rather grandly.

Bernie rolled her eyes. "Spare me."

"Did you take the fall for Sweeney?" Libby asked, continuing to press him.

Duncan gave her a wounded glance. "I thought you were my friend. You're supposed to be helping me."

"I am your friend," Libby said. "And so is Bernie."

Duncan flared his nostrils, crossed his arms over his chest, and hunched himself forward. Libby decided he looked like a small child.

"No, you're not," he told them.

"Yes, we are," Bernie snapped. "This is ridiculous."

Duncan slid down in his chair. "Well, you guys certainly don't act as if you are."

"We are," Bernie said, fighting her rising desire to place her hands around Duncan's neck and throttle him. "Honestly. That's why we need you to tell us what happened."

Duncan put his hand up again. "That I can not do since I am sworn to secrecy. If I did I would have to kill you."

"Me or Bernie?" Libby asked.

"Everyone," Duncan said.

"Okay." Bernie made a space on the coffee table and set her beer down. "Maybe you can tell us this then. Why did you lie about it? Why did you pretend to be going to work when you weren't?"

Duncan looked at her through bleary eyes. "Truth?"

"Truth," Bernie said, although by this time she wasn't sure that Duncan was capable of recognizing it, let alone saying it.

"Obviously because I didn't want anyone to know about it."

"And why was that?" Bernie asked.

Duncan looked around to make sure no one else was in the room. Then he leaned forward and whispered, "You want the truth?"

Bernie took a deep breath and let it out. "Yes, I want the truth," she replied through gritted teeth.

"The truth is I lied because I didn't want my mother to find out because she would have flipped," Duncan confided. "And that is not a good thing because she's one seriously crazy lady." Duncan lowered his voice even more and leaned farther forward to the point where Libby was afraid he was going to fall. "She even has a diagnosis," he confided to Bernie before sitting back in the chair. His eyelids dropped slowly, as if he had expended his last bit of strength.

"And Liza. What would she have said?" Libby asked, trying to extract a few shreds of useful information out of the conversation.

Duncan let out a sigh, the beer bottle in his hand precariously close to slipping and spilling its contents. Libby extracted it and put it on the table beside his chair. "Duncan?" she said.

But Duncan didn't answer her. He couldn't. He was totally and completely passed out. Bernie looked at him, with his head lolling on the pillow and decided he was down for the count. Or at least until tomorrow morning. Then she looked at Libby. "You know," she said, "as long as we're here, I think we should have a look around this place."

"I thought we agreed not to do that," Libby replied.

Bernie brushed a piece of lint off her designer denim shirt and rebuttoned a button that had come open before answering. "No. We agreed not to break into the guest cottage, but since we're already here, it's not the same thing."

"That's parsing it rather finely," Libby observed.

Bernie grinned. "That's why Mom used to say I should be a lawyer."

"She didn't mean that in a nice way, Bernie."

Bernie grin grew. "Seriously? I always took it as a compliment."

Libby rolled her eyes.

"Listen," Bernie continued. "We're here. Duncan's out cold. We didn't get a chance to ask him about the Oxi."

"What if he wakes up?"

"He won't, but just to make sure, you watch Duncan and I'll do the looking. If he wakes up call me."

"Fine," Libby said. "But don't take too long."

"Me?" Bernie pointed to herself. "Miss Speedy Gonzalez."

"You know," Libby said as Bernie headed for the bathroom, "even if you do find them, that doesn't mean Duncan's story isn't true. Lots of people get off on Oxis."

"This is true," Bernie replied. "But it would be good to know."

"I guess it would," Libby agreed.

The sisters walked out of the guest house thirty-five minutes later. Duncan was snoring.

"Maybe Duncan has Oxi," Bernie told Libby as they headed to the van, "but if he does I'll be damned if I know where it is. The guy doesn't even take aspirin, for heaven's sake. Just lots and lots of supplements."

Chapter 26

It was gray and drizzly out at six the next morning and according to the weatherman it was going to stay that way for the next two days. As Sean happily inhaled the odors of coffee and yeast and butter and garlic swirling around the kitchen of A Little Taste of Heaven, he thought about how it would soon be light at this time of the day and about how the birds would be singing.

Sean had spotted his first robin yesterday morning. It had been hopping around on the pavement outside the shop, pecking at a piece of corn muffin someone had dropped as he'd been sweeping up. Spring was definitely on its way. He could smell it when he stood outside. He liked getting up when it was lighter outside, although he got up when it was dark too. In fact, he got up at the same time every day. Between his job and Rose's, he'd been rising early for so long that he probably couldn't sleep in even if he wanted to. Which he didn't.

As far as he was concerned early morning was one of the nicest parts of the day. When his wife was alive he'd loved coming downstairs and watching her get ready for the day before he went off to work. And the same held true for his daughters. He loved watching them work. It was so quiet and peaceful down in the shop before the store opened.

No traffic. No customers. No delivery guys stacking cartons in the backroom. No sales reps trying to get his daughters to buy something they didn't want. No linen guy changing mop heads and counting out aprons. No Amber. No Googie. Just nice smells and the hum of the washing machine and the clank of the mixer and the sound of wooden spoons against sauce pans. And, of course, the sounds of his daughters talking. Sean liked those sounds best of all.

Sean sipped his coffee, a fresh roasted mocha-java made in a press pot, sat on a stool by the counter, and watched as Libby and Bernie finished making the featured soups of the day—a minestrone with almond pesto, and a French-style fish soup featuring haddock, clams, mussels, anise, garlic, fennel, tomatoes, and white wine. He enjoyed watching his daughters chop and sauté while he inhaled the aromas of the onions and the fennel and the basil and the rosemary as they hit the warm olive oil and released their fragrances.

When Libby and Bernie were done and the soups were on the cook tops, they moved on to the new bread they were trying out. They'd started last night before they'd gone to bed because the dough needed two risings. First they'd proofed the yeast, then they'd added a bit more sugar, the whole wheat and white flour, butter, salt, chopped walnuts, and yellow raisins to the bowl.

When they were finished mixing the ingredients together, they cut and weighed the dough, kneaded each piece, and laid them down on the white, plastic dough trays. They got eight dough balls to a tray. Then they'd stacked the trays in the cooler and left the dough to rise overnight. Now they were taking the trays out of the cooler. Next they'd knead the dough again, form it into loaves, and put the loaves in pans for their second rising, after which they'd put them in the oven to bake.

Watching Libby and Bernie, Sean was once again filled with amazement at the grace both his daughters exhibited as they moved around the kitchen. Every movement they made had a purpose. They didn't dither. They worked like their mother had. With style and grace and economy.

As he watched them forming the dough for the whole wheat bread into loaves and slashing designs on the tops of the bread with razors, he made up his mind not to disturb them—well, not to disturb Libby, really—with the details of last night's meeting with Orion. He'd been asleep when Bernie and Libby had come in, so he hadn't had the chance to tell them about Orion's visit, and now that he did have the opportunity, he didn't want to shatter the morning's peace. Just hearing Orion's name sent Libby into a tizzy. And really what was the point? It wasn't as if Orion had given him any useful information about the investigation, because he hadn't. In fact, Sean was beginning to believe that, truth be told, Orion had no useful information to give. If he did come up with something, Sean would tell Libby about it then.

"So," he said to Libby and Bernie, that decision having been made, "how did last night go?"

"Interesting," Bernie said. She stopped, painting melted butter onto the tops and sides of the loaf pans they were using, and told her dad about Duncan and Patrick and Patrick's trip to Connor's parents' house and what Libby had found in Connor's parents' bathroom and hadn't found in Duncan's.

Sean raised an eyebrow when Bernie got to the last part. "Interesting indeed," he murmured.

Libby rolled a portion of dough out, folded it into three, sealed the edges, plopped it in the pan, and cut three horizontal lines on the loaf's top. "I thought so," she said when she was done.

"So we don't know if the Oxis belong to Connor or Priscilla," he said. "Not that it really matters—since the bottle was in the medicine cabinet either one had access to it."

"They're definitely not that hard to get these days," Bernie observed.

"I wonder if Brandon would know," Sean asked.

"Why would Brandon know anything?" Bernie demanded. "What are you saying?"

Sean raised a hand. "Peace," he said. "All I'm saying is that Brandon is a bartender and bartenders know things. Call him up and ask him."

"But he just got to sleep," Bernie protested.

"So, he'll go back to sleep," Sean said. "Seriously. Call."

Brandon answered on the fourth ring. "What?" he rasped.

"Quick question," Bernie said.

"It couldn't wait?"

"My dad wanted me to call," Bernie said, laying the blame on Sean.

There was a moment of silence, then Brandon said, "Go ahead."

"Dad wants to know if you know who was dealing Oxis to Connor."

"Probably Liza," Brandon said promptly. "She offered some to me too, but I could be wrong."

"Ask him if the other guys bought them too," Sean prompted, having been following the conversation.

"You ask him," Bernie said, handing him the phone.

"No," Brandon said when Sean was on the line. "Connor was the only one. The others just drank and did a little weed."

"Do you know where Liza got the stuff from?" Sean asked.

"Some guy in Staten Island."

"Do you know his name?"

"Nope. He used to just roll through here once in a while. Haven't seen him lately."

"Thanks," Sean said, and handed the phone back to Bernie.

"Did that help?" she asked her dad after she'd hung up.

"I'm not sure," he said. "Maybe." He rubbed his hands together. "I'm thinking that maybe we might want to explore Conner's relationship with Liza a little more deeply. Also I think it's significant that Patrick responded to what you said to him at the bar. I wonder if he went and visited Liam as well after you lost track of him."

"That's what I was wondering too," Libby said. "I'm thinking that maybe one of us should go ask him."

"Patrick or Liam?" Bernie asked.

"Liam," Libby said promptly. "He's the only one we haven't talked to yet."

Sean nodded. "It would be interesting to see what his reaction is. Nothing like stirring the pot a little more and watching what happens, I say."

"It couldn't hurt," Libby allowed.

Sean took another sip of his coffee. "In my experience, catching someone first thing in the morning works pretty well in that regard."

"You mean like now?" Libby asked uneasily, thinking of the rest of her to-do list. After she got done with the bread, there were still cookies and cheesecakes to be baked, quiches and salads to be prepared, and vegetables to be chopped.

Sean put down his mug on the counter. "Like my mama always used to say—ain't no time like the present to do what you got to do."

"Grannie Simmons did not say that," Bernie protested. Her dad's mother had been a grammar Nazi, constantly vigilant for any infraction.

Sean laughed. "Well, maybe not in those words, but the intent was the same."

Bernie looked at the clock on the wall. "I think Liam takes the six fifty-eight into Grand Central."

It was now 7:15.

"You think?" Sean asked.

"I know," Bernie said, correcting him.

Sean shrugged. "Oh well," he said, clearly disappointed, having had visions of charging over there. "There's always tomorrow morning. Or we can talk to him tonight when he gets back."

"We could," Libby said. "Or we could do this."

Sean and Bernie turned to look at her.

"What's 'this'?" Bernie asked.

"'This' is that Liam's wife works out at the gym in the morning," Libby continued. "I know Katrina takes a nine o'clock Strength and Power class on Tuesday and Thursday mornings and today is Tuesday."

"How do you know?" Bernie demanded.

"Misha mentioned it to me when she was telling me about the class and what jerks Katrina and her friends were."

Bernie grunted. Misha was a gym rat who took every class the place had to offer. "That's no big surprise," she said, speaking of Katrina, who in Bernie's humble opinion thought way more of herself than she should.

"So," Libby continued, "since we can't get Liam maybe it would be good to talk to his wife and see what she has to say. Who knows? It might be interesting."

"I think that's an excellent idea, Libby." Sean finished his coffee and went over to fill his cup back up from the thermos, but before he could Bernie beat him to it.

"I think it's an excellent suggestion too," Bernie said, smiling. "Katrina is definitely a Chatty Kathy."

Libby did not like Bernie's smile.

"I'll make the muffins so you can get ready for class," Bernie said.

"Me?" Libby squeaked. "I don't do gyms."

"Well, it was your suggestion," Bernie pointed out, all sweet reasonableness. "And you surely can't expect Dad to go."

"Hardly," Libby said, while her dad laughed at the suggestion. "I was thinking you would. This is your kind of deal."

Bernie sighed. "If I could I would. But I can't. So sorry."

"And why is that?" Libby demanded.

"Simple. Because Liam's wife doesn't like me."

"Since when?" Libby asked.

"Since she almost ran me down in the Target parking lot and I told her to watch where she was going—only a little less politely. Remember, Libby? I told you about it."

Libby vaguely recalled the incident. However, she didn't think the interaction between the two was as bad as Bernie made it out to be. It couldn't have been. Otherwise she would have remembered the story. Or heard about it from someone else.

"Anyway," Bernie continued before Libby had a chance to frame an adequate reply, "going to the gym will do you good."

"Do me good? Are you saying I'm getting fat?" Libby demanded, immediately making the worst possible interpretation of Bernie's comment.

Bernie shook her head in disgust. "No. I'm not," she told her sister.

"Then what are you saying?"

"Let's not have this conversation, Libby."

Libby put her hands on her hips and began tapping one of her feet on the floor. "No. I want to know."

"Fine. As long as you asked, I don't think it would hurt you to get into a little better shape."

"I didn't ask you," Libby retorted.

Sean quickly inserted himself in the conversation before things totally unraveled. "Your sister just means that it's good to exercise, isn't that right, Bernie?"

Bernie didn't reply immediately.

Sean gave Bernie the evil eye. "Well, isn't it?" he repeated more loudly.

"Yes," Bernie reluctantly said after waiting a few seconds longer than she should have to reply.

"That's right," Sean said. "It's a well-known fact. Exercise gets the blood flowing. It puts one in a better mood."

"Not me it doesn't," Libby declared with absolute certainty. "The last time I went to the gym I pulled my hamstring and it took weeks for it to heal."

"The last time you went to the gym was when you were in college," Bernie pointed out.

Libby sniffed. "So?"

"So things change, Libby."

"Not in this case," Libby told her sister. "I hate the gym," she continued. "I hate everything about it."

Bernie threw her arms up in the air. "I get it," she said. "Really I do. But we're talking about a forty-five minute class here. How bad could it be? Just hang out in the back and do a little something, then strike up a conversation with Katrina. That's it. That's all we're asking you to do."

"Please, Libby," Sean said, weighing in. "Maybe you'll get something out of her—which would be a good thing—because we're definitely getting nowhere fast here. This case has been like walking through a field of molasses."

"A fact that Bree is sure to bring up," Bernie threw in as the clincher.

Which Libby knew to be true since they'd been getting calls from Bree for the last four days demanding to know what progress they'd made on the case. Unfortunately, there hadn't been much to report. Libby sighed while she tried to think of an argument to get out of going to the gym, but she couldn't, especially since on top of everything else the whole thing had been her idea in the first place. Which totally rankled. And that is how she found herself at the gym at 8:45 that morning. In Libby's mind it wasn't a fate worse than death, but it was coming pretty darn close.

Chapter 27

Libby had taken Bernie's advice about being in the last row to heart, actually going her one better by skulking around in the room's back corner. She'd gotten there fifteen minutes early but there'd been no Katrina in sight, leaving Libby nothing to do but try to avoid catching glimpses of herself in the mirror and fight down a rising tide of irritation. Finally, just as Libby was beginning to give up hope and the class was about to start, Katrina sashayed in.

Katrina was tall and thin and blond. Statuesque was the word Marvin had used, much to Libby's chagrin, when he'd seen her at RJ's. She had no bulges anywhere, as the T-shirt and leggings she was wearing made abundantly clear. Her hair was always perfect and her makeup skillfully applied. Actually, she was a little like Bree in that regard. Both women spent way too much time and money on their appearance for Libby's taste, but then her sister would say she didn't put enough time in in that area. And like Bree, Katrina definitely thought she was entitled to first-rate treatment. At least that's what it seemed like to Libby whenever Katrina came into the store to buy anything. Amber and Googie both referred to her as She Who

Would Like to Be Obeyed, as opposed to Bree, whom they called She Who Must Be Obeyed.

Libby had just finished counting the number of women in the class waiting for it to begin. There'd been fifteen the first time she'd counted and there were fifteen the second time. Just then Katrina made her entrance. Unlike Libby, who had positioned herself as far out of everyone's line of sight as possible, Katrina went over to the side, where she picked up her mat and her weights and her step and carried them off to the front row, greeting everyone as she went.

Naturally, Libby thought as she watched her progress. She should have realized Katrina would pick the front row. So much for the whole being in the same row and leaning over and exchanging casual comments while doing the bicep curls thing. Libby would have to move up if she wanted to talk to Katrina. But then Libby realized that even if she were in the front row, the scenario she'd been imagining wasn't going to happen anyway. The truth was she and Bernie hadn't really thought this whole thing through. At all.

How was she going to talk to Katrina? When was she going to talk to Katrina? She certainly couldn't do it in class. At least not the kinds of questions she wanted to. Now that she thought about it, she'd be better off cornering her in the locker room. No. This was definitely going to be one of those "seemed like a good idea at the time" kind of deals.

In fact, Libby decided maybe she could just wait for Katrina in the locker room and not even take the class. That would be even better. But that would be wasting the fifteen dollars she'd paid to take the dratted class and she hated wasting money. She hated wasting money even more than she hated being in the gym.

And talking about waste, it was definitely a waste of

time for her to be taking a strength and power class. It really was totally ridiculous. This was the last kind of class she needed, given what she did for a living. If anyone wanted to bulk up, let them try lifting fifty-pound boxes of supplies in and out of the van, like she and Bernie had to do every day. Or let them empty forty pounds of dough out of the mixer once or twice a day. Hey, maybe people could pay them to do that. Maybe they could start a new fitness craze called Cooking Your Pounds Off. Now that was an idea.

Libby laughed out loud at the thought. No. Her being here really was absurd. She'd just decided she was going to wait for Katrina in the locker room, fifteen dollars be damned, when the class instructor strode in and took her position in the front. Everyone stopped talking and snapped to.

Libby was still thinking it wasn't too late to quietly sneak out of class when the instructor spotted her in the corner. First she welcomed her, which in Libby's mind was bad enough, and then she made her introduce herself, which was even worse. In truth, Libby hated the idea of being the center of attention. She always had. That's why she'd made sure she sat in the last row in class in school.

And it was especially true in this situation since all the other women in the room had on cute little matching outfits and she was wearing a T-shirt that was three sizes too big and a pair of sweats that even she admitted should be torn up for rags. And on top of that she needed to wash her hair. She should have listened to Bernie and worn something halfway decent—not that she would ever tell her that.

As the class started doing their warm-up exercises, Libby found herself staring at Katrina's hands. In fact, she couldn't take her eyes off them. After about five minutes, when the class had graduated to squats, Libby's personal bête noir, Libby realized why she'd been staring at Katrina's hands. Her fingers were bare. She wasn't wearing her wedding band or engagement ring.

Libby remembered hearing from Bree that they'd been expensive. According to her—and Bree was never wrong in matters like this—the engagement ring was a perfect two-carat pear-shaped number, while the wedding band had been platinum, studded with small diamonds.

There might be a benign explanation for the rings not being on Katrina's hand, Libby thought. For example, they could be at the jeweler being resized, but in Libby's experience that usually wasn't the case. Like practically never. So maybe coming here wasn't going to be such a waste of time after all.

Between the weights and the bands and the running in place and the hopping on and off her step and the jumping jacks and the sit-ups, Libby was ready to collapse by the time the class came to an end. Clearly she had made a mistake in her assessment of this class, she thought as she gulped down air. She was hot and sweaty and she had a headache and her arms and legs ached and her stomach felt as if someone had punched her in it. In short, she felt as if she was going to die. Or at least throw up.

At the moment, the only thing she wanted to do was take a long, hot shower and then eat half a pint of chocolate-chip ice cream and take a four-hour nap. The one thing she did not want to do was talk to Katrina. Actually she didn't want to talk to anyone. She didn't have the energy. But after all, she reminded herself, that's why she'd come. So she'd better. Otherwise she'd never hear the end of it from her sister and her dad. And, in addition, if there was one thing she knew, it was that she wasn't going to do this again. Ever. For any reason.

Libby told herself that she'd just have to dig deep and find the reserves to carry on, although she was convinced that as far as reserves went she was pretty clearly running on empty. Especially since she didn't have any chocolate with her. While Libby was waiting for Katrina to come out of class, she pictured herself slogging across the desert under the burning sun, dragging a suitcase behind her, her lips parched, her body burning up. Maybe Bernie was right, Libby decided as Katrina came out and Libby fell in step beside her. Maybe she did have a tendency to over-dramatize things.

"This was my first class," she said to Katrina, trying to make conversation as they both walked down the hallway toward the women's locker room.

Katrina didn't say anything.

"It's a hard class," Libby continued.

Katrina gave a slight nod of agreement.

"So how do you do it?" Libby asked her.

"Do what?" Katrina inquired, looking at Libby for the first time.

Libby decided Katrina didn't like what she saw because she wrinkled her nose ever so slightly. "Keep from sweat-ing," Libby said.

Katrina flashed her teeth and laughed as she reached up and gave her ponytail a tweak. "I never sweat. It's just not something I do."

"Ever?"

"Ever. Not even when I was a child."

Libby wished that she could say that. Right now she was positive she could wring out her T-shirt and leave a puddle on the carpet—a disgusting thought if there ever was one.

"Lucky you," she said to Katrina.

Katrina nodded to show she'd heard and started pulling away from Libby.

Libby picked up her pace. "Listen," she said to her. "Can I talk to you for a moment?"

"You already are," Katrina pointed out.

"About something else."

Katrina arched a well-plucked eyebrow and looked down at her. "If you want to talk to me about catering, this is not a good time. In any event, I'm not in charge of the Junior League lunch anymore. You'll have to call the president and get the name of the person who is. I'm sure she'll be happy to speak to you. Although, frankly, I should tell you that I found your prices to be a little on the high side."

"That's not what I wanted to talk to you about," Libby told her as she resisted the temptation to discuss the shop's price points. In truth, they were not high. If anything they were too low.

"Then what do you want to discuss?" And Katrina cocked her head and waited for Libby to speak.

"I want to talk to you about Liam."

Katrina's eyes narrowed. "I have nothing to say," she growled, and with that she started walking again.

Undeterred, Libby continued tagging along beside her. She pointed to Katrina's bare hands. "I can't help but notice that your rings are gone."

Katrina stopped again. "What's your point?" she snapped.

"I just wondered if you and Liam were still together, that's all."

"And that would be your business why?" Katrina asked.

Libby got the word "because" out before Katrina held up her hand and stopped her. "Wait. Don't tell me. I know. This is about the Mike Sweeney thing."

"Yes. As a matter of fact it is," Libby said.

Katrina leaned in toward Libby and put her hands on her hips. "Well, you can leave me out of it. As far as I'm concerned Sweeney got exactly what was coming to him. I'm only sorry I didn't do it myself."

"Did you?" Libby asked.

Katrina snorted and moved back. "Don't be even more idiotic than you already are. Do I look like someone who could hold Mike Sweeney's head under water . . . ?"

"Beer," said Libby. "Not that it really matters. Liquid is liquid."

Katrina's nostrils flared. "Well, do I?" she demanded of Libby.

"No," Libby admitted. "But maybe your husband did."

"First of all, Liam is no longer my husband, and second of all, he wouldn't have the guts to do something like that."

"Are you divorced?" Libby asked.

"Go to hell," Katrina told her. And with that statement, Katrina swept off to the locker room.

"Wow," Libby said out loud to no one in particular as she started walking again. "That was intense."

"You'll have to forgive Katrina. She's a little on edge these days," a voice behind her said.

Libby spun around. Her friend Misha was standing in back of her.

"That's one way of putting it," Libby said.

"Well, I would be too in her position," Misha said.

"And that is?"

Misha wrinkled her nose. "I don't know if I should tell you."

"Of course you should," Libby said.

"But she told me in confidence," Misha answered.

"You mean about what Liam did?" Libby turned to see that the speaker was the instructor of the class she'd just taken. Libby had been so wrapped up in talking first to Katrina and then to Misha that she hadn't heard her come up. "She told everyone in confidence," the instructor continued. "It's no big secret. Liam borrowed a lot of money from Katrina's parents to invest in a business. At least that's what he told her parents. But instead he invested with Sweeney, who lost it all. And now things are a total mess."

"That's awful," Libby said.

"Well, it's certainly not good," the instructor agreed before she walked off, leaving Libby and Misha standing in the middle of the hallway.

"Why did she tell me that?" Libby asked Misha.

Misha shrugged. "Because Katrina made a move on her boyfriend. I guess she figured tit for tat."

"I guess so," Libby agreed. "So what happened to Katrina's rings?" she asked Misha.

"Katrina told me her dad demanded them to help repay some of the money Liam had lost."

"And she gave them to him?" Libby asked.

"I don't think she had any choice. He threatened to sue her if she didn't."

"That's really hard core," Libby said.

"Hard core is right," Misha replied. "I don't think her dad is a very nice guy. I think he has ties."

"Ties?" asked Libby. "Like lots of ties?"

Misha giggled. "Not those kind of ties. The other kind of ties."

"Oh," Libby said, feeling like a fool. "I get it."

"I thought you might," Misha said.

"I'll say one thing for Sweeney," Libby commented.

"Yeah?"

"He sure made a lot of enemies."

"Hey," Misha said. "For once I have to agree with Katrina. Sweeney definitely got what was coming to him. I think someone should pin a medal on Duncan for doing what he did."

"Duncan didn't do it. He was framed," Libby told her.

Misha shook her head. "Yeah. Right."

"It's true," Libby insisted.

"Well, good luck proving that."

"He was," Libby told her.

Misha patted Libby's shoulder. "I'll believe it if it'll make you feel better."

"It's true," Libby repeated.

"If you say so." Tired of the conversation, Misha looked at the clock on the wall. "Spin class is starting in ten minutes. You want to come with me?"

Libby shook her head. "I've got to get back to the shop," she told her. She didn't feel it necessary to inform Misha she was going to have enough trouble walking to the van; spending another forty-five minutes riding a bike simply wasn't a possibility.

Katrina was nowhere in sight by the time Libby made it to the locker room. Libby assumed she'd left, which at that moment was fine. She took a shower and dressed. Then she called her dad and told him what she'd found out.

Sean listened carefully to what his daughter had to say. He was smiling as he hung up. Now he had a direction to go in.

Chapter 28

It was a little after two in the afternoon by the time Marvin came over to pick up Sean and drive him to Katrina's parents' house.

"No hearse?" Sean said, looking at the green Taurus.

Marvin grinned. "Nope. It's in the shop. This is my dad's car."

"I used to have one of these," Sean said as he got in and closed the door. Then he told Marvin how to get there. Sean had known Katrina's parents to say hello to when he was still on the police force, but that had been a long time ago and he hadn't run across them in quite a while. Back then Katrina's mother, Gertrude, had been a lunch lady in the Longely high school cafeteria while her husband, Bob, had been a long distance truck driver.

At least that had been the official story. The unofficial story was that Bob had something to do with the Gambino family. Sean had never believed the rumor. And in fact, one day while he and Bob were both pounding down a couple of beers Bob had explicitly told him that the story wasn't true. Sean had believed him then—not that he had really cared one way or another as long as nothing went down in his jurisdiction, a fact he'd mentioned to Bob. But now he wondered if Bob had been snowing him, going on the offensive.

Which is what Rose had believed. After all, the trucking industry was nothing if not mobbed up and Bob seemed to have a fair amount of flash cash. But who knew? On the other hand, maybe Gertrude was a good household manager. Maybe Bob didn't believe in banks. Maybe they played the lottery and won.

About ten years ago Bob and Gertrude had sold their house and moved down to Florida. Boca specifically. One version Sean had heard said that they both had retired, while the second version said that Bob had gotten into some sort of trouble with the Gambinos and had had to lie low for a while until everything blew over.

But whatever the truth, Gertrude and Bob had come back a couple of years ago and bought a neat little three-bedroom cottage on the edge of town. One of those classic white picket fence and red roof jobbies. Sean had heard through mutual acquaintances that neither Bob nor Gertrude had been fond of the alligators, the bugs, the humidity, or the white shoe brigade.

"Don't go anywhere," Sean told Marvin as Marvin pulled up in front of Gertrude's and Bob's house.

Marvin turned off the ignition. "Where would I go?" he asked.

Sean shrugged. "To get some coffee, maybe? I don't know. I just don't want to be left standing here in case they don't want to talk to me."

"Of course, they'll want to talk to you. They invited you over," Marvin replied. He reached for his phone, figuring that he'd stay in the car and catch up on some of the calls he had to make.

"Not really," Sean said.

Marvin put his hand down and turned to look at Sean. "What do you mean 'not really'?"

Sean took a cigarette out of his pack and lit one. "Not

really as in they don't know I'm coming," he told Marvin
as he rolled down the window to let the smoke out.

"How come?"

"Because I didn't tell them," Sean replied, watching the
wind take away the plume of smoke he'd just exhaled.

"But why?" Marvin persisted. This seemed like a coun-
terproductive approach to him.

"Think about it," Sean told him.

Marvin did. Nothing surfaced.

"The element of surprise," Sean prompted.

Marvin's face lit up. "Now I get it." But then he said, "I
still don't see how that's going to help."

Sean restrained himself from saying what was on his
mind. As he did, it occurred to him how much easier life
would be if he could go places by himself. Instead he explained his strategy as patiently as he could. "Obviously,"
he said to Marvin, "they might not want to talk to me
about what I want to talk to them about. This way they
won't get the opportunity to refuse."

Marvin thought about turning the ignition back on and
decided not to. "They can still refuse," he said, stating the
obvious.

"Yeah," Sean countered. "But in my experience," he
said, pulling out the age card—after all, what was the
point in being old if you couldn't use it once in a while?—
"it's harder to do that when you talk to people in person.
It's way easier to hang up the phone on someone than to
slam the door in his face."

"So you do know them," Marvin said, meanwhile thinking about all the paperwork he'd left behind and the time
he was going to spend driving Sean here and back when he
could have been in his office clearing off his desk and how
this might turn out to be a waste of time investigation-
wise. Unfortunately, this month was turning out to be a
busy one for the funeral home.

Sean took another puff of his cigarette, then nodded. "I

did and I do. But even if I didn't the dynamics remain the same."

"Is this going to take a long time?"

"Not to state the obvious, but I guess that depends on whether or not Gertrude and Bob will talk to me."

"If they're home," Marvin said.

Sean pointed to the green Subaru parked in the driveway. "They're home."

And with that Sean flicked his cigarette out the window and got out of the hearse, using his cane to lever himself up and off the seat. Then he made his way over the grass verge, onto the sidewalk, and up the flagstone path. He walked up the concrete steps and rang the bell.

While he waited he took note of the excellent paint job on the front of the house and the wreath of dried flowers and twigs on the door. It looked like something Gertrude had either bought at a crafts fair or made herself. A moment later Gertrude answered the door. She was wearing an immaculate flowered apron over her jeans and a stretched out, long-sleeved pink polo shirt. No one wore aprons anymore, Sean reflected as he wondered what Gertrude was making. Judging from the aroma, Sean was guessing tomato sauce.

"Yes?" Gertrude said as she squinted at him.

Sean reflected that she'd aged since he'd seen her last. Her hair had gone gray and she'd developed jowls, bags under her eyes, and a tire around her waist, all the accessories of age, as his friend Inez liked to say. But then he supposed—no, he knew—that the same could be said of him. Probably even worse, if the last picture Bernie had taken of him was to be believed.

Sean extended his hand. "Sean Simmons, ma'am. I don't know if you remember me but I used to be—"

"Oh yes." Gertrude cut him off. "The chief of police."

Sean nodded.

"And your girls baked those wonderful cinnamon

rolls," Gertrude continued, her smile widening. "The ones with the filberts."

"They still do," Sean told her.

Gertrude beamed and patted her middle. "I'm trying to stay away from them. They're too good."

Sean patted his middle in turn. "Unfortunately, I can't."

"So what brings you here?" Gertrude asked, changing the subject.

"I'm working on the Mike Sweeney case," Sean began, but Gertrude cut him off before he had a chance to finish.

"I thought you were retired," she asked, her voice going cold.

Wow, Sean reflected. Talk about a change in attitude. Could we use the word *hostile*? Although, he reflected, the hostility made sense given what Libby had told him had happened to Katrina's parents.

"I am retired," Sean told her. "I've gone private."

"As in private detective?" Gertrude asked, smoothing down her apron.

"Exactly. And my daughters help me."

Gertrude raised both eyebrows, giving him a quizzical look. "They cook and detect? That's rather an odd mixture, don't you think?"

"Possibly, but they're really quite good at this kind of thing," Sean told her. And they were. Not that he was prejudiced or anything.

"Are they as good at detecting as they are at baking?" Gertrude asked.

"Not quite," Sean conceded. "But almost. Give them another couple of years and I'll match them up with anyone."

Gertrude pressed her lips together while she thought about what Sean had said. Then she asked for clarification. "You said private, didn't you?" she inquired after a minute had gone by.

"Yes, I did," Sean replied, not liking the direction things were taking.

Gertrude smiled unpleasantly. "Good. So that means I don't have to speak to you if I don't want to, doesn't it?" Gertrude hadn't spent hours watching reality TV crime shows for nothing.

This was not what Sean wanted to hear. "That's correct," he said, because he couldn't think of a way to spin the truth and make it sound plausible. Unfortunately. "But I was hoping that you would want to."

Any trace of the sweet old lady who had answered the door vanished. "Why?" Gertrude spat out. "That son of a bitch got what he deserved."

Sean was slightly taken aback by her virulence. He moved his cane slightly to ease the pressure on his shoulder. "I can see why you would say that given the situation," he told her in his most soothing tone of voice. "But I'm working on behalf of Duncan Nottingham."

If Sean thought that was going to bring Gertrude around to his side, he had another think coming. It did quite the opposite, in fact. Gertrude's scowl grew.

She said, "Frankly, I don't care if Duncan fries."

"He may be innocent," Sean protested.

Gertrude waved Sean's objection away. "No. He's not. He's a scumbag. Between him and Mike Sweeney and Liam, Katrina's worthless husband, they may as well have shot us. It's lucky Bob and I have the shirts on our backs left and aren't out on the street begging. In fact, that whole group can go to hell. They're all responsible. I don't care what happens to any of them and you can tell them I said so. Corned Beef and Cabbage Club, indeed." She sniffed. "They should call themselves the Worthless Pieces of Garbage Club."

"Okay," Sean said, changing tactics. "But I bet you care about your daughter." He had one gambit left and he was determined to use it.

"My daughter?" Gertrude said.

"Yes. Your daughter," Sean replied.

Gertrude tried to stare Sean down. "She doesn't have anything to do with this," she stated in a hard, flat voice. "And don't even intimate that she does."

"That's what I want to talk to you about," Sean said, taking a step inside the house before Gertrude could stop him. "After all, she was part of this."

Gertrude went into full glower. "That's a horrible thing to say," she told Sean. "How can you even imply something like that? In fact, I'll sue you for libel if you do."

Now it was Sean's turn to raise an eyebrow. "Have I touched on a sore spot?" he asked. "Because it seems as if I have."

But before Gertrude could reply, her husband did.

"What's this I hear about Katrina?" Bob demanded, his voice preceding him as he charged out of the back of the cottage. "What's she done now?"

A second later he'd joined his wife in the hallway. Time had been even unkinder to Bob, Sean reflected. Bob had lost most of his hair and gained about fifty pounds, making him look like a bowling ball with a head and skinny arms and legs attached to it. Actually Sean thought he looked like one of those figures Bernie used to draw when she was eight. Art had never been her forte. There had been a small circle on top of a bigger circle with lines for arms and legs sticking out. But Bob's fat was hard fat, biker fat, and despite all the padding, Sean could sense that the strength that Bob had had was still there and that being on the receiving end of one of his punches would put him down and out.

"She hasn't done anything, Bob," Gertrude told him.

"Really?" Bob said to his wife.

"Yes, really," Gertrude replied.

"I'd say that bankrupting us is something."

"That's not her fault," Gertrude protested.

"If you don't mind, Gertrude, I would very much like to hear what Mr. Simmons here has to tell us. Hey," Bob said when Sean didn't say anything. "I asked you a question. What's Katrina done now? She's my daughter and I think I have the right to know."

"Nothing, as far as I know," Sean confessed. "That is, other than exercising poor judgment in picking out a marital partner."

Bob's jowls quivered. "Then why did you say what you did?"

"I was merely positing a possibility," Sean said, taking a leaf from Bernie's book of infuriating phrases.

"Positing a possibility? What does that mean?"

"It means he's guessing, Bob," Gertrude said.

Bob took a deep breath and let it out. "I know what it means, Gertrude."

"You said you didn't."

Bob raised his eyes to the heavens. "God, grant me mercy."

Gertrude's shoulders sagged. "I was just trying to help, Bob," she told her husband in a voice that quavered slightly.

"Well, don't," Bob said, turning to Sean. "So you lied?"

"Exaggerated," Sean replied.

"Are you here to cause trouble? To maybe stir things up?" Bob demanded of him.

Sean shook his head. "Hardly. That's a younger man's game. Don't have the energy anymore," he said regretfully.

There had been a time when he would have grabbed Bob, jacked him up against the wall, and got what he needed. But those days were long gone. And besides, Bob had been thinner then. Now it would take a forklift to accomplish that maneuver.

Bob crossed his arms over his chest. "Then why are you here? Exactly."

As Sean looked around he noticed a stack of clothes

that could only be Katrina's in the corner. "I guess Katrina's moved back home," Sean said, going off on a tangent and annoying Bob even more because if there was one thing that Bob hated it was someone not answering the question he'd asked.

"So?" Bob growled. "What do you care?"

"I don't. I just feel bad for Katrina, seeing what happened and all," Sean told him. As he spoke it occurred to Sean that all Bob had to do to hurt him was lean on him and he was a goner.

"It's horrible," Gertrude said.

"Gertrude, be quiet," her husband snapped.

"Why, Bob? What's wrong with saying that? It is horrible."

"I'm not feeling sorry for her," Bob answered his wife. "What happened to us is worse. In the end the responsibility rests with her."

"But I bet she felt bad about you taking her wedding rings," Sean interjected.

"Bad?" Bob said. He blinked. He began to get red in the face. "Bad? Giving us those rings was the least she could do after all the money she lost us."

"Well, it's not as if she had a direct hand in this," Sean said. "Or did she?"

"Of course she didn't," Gertrude told Sean. "What an absurd thing to say. I told you, it was Mike Sweeney and his crew who were responsible for the mess we're in."

Bob punched his right hand into his left. "Yeah, Gertrude, but your daughter was the one who married Liam. Your daughter was the one who convinced us to invest with Sweeney and his crew." Bob mimicked his daughter's voice. "Such a good opportunity, Dad. You can't pass it up, Dad. Liam's friend is brilliant.'" Bob drew out the word *brilliant*. "Absolutely brilliant. Which is more than I can say for her."

"You're always blaming Katrina," Gertrude told her

husband. "Either blaming her or ignoring her. That's the reason she is the way she is."

Bob rolled his eyes. "Spare me your psychobabble," he said to Gertrude. "If we had reined her in when she was younger we wouldn't be in this position now," Bob countered.

"Your idea of reining in involved your belt," Gertrude retorted.

"And yours involved turning a blind eye to everything," Bob told Gertrude before turning toward Sean. "Katrina's never listened to anyone," he explained to Sean. "She always did exactly what she wanted to do because she knew her mommy would protect her when she did anything stupid."

"That's not true," Gertrude cried.

Bob ignored her and continued talking to Sean. "I told Katrina that Liam was no good. I told her from the minute she brought him home. I told her Liam ran around with a bunch of scum buckets. But that just made her like him more."

"You're wrong, Bob," Gertrude said, interrupting.

Bob glared at her. "I most certainly am not. Your daughter always thought she knew everything. And now look what's happened. We've lost every cent we ever had thanks to Mike Sweeney and his crew."

"From what I've been told, so has Liam and all the remaining members of that group," Sean pointed out. "Everyone took a hit."

"So?" Bob flushed with indignation. "Am I supposed to be crying about that?" he demanded. "Is that supposed to make me feel better? Liam is young. Liam can make it back. We can't. Meanwhile I have another mouth to support on top of everything else. I'd like to wring Mike Sweeney's neck."

"Did you?" Sean asked, the thought having already occurred to him when Bob's name came up. He'd just been waiting for the opportunity to broach the subject to see Bob's reaction.

"Do I look like I can go up against someone like Sweeney?" Bob demanded.

"No," Sean replied. "You don't. But maybe you know some people who could."

"And what would I pay them with?" Bob sneered. "Chocolate-chip cookies and pasta sauce? People don't do that kind of work for nothing. Or have you forgotten?"

Sean shrugged. "No. I haven't forgotten. But some people will do it as a favor. Maybe someone owes you one from the old days. Maybe you have money stashed away someplace. There are all sorts of possibilities."

Bob shook his head in disgust. "That crap again."

"Are you telling me it isn't true?" Sean asked.

"I already have."

"I know you did. And I believed you then, but when I think back I wonder if you were snookering me."

Bob gestured toward the interior of his house. "Look at this place. Does it look like I'm livin' large to you?" he demanded.

"No. But that doesn't mean anything. Not everyone has a mansion in Staten Island." Sean remembered one mobster he knew who'd lived in a small ranch off Euclid and had had a cool couple of mil stashed away in the crawl space under the house.

Bob took a step closer to Sean and wagged his finger in front of his nose. "Don't you be saying that stuff again."

"And don't you be wagging your finger under my nose like that," Sean told him. "Otherwise I might have to break it off. "

Gertrude put her hands on her hips and looked from one man to another. "How old are you two anyway?" she demanded of Sean and her husband. "I'll tell you. Old enough not to do this. That's how old."

Both men looked sheepish.

"Your wife's right," Sean said to Bob.

Bob let out a sound of disgust while he dropped his hand to his side and took a step back. "I don't need this," he told Sean. "I have enough to worry about at the moment. You want to talk to someone about Sweeney, don't talk to me, talk to your daughter's friend."

"Which daughter?" Sean asked him.

"The dark-haired one," Bob replied.

"They both have dark hair. Do you mean Bernie?" Sean suggested because Bernie was more likely to be out and about.

"I guess," Bob said. He'd never been good with names and faces and had never been able to keep the girls straight, even though neither of them looked remotely alike. Not that he would admit this to anyone, especially not their father.

"Are you talking about Brandon?" Sean asked. "He's the redheaded guy who bartends at RJ's."

"No. The other one."

Sean wrinkled his nose. "You mean Marvin?" he asked. Now there was a ridiculous thought if there ever was one. The only things that Marvin was involved with were the funeral home and Libby.

Bob shook his head impatiently. "No. No. Not Marvin. This guy's name begins with a P. Or is it an S? Let me think." A moment later Bob snapped his fingers. "I got it. His name begins with a C."

"C?" Sean said. "Could you be more specific?"

"Casey."

"Casey Murphy?" As far as Sean knew, Libby never had anything to do with him. Ever.

"Yeah. That's it."

"Are you sure?"

Bob drew himself up. "Of course I'm sure," he said in an offended tone of voice. "I just said it, didn't I?"

"I'm just asking," Sean said.

"And I'm just saying," Bob snapped.

"Bob," Gertrude chided her husband. "You're behaving very rudely."

Bob glared at his wife. "Like you're one to talk."

"What do you mean?" Gertrude demanded.

"I'm referring to the way you were talking to Sean earlier."

"I was not impolite. Maybe I was a little forceful with Sean, but given the circumstances, I don't think I was out of line."

"Yeah, Gertrude. When you do something, it's fine. When I do it, it isn't. This is exactly what she was like with our daughter," Bob told Sean. "Whatever I said was one hundred percent wrong."

"That is not true," Gertrude told him.

"Isn't it?" Bob said. "What about that thing with Liza?"

"Liza Sepranto?" Sean asked, coming to attention. "She and your daughter were friends?"

"Yeah, they were," Bob said. "Despite my objections. When you see a car about to slide down a steep hill you try and stop it, right? You don't sit there and let it happen if you can help it."

"I tried," Gertrude retorted.

"Not hard enough," Bob countered.

Gertrude began tapping her right foot on the wood floor. "And what did you want me to do, Bob?" Gertrude demanded. "Liza's mother is my best friend."

"I don't care if she was your sister, Gertrude. Her daughter got Katrina arrested for shoplifting. They shouldn't have been allowed to see one another."

Gertrude turned to Sean. "He's exaggerating. There was just this misunderstanding."

"Misunderstanding my ass," Bob said. "Both of them

ripped off a thousand dollars worth of merchandise each at Bloomingdale's," he said to Sean. "If I hadn't got someone over there and made nice and paid everything off, they would have gone to jail."

"You always make such a big deal out of everything," Gertrude told him.

"And you look the other way," Bob said.

"Maybe because I've had to," Gertrude replied. "Maybe instead of yelling at me all the time you should think of the example you set for your daughter."

"My example is fine, thank you very much," Bob snapped back.

"Is it?" Gertrude said.

Bob blinked. He opened his mouth to say something else and shut it, at which point Gertrude turned to Sean.

"You'll have to forgive my husband," she said. "He's having a slight tummy upset." And Gertrude patted her stomach. "I told him he shouldn't be eating all those hot peppers, but he doesn't want to admit he can't do it anymore. Actually, he doesn't want to admit he can't do lots of things anymore, isn't that true, snookums?" And she puckered her lips and gave him a mock kiss.

Bob probably would have preferred a punch in the jaw, Sean reflected as he watched Bob flinch. In truth, there was nothing like a wife to know where to stick it to you. Bob looks like a balloon with the air let out of him, Sean thought as he watched Bob raise his hands in a gesture of disgust. Well, one thing was true. Gertrude and Bob were definitely a matched pair.

"That's it," Bob said to Gertrude. "Deal with this yourself. I've had enough." And he stalked back to where he'd come from, leaving Sean and Gertrude standing in the vestibule.

Sean sighed. The reason that Katrina behaved the way she did was fairly obvious. It was called playing one parent against the other and getting away with it. Thank heavens he and Rose hadn't done that. It's true they used to fight, they used to fight a lot, but when it came to the core stuff like the girls' friends, they'd always been in agreement, and even if they hadn't been, they'd backed each other up.

He and Rose had been a good team. God, he missed her. He banished the thought and concentrated on what he'd just learned. When he thought about it, it really didn't surprise him that Liza and Katrina were friends and that their mothers were too. After all, when you got down to it, Longely was a small town and the people who lived here had long memories.

And speaking of memories, Sean wondered if maybe Bob had meant Orion instead of Casey. That at least made a little more sense. Because Bob had never been good with names. And both Casey and Orion looked alike in a general kind of way. Or they used to. Before Orion had gotten downright skinny.

For a moment, Sean debated going after Bob and trying to get a little more information out of him, but then he decided it would be a waste of time. Bob was probably knee deep in gin by now, pondering his humiliation at his wife's hands. It was definitely time to move on. He said good-bye to Gertrude and left.

On the way to Marvin's vehicle he took out his cell and tried to call Casey, but his call went straight to voice mail. The same was true of Orion. Okay. That left Liza's mom to talk to. He'd put off doing that for longer than he should have. He thought about having to convince Marvin to drive him. And then he thought about how much simpler it would be if he could go there by himself. If Marvin didn't have to drive him. If no one had to drive him.

After all, he had gotten better. A lot better. His hands didn't shake anymore. He could walk okay. Well, almost okay. He wasn't slurring any words. His judgment was as good as it had always been. No. Despite what Bernie and Libby would say, he was ready to drive. And Marvin's father's car was the perfect vehicle for his first time out. After all, he'd driven one like it before. The trick was going to be persuading Marvin to see it that way.

Sean smiled. He'd always loved a challenge.

Chapter 29

Libby was taking a rare but well-earned nap when Orion walked into the Simmonses' flat and woke her up. She had been dreaming of a loaf of cinnamon-raisin bread with a diamond ring baked inside it. Somehow the ring had belonged to one of their customers and Libby wasn't sure how it had ended up in the batter, but there it was winking away.

Libby was in the middle of hearing why that was important from a voice coming out of the oven—it had something to do with being able to forecast the advent of the hurricane season and how bad global warming was going to be—when another customer came into the shop and slammed the door behind her. She thought the sound was in her dream, but then she realized it was real. She opened her eyes. A moment later she screamed. A man was standing by the door. It took her thirty seconds to realize it was Orion. She bolted up, instinctively smoothing down her sweatshirt as she did.

"Sorry if I scared you," Orion said apologetically. "I didn't mean to."

"What are you doing here?" Libby demanded, now wide awake.

As she looked at Orion it suddenly occurred to her that a miracle had happened. All the anger she felt toward him had slipped away. She didn't feel sad that she wasn't with him anymore. She didn't feel hurt thinking about all the lies he'd told her. She wasn't wondering whom he was going out with.

In fact, she didn't feel attracted to him at all. Her heart wasn't beating faster. She wasn't blushing. He was just a guy. A skinny guy with a bad haircut, a big nose, and ears that stood out from his head. She remembered she used to find those ears cute—she'd liked to tug on them gently—but not anymore. Now they just looked goofy.

Orion looked at the floor, then back at Libby. Clearly, she thought, he's uncomfortable. And that also made her feel even happier because she was usually the one feeling that way. Or maybe he'd always felt that way and she'd been so consumed with her own feelings that she hadn't noticed. Bernie was always telling her to get over herself. Maybe she was right, Libby thought.

"The door was opened and I just walked up," Orion stammered as Libby continued to study him. "I was looking for your father."

Libby gave her sweatshirt a final tug. Even though she was over Orion she was still glad she'd washed her hair last night.

"He's not here," she told him. "He's with Marvin."

"I guess I should have called," Orion said, turning to go. "I would have but my phone is on the fritz. I'll come back later."

"I guess you should have called first," Libby agreed. "What do you want with him anyway?"

"Nothing, really," Orion said. "Your dad asked me to get him some information."

Libby cocked her head and looked at him. "Information?"

"Yeah. About Sweeney and those guys."

"Oh, yes." Libby remembered that her Dad had said he was going to talk to Orion, but then he hadn't mentioned anything about it and it had slipped her mind.

Orion ran his fingers through his hair, and Libby noticed with a certain amount of pleasure that it was thinning on top.

"I've got the financial stuff he asked me about," he said. He corrected himself. "Well, some of it. I managed to get him a couple of lists. There's a lot more out there but this is all I could lay my hands on."

"Why don't you give the info to me and I'll give it to him," Libby suggested.

Orion hesitated.

"I'm working on the case too," Libby told him.

"It's not that. I just figure your dad might need an explanation for what I've come up with."

"Well, if he does he can call you. Unless you want to come back later, that is," Libby said.

Orion thought it over for a minute, then said, "No offense, but I don't think I do."

"No offense taken," Libby answered.

She watched as Orion slipped his messenger bag off his shoulder and began rummaging around in it. "So how have you been?" she asked him.

"Fine. And you?"

"Fine," Libby said. "You like your work?"

"It's fun," Orion said. "Or as much fun as work can be. And you?"

Libby smiled. "The shop is the shop."

"You ever think of doing something else?"

"Not really," Libby said, shaking her head.

Orion fell silent, as did Libby. There didn't seem to be anything else to say. A moment later Orion extracted a sealed, standard, twelve-by-fifteen-inch manila envelope from his messenger bag and handed it to Libby.

Libby looked down at it. "What's in here anyway?" she

asked. Somehow she felt it would be wrong to unseal the envelope since it was addressed to her father.

"Nothing that earth shattering. Basically it's a list of Mike Sweeney's and Duncan's clients."

"Duncan said they'd worked together."

Orion nodded. "Yeah. For the past four years. It's all about teamwork these days."

"How did you get the info?" Libby asked.

Orion shrugged. "The way you find out anything these days. I called in a few favors."

"It doesn't sound like a nice world," Libby noted.

"It's not," Orion agreed. "Just be happy you have the shop." He turned to leave and then turned back again. "I just want you to know I'm sorry about the way I acted," he told Libby. "Honestly, I never meant to hurt you. I know that doesn't mean much but it's true."

"No. It does." She swallowed. "It was my fault as well," she told him.

"No it wasn't," Orion protested.

"That's very sweet of you to say, but you and I know the truth. I knew you wanted to go. I knew we weren't right for each other. You were trying to tell me that in all sorts of ways but I refused to listen. So you acted out, hoping that I would throw you out. But I didn't. I overlooked everything, which was when you left." Libby extended her hand. "No hard feelings."

Orion took it and they shook. "Maybe we could have a drink sometime," he said, more out of politeness than desire.

Libby shook her head and smiled. "I don't think so."

Orion smiled too. "You're right," he said.

"I know," Libby told him.

She stood holding the envelope to her chest as he turned and walked out of the flat. All those years, she thought. All that anguish. All that anger. All those hurt feelings. All those nights crying and imagining revenge. And now she felt nothing. It was as if someone had turned the water tap off. It was odd, but she kind of missed hating him. Now that that feeling was gone, she realized how much time it had taken up. Oh well. As Bernie would say, on to the next thing.

Libby was just about to call her dad and tell him that Orion had dropped off the information he wanted, after which she was planning on going downstairs to the shop and starting in on a new batch of the smoked trout, walnut, apple, and frisée salad—the stuff was flying out the door—when Bernie came dashing up the stairs.

"Libby, we need you," she cried as she ran into the flat. "The cooler is on the fritz."

Libby cursed under her breath, threw the envelope Orion had given her on the coffee table—all thoughts of the investigation now out of her mind—and ran down the stairs after Bernie.

"Did you call Isaac?" Libby asked Bernie.

Isaac was the repairman.

"He can't come until later tomorrow. We're going to have to empty the cooler out."

Libby groaned. The cooler was packed full of bread dough, eggs, butter, cream, milk, cheese, tuna and egg and salmon salads, as well as plastic containers of chicken and beef waiting to be turned into tomorrow's feature of the day.

"The guys at A La Carte said we could use the cooler they have in the basement to get us through," Bernie said.

Libby groaned again. "Damn. What a pain."

"I know," Bernie told her. "I called Brandon and he's going to help us schlep."

"Thank God," Libby said gratefully.

But even with Brandon helping, it was going to be a pain in the butt. It meant unloading the contents of the cooler and packing it up, putting everything in the van, unloading it all, carrying the cartons down the steps, which were incredibly steep and narrow, putting everything in A La Carte's cooler and then reversing the process the next day. Not to mention dashing over there when they needed something.

And on top of that, she still had the Baums' dinner party to get ready. Risotto with Parmesan cheese and asparagus. Chicken sautéed with white wine and rosemary. A tossed green salad of watercress, radicchio, and romaine lettuce, sprinkled with toasted walnuts and dressed in walnut oil. And a chocolate panna cotta with raspberries for dessert. Nothing fancy, but still a dinner for eight took time to assemble. Libby decided it was going to be a long and not particularly pleasant afternoon.

Chapter 30

Marvin looked at Sean sitting behind the steering wheel and thought, what have I done?

"No," he said. "Absolutely not. No way. No how."

"It'll be fine," Sean assured him as he moved into the right lane to allow the car in back of him to pass.

"It won't be fine," Marvin retorted. "It won't be fine at all."

Marvin felt like burying his head in his hands. He should never have allowed himself to be talked into letting Mr. Simmons drive in the first place. But how could he have said no, especially when Mr. Simmons had smiled and said he just wanted to have one more chance to get his hands on the wheel.

"For old time's sake," he'd said, smiling sweetly.

And Marvin had obliged. God, what a sucker he was.

"I mean it's not that much farther," Sean pointed out as he turned into Mulberry Street. He pulled over and parked.

Marvin let out an audible sigh of relief. Sean looked annoyed.

"I've already driven two blocks. Have I had an accident?" he asked Marvin.

"No," Marvin replied.

"Have I dented anything?" Sean asked.

"No," Marvin muttered.

"Have I even come close to doing anything dangerous?"

"No," Marvin admitted reluctantly. He could see the way the conversation was going and he wasn't happy about it.

"Then what's the problem?" Sean asked.

"The problem," Marvin told him, "is that you're not supposed to be driving."

"Not true," Sean said. "I have a valid license. Do you want to see it?"

"That's not what I'm talking about and you know it."

Sean held up his hands. "Are they shaking?"

"No," Marvin allowed.

"That's because I'm in remission. I'm not irresponsible, you know. I wouldn't drive if I didn't think I could."

"But—" Marvin said.

Sean interrupted. "No buts. That's the truth. This may be my last opportunity, my last hurrah. I may get sick again. In fact, I probably will get sick again. That's what remission means." Sean clapped Marvin on the back. "Listen, don't think I don't appreciate all the time you've taken driving me around, because I do, but it makes me feel like I'm two."

"Then why—?" Marvin began, but once again Sean swooped in before Marvin had a chance to finish his sentence.

"Then why don't I discuss this with Bernie and Libby?" Sean asked. "Why don't I use the van? Why am I picking this time and place?"

"Exactly," Marvin said.

"A number of reasons." And Sean began to enumerate them. "First of all, I don't want Bernie and Libby to worry, and you know that they will."

"I guess you're right," Marvin agreed reluctantly.

Sean snorted. "Of course I'm right. Bernie and Libby worry when I'm fifteen minutes late. I can't imagine how they'd feel about this."

"I guess they are a little overprotective when it comes to you," Marvin replied.

"Just a tad." And Sean held up his thumb and forefinger. "And then we come to reason number two. The simple truth is that the Taurus is easier for me to drive than the van. This will be like a test run. If things go well I'll talk to Bernie and Libby and tell them."

"Like you told them about your smoking?"

"Ha. Ha. That's different." Sean turned and smiled at Marvin. "Just think. You won't have me yelling at you anymore. How nice will that be?"

Marvin had to admit it would be nice indeed. But that wasn't the issue. The issue was that Libby would skin him alive, and so would his dad for that matter, if they found out. Just thinking about what his dad would say made Marvin cringe.

"But this isn't my car, Mr. Simmons," Marvin wailed.

"So you've said. I know. It's your dad's. Relax. He'll never know. He's gone until seven o'clock tonight, remember?"

"He'll know," Marvin said, cursing himself. Why had he told Mr. Simmons that his father was away on business? God, he had a big mouth. "My dad knows when a pin is out of place."

"The car will be fine," Sean assured him. "I'll take care of it as if it was my own."

Marvin was not reassured. He was thinking about what to say when Sean looked him square in the eye.

"Listen," Sean said, summoning up his most confidence-inspiring expression. "Your dad is not going to know because you're not going to tell him. If you don't tell him there's no way he will know. Last I knew, being psychic wasn't one of his abilities. He's not coming back till seven o'clock tonight, and by that time the Taurus will be safely back in the garage."

"Someone will see you and tell him," Marvin said.

"Like who?" Sean asked.

"I don't know. Someone."

"Most people are at work right now. And anyway, do you really think that people will identify this car as your dad's? It's one of the most common cars on the road today. If this was a chrome yellow Jeep I could see your point. But it isn't."

Marvin had to agree that that was the case.

"I'll drop you off," Sean continued. "You'll do your paperwork and I'll drive over and visit Rose at the cemetery. I haven't been there in a while." Which was true. He was leaving out the part about visiting Liza's mom just in case Marvin objected. "And then," Sean continued, "I'll come back and you'll take me home. It's a win-win situation. I get to do what I need to do and you get to do your tasks. No one will be any the wiser." Sean raised his hand, palm outward as if he were taking an oath. "I promise. I'm driving a total distance of what? Maybe five miles at the most? I'm using surface streets. I mean it's not as if I'm telling you I'm going to drive into Manhattan. Think about it."

Then Sean sat back and waited for Marvin's reply. He actually felt sorry for Marvin. He looked one hundred percent miserable. Probably because Marvin *was* miserable. He was thinking that he was damned if he did and damned if he didn't. If Libby and/or his dad found out, if God forbid Mr. Simmons got himself in trouble, then it was his fault and he was to blame.

On the other hand, if he said no to Mr. Simmons, Mr. Simmons would never forgive him and that was not a good thing. Especially when he planned on having a long, possibly permanent, relationship with his daughter. And what made it worse was that Marvin strongly suspected that Mr. Simmons was fully aware of the situation he'd placed Marvin in. But really, how could he say no to a man who wanted to pay his respects to his beloved wife? How could he be that heartless?

"So," said Sean after a moment had passed, "what's it going to be?"

Marvin blushed. He felt silly asking the question he was going to, but he really wanted to know. "If you do end up driving, does this mean I can't come with you anymore when you do your investigative stuff?"

Sean grinned. "Of course you can come with me. I wouldn't think of leaving you out. I'd miss your observations."

Marvin grinned back. "Okay then," he said. He straightened himself up. "But I'm driving back to my place."

"Not a problem," Sean said.

"And please, Mr. Simmons . . ."

"Yes, Marvin."

"Don't be late."

"I won't," Sean assured him. "I swear."

As Sean changed seats with Marvin he had the good manners not to gloat. He was a man who was always magnanimous in victory.

Sean sat on the bench in front of Rose's tombstone and thought about his wife. He hadn't expected her to die first. He'd been the one with the dangerous job. He'd been the one who was always getting sick. She was the one who was always fine. She used to joke she was just like a mule on the Erie Canal. She'd just kept going and going.

Until the day she didn't. Until the day she'd just dropped dead right in front of him. An aneurysm. Nothing he could have done. Nothing anyone could have done. The only saving grace was that the girls had been in school when it happened. Telling them their mom had died had been one of the hardest things he'd ever done.

He liked Inez. He'd met a few women he'd liked since Rose had died. But it wasn't the same. He should come here more often, he reflected. Now that he could drive himself, he would. Somehow, it wasn't the same coming here with the girls. He lit a cigarette—he knew Rose wouldn't mind—and let his mind go blank. After a few minutes he found himself looking at the tombstone of the person buried in the next plot over. He remembered when Jennifer Marie Strunk had died. She'd been twenty-seven, Liza Sepranto's age.

Six months later Sean had arrested the man who'd killed her. And that got him thinking about Liza's death. He took another puff of his cigarette and decided that somehow she'd gotten lost in the investigation. He probably should have talked to Anne before this, but he hated talking to the recently bereaved. He always had, and now he disliked it even more since he knew what it felt like.

Sean looked at his watch. He was right on schedule. Plenty of time left to talk to Anne and maybe take a quick peek at Liza's room. And if he was a little late, so what? It wouldn't be such a big deal. An idea was beginning to take shape. One he really didn't want to entertain. But it would explain everything. He just hoped he was wrong. Sean sighed, took a last puff of his cigarette, ground it out under his heel, then picked the butt up so he could throw it away later. He'd always done his best thinking around Rose. Looked like that was still the case.

"Bye for now," he said, blowing a kiss in the direction of Rose's grave. He expected to be there soon. He'd reserved the adjoining plot for himself. But not yet.

Pat and Anne Dwyer's house was in a small cul-de-sac off Euclid. It was one of those places that had fallen off the Longely map. Marked as a development in the thirties, it had been a nonstarter after three houses had been built, plans for the next seven having been abandoned when the developer had gone broke.

At the present time the Dwyers were the only people living there, the residents of the other two houses having not come back from Florida yet. Which suited Pat Dwyer fine. He liked the privacy, although his wife and his stepdaughter didn't feel the same way. But since he was paying all the bills, what they thought didn't really matter.

Sean pulled up in front of the Dwyers' house and sat for a moment, enjoying the sound of the car's idling. He was extremely pleased with himself. The drive over here had gone very well, if he did say so himself. He felt like a teenager right after he'd gotten his license. Odd but true. Free at last. It was wonderful to be out and about on his own. He was thankful for each disease-free moment he got. For each moment where his hands weren't shaking so bad he had trouble feeding himself. For each moment when he didn't have trouble walking.

Of course, he wasn't exactly as good as new. He'd lied to Marvin a little bit about that. It had taken all of his concentration to drive here. He had to stay superfocused, and judging by the way he was feeling at the moment, he figured that short runs were about as much as he could manage in the near future. He'd done it though. He had managed it quite well, in fact. And he could always build up his endurance. He'd just go a little farther every day.

Then Sean thought that if this was the best it was going to be, that would be okay too. In fact, he'd do everything short of sacrificing his first and second born if he could stay this way. He sat back, reached in his pocket, took out a cigarette, and lit it while he studied the Dwyers' house. The word that came to mind was *modest*. Like Dwyer's office. This was a man who had money but didn't spend it. He evidently didn't feel the need to let everyone know how well he was doing. It was enough that he knew.

The house had been added on to as the decades had passed. The original house had been compact; now it rambled due to the additions of a garage and a den. But it had retained its small lawn and a neatly clipped privet hedge, which had bordered the house for as long as Sean had driven by it. From where he was parked, Sean could see the yellow tips of daffodils beginning to break through the soil in the flower bed. He rolled the window down a little and tapped the ash from his cigarette onto the street.

He was here because he needed to speak to Anne without Pat, if at all possible. He'd get more information that way. Pat disapproved of Liza, that had been obvious when he had spoken to him at his office, so Anne would naturally hold back on any information that didn't reflect well on her daughter if her husband was present. There was nothing wrong with that. It was simply what a parent did. It was what he would do if he found himself in that sort of situation.

Sean finished his cigarette, turned off the Taurus, and carefully pocketed the keys. Then he closed his eyes, took three deep breaths, slipped into a meditative state, and focused on the case at hand. Everyone in the force thought he was nuts doing this, but he'd found it to be extremely helpful.

He found it helped him hone in on the questions he needed to ask. Sometimes the small things, the easily overlooked things, were the things that pointed the way to a solution. He ran through Brandon calling up Bernie, and what they'd found in the alley behind RJ's. He thought about Duncan's arrest and Libby and Bernie meeting Connor, Liam, and Patrick at RJ's. He thought about Bree and Duncan and about finding Liza. And then it occurred to him that there was a tiny piece of information from Brandon that he needed.

This particular fact was probably irrelevant, but if there was one thing Sean had learned from his years on the force, it was that it definitely paid to dot all your i's and cross your t's. He opened his eyes, took out his cell, and called Brandon. Brandon didn't answer. As Sean looked down at his cell, he realized that it was about to die. He'd forgotten to charge the dratted thing again.

Oh well. Not exactly a catastrophe in the scheme of things, he thought as he slipped it back in his pocket. After all, he'd gotten along for how many years without one? And as for his question, it could wait. He'd stop at RJ's on the way back to Marvin's and ask Brandon. Face to face was always better anyway.

And on that note Sean reached over to the passenger side, grabbed his cane, and opened the Taurus's door. Then he swiveled around and, using the cane and the door frame for support, pulled himself up and out of the car. He stood on the curb for a moment and looked up.

It had stopped raining. He could see the sun, and the branches on the willow tree above him were beginning to fill with buds. Winter was over, spring was ahead. Life was good. On that note, he carefully closed the Taurus's door, turned, walked up the path to the Dwyers' house, and rang the bell. He stood there admiring the gleam of his cane's silver handle while he waited for the door to open. A moment later it did.

"What a nice surprise," the person answering the door said. "Come on inside."

"Thanks," Sean replied, even though the tinkle of warning bells was going off in his head. "I think I will."

Chapter 31

It was a little after four o'clock in the afternoon and Marvin was officially in panic mode. It had been over an hour and a half since Libby's dad was due back with Marvin's father's car and Mr. Simmons still hadn't returned. Marvin had tried calling Mr. Simmons several times—every five minutes in fact—after the first hour had elapsed, but his calls had gone straight to voice mail.

Marvin told himself that that didn't mean anything. Mr. Simmons had either shut off his phone or forgotten to charge it, both of which were common occurrences. He told himself that there was a perfectly good reason Mr. Simmons was late returning the Taurus. But it didn't help. He got more and more nervous.

Half an hour after Mr. Simmons was supposed to be back, Marvin couldn't stand the waiting and not knowing anymore, so he took the hearse and drove over to the cemetery. But Mr. Simmons wasn't at his wife's gravesite. Marvin got out and walked down the footpaths hoping to spot him, but he didn't. He got back in the hearse and drove around some more. The only people that he saw were two grave diggers manning a backhoe. He stopped and asked them if they had seen a Taurus. Both of them shook their heads. They hadn't.

The cemetery wasn't huge but it was big enough, and Marvin started systematically driving up and down the roads, but the only things he saw were a couple of deer who were eating the lilies decorating a freshly dug grave. They didn't even flinch when he drove by, just watched him with their large eyes.

Marvin's stomach was doing flip-flops as he drove. He covered the cemetery again and then he went in and talked to the caretaker, who also hadn't seen a Taurus or Sean, but promised he'd call Marvin the minute he did.

Having done everything he could think of there, Marvin got back in his car and started cruising around Longely. He drove down Ash and Bell and Oak and Main Street; he drove up Elsworth and Fern and Hemlock and Houston. He drove by RJ's, cruised the mall parking lot, as well as the lots of the local supermarket and liquor store. He even checked out Bree Nottingham's house in case Mr. Simmons was there talking to Mrs. Nottingham or Duncan about the case. No luck.

He drove by Mr. Simmons's friend Inez's house, even though he knew that Inez was in Brazil visiting a relative and hence would not be home. He even drove by A Little Taste of Heaven on the unlikely possibility that the Taurus was parked in front of the shop because Sean had decided to tell Bernie and Libby about what he was doing after all.

As Marvin drove around he imagined the worst. Mr. Simmons in a ditch somewhere. Mr. Simmons in the hospital with a massive brain injury. Mr. Simmons rear-ending someone in a parking lot or driving into someone's house like that eighty-year-old guy had done on Seward Street last week. Or Mr. Simmons going into Manhattan for some reason that Marvin couldn't begin to fathom and getting lost and ending up in a bad part of the Bronx. Or

Mr. Simmons lying to Marvin and not really having a valid driver's license after all.

This proved to be the worst thought of all. Or maybe it was the cumulative possibilities swarming around in Marvin's head, but in any case that idea proved to be the coup de grâce, and Marvin had to pull over to the side of the road and take several deep breaths to calm himself down and prevent himself from hyperventilating.

Marvin told himself that Mr. Simmons would not do something like that to him. Ever. And that he had to stop his imagination from running wild. He told himself that there was a perfectly simple explanation for Mr. Simmons not showing up with the Taurus. But what was it? Marvin couldn't imagine one. Or he could imagine one and all the images were bad. He took his cell out of his front pocket and called the ER. No Sean Simmons had been admitted in the last five hours. Marvin let out the breath he didn't know he'd been holding as the person at the admitting desk suggested he call the police.

Marvin thought about doing that for a moment and then deep-sixed the idea. If he did that, there was a strong possibility that Sean's friend Clyde would hear about the call—or even take the call himself—and then Clyde would ring up Libby and Bernie and ask them what the hell was going on before Marvin had a chance to tell them what had happened. And that would be bad. Of course, there was no good in this situation. There was only terrible and more terrible.

Marvin took another couple of breaths and started the car. As he drove toward A Little Taste of Heaven, he decided that this was going to be very, very bad. His hands were sweating and he was having trouble breathing. I mean, really, how do you tell someone that you've misplaced their father?

*   *   *

Libby was in the kitchen finishing up the risotto that went with the dinner she was catering tonight for the Baums and thinking about how the business really needed to buy another cooler as well as get the broken one fixed, when Marvin walked in.

Libby looked up from the Parmesan cheese she was grating, took in his expression, and said, "You look terrible. What's wrong?"

Marvin stopped in front of her. He didn't say anything.

"Seriously," she said. "Are you sick?"

"No," Marvin told her.

"Then what?" She put down the cheese grater. "Wait. I know. You've lost a body," she joked.

"Worse than that," Marvin answered. "Way worse." He moistened his lips.

Libby laughed. "What could be worse than that?"

"I've lost your father," Marvin replied.

Libby looked at him blankly. "Excuse me?" she said.

Marvin took a deep breath and let it out. And then he told her. "I lent your dad my dad's car and he hasn't come back and I can't find him."

"Say again?" Libby said.

Marvin repeated himself.

She shook her head. "I don't believe you."

"It's true."

"What's true?" Bernie asked as she walked into the kitchen. She'd been out front manning the cash register until Amber got back from her bathroom break.

"Evidently, Marvin's lost Dad," Libby told her.

"Right. And I'm the Queen of Sheba," Bernie said.

"It's true," Marvin said.

Bernie studied his face for a moment. Then she said, "Bad joke."

"It's not a joke," Marvin replied.

Bernie wrinkled her nose. "I don't get it. What do you

mean you lost Dad? What did you do? Misplace him at the mall? Lose him at the checkout line at the supermarket?"

"I wish," Marvin said, looking everywhere but at Bernie.

Libby explained. "Evidently, he let him drive his car. . . ."

"My father's Taurus," Marvin interjected.

"And Dad hasn't come back when he was supposed to," finished Libby.

"Where did he go?" Bernie asked.

"To visit your mom at the cemetery."

"And how late is he?" Bernie asked.

"Over an hour," Marvin whispered.

"Why didn't you call us immediately?" Bernie demanded.

Marvin looked even more chagrined than he had before, if that was possible. "I thought I could find him. I've looked everywhere," Marvin said, wringing his hands.

"Exactly where . . ." Bernie began, and then she stopped and grinned. "You guys are good. You really are. You almost got me." She looked from Marvin to Libby and back again, and the grin faded. "This is a joke, right? Right?"

Marvin hung his head.

"Tell me this is a bad joke," Bernie pleaded. "Please."

"I wish I could," Marvin mumbled, unable to look Bernie and Libby in the eye.

"What were you thinking lending Dad the car?" Libby asked Marvin.

"Obviously I wasn't," Marvin answered. "But he promised to bring it back and he sounded so convincing. If you had been there—"

"If I had been there this never would have happened because he never would have asked me," Bernie answered.

Marvin didn't argue the point. He couldn't because he knew Bernie was right. "I should never have let it happen," he said, apologizing again. "I just . . ." He bit his lip. "Your dad wanted . . . I just felt bad for him and I was in this weird position . . . I don't know." Marvin's voice trailed off. "There is no excuse for doing what I did," he said in a voice so low Libby and Bernie had to strain to hear it. "None at all."

He looked close to tears and Libby mastered her outrage enough to imagine how bad Marvin was feeling. She could also imagine how it had happened. Her father could be very persuasive when he wanted to be.

"He's probably fine," Bernie said, trying to stall off the panic rising in her chest by convincing herself that everything was okay. "He's probably off on some weird errand or other."

"But then where is he?" Marvin asked.

"Tell me where you went," Bernie ordered for the second time.

And Marvin did.

"Did you look in the park?" Libby asked when he was through.

Marvin shook his head.

"Maybe he's there. He used to like to go there."

"Or that old cigar store over in Castlebrook," Bernie suggested.

"That closed about two months ago," Libby said.

"Maybe Dad doesn't know that."

"True," Libby said. "Or there are the greenhouses out on Route Eighty-two. That's another possibility. Dad used to love to go out there."

"I think they open in April," Bernie said.

"It wouldn't hurt to check," Libby said.

"No. I guess it wouldn't," Bernie agreed. Then she turned to Marvin and asked him if he'd called the ER and the police.

"I called the ER," Marvin told her. "They don't have him."

Libby called again, just to make sure. But the answer was the same. Then she called the police and got Lucy— just the person she didn't want to speak to. She shook her head when she got off the phone. Her face was bright pink with anger.

"They don't have him and they're not going to look for him. Lucy said, and I quote, 'Call me if he hasn't shown up in a week or so.'"

"Where's Clyde?" Bernie asked.

Libby answered. "He and Mrs. Clyde went to Sarasota to babysit for one of the grandbabies. They'll be gone for another couple of days."

"Great," Bernie said as she pressed her cheeks together with the palms of her hands. "Just our luck."

"I think I'm going to kill myself," Marvin said.

"Stop whining," Bernie told him. "We have enough to worry about. If you want to, you can kill yourself after we find my father. But not before."

Marvin bit his lip. He looked perilously close to tears. "I'm sorry," he said.

"Do not say you are sorry again," Bernie snapped at him, what little patience she had gone. "Otherwise I'm going to kill you myself."

"Bernie," Libby remonstrated.

Bernie held up her hand. "You're right, Libby. I'm totally out of line." She turned to Marvin. "Now it's my turn to apologize. Sometimes I get a little carried away. You do know I didn't mean the whole killing you thing, right?"

Marvin nodded but he didn't look convinced. Libby went over and gave him a hug. "Everyone makes mistakes," she told him.

"But not like this," Marvin pointed out.

"What is it they say about no good deed going unpunished?" Libby said.

Marvin brightened slightly. "I hadn't thought of it that way. I was just trying to be nice to your dad."

"Yes, you were," Libby reassured him.

Libby was about to say something else when Bernie clapped her hands. Libby and Marvin turned toward her. "People," she said, "we can do this later. Right now let's concentrate on the important thing. Let's concentrate on finding Dad. He has to be somewhere, right?"

"Right," Marvin said.

"He couldn't have just disappeared. I'm going to call Brandon and get him to help us look. If we divide the town up into four areas it shouldn't take that long. Now let's coordinate this and get going."

An hour later they were all back at the Simmonses' flat Seanless.

"There has to be something we're overlooking," Bernie said to Libby, Marvin, and Brandon as they all sat slumped on the sofa and armchairs.

She hadn't offered anyone anything to eat or drink and no one had asked. Everyone was too upset. Which had to be a first.

"Like what?" Brandon asked despondently.

"I don't know," Bernie said. "Something."

Brandon sighed and began to fiddle with the hem of his T-shirt. "We could go out and look again."

"Yes, we should," Bernie agreed.

Brandon's foot began jiggling up and down. "At least we'll be doing something, and doing something is a hell of a lot better than sitting around waiting for the phone to ring."

"Agreed," Libby said.

But she didn't make a move to get up. Neither did anyone else.

"Does your dad ever keep notes?" Marvin asked.

"Unfortunately no," Bernie answered. "He keeps it all up here." And she pointed to her head. "You're assuming," she said to Marvin, "that his being missing has something to do with the investigation."

"I guess I am," Marvin allowed.

"But we don't know that's the case," Bernie told him.

"We don't know it's not," Marvin argued. "If we proceed along those lines at least it gives us a direction." Not for nothing had he spent as much time with Mr. Simmons as he had.

"You're right," Libby said to Marvin.

"Yeah," Brandon said. "What would your dad be doing if the situation was reversed?"

Bernie brightened. "That's easy. He would go over the information we have again. Every little detail."

"Because it's always the little things that point the way," Bernie and Libby said together, paraphrasing their dad.

Brandon leaned forward, replanted his legs on the floor, clasped his hands together, and rested them on his knees. "Okay, Marvin," he said. "Tell us everything you said and did from the time you picked up Sean."

"But I've already done that," Marvin wailed. "Multiple times."

"Well, do it again," Bernie instructed. "There has to be something we're missing here."

And there was, Libby thought. Something that had happened. Something that was potentially important. But she couldn't remember what. It was floating in the forefront of her brain but she couldn't verbalize it. It bothered her. It bothered her enough so that as Marvin talked, despite her best intentions, Libby found her attention drifting off as she tried to remember.

She studied the branch of the budding ginkgo tree bowing in the wind outside the living room window. She watched a car across the street back into a parking space. Her glance lit on the clock on the wall and the empty armchair her dad would have been sitting in if he'd been here and the neatly folded paper he'd gone through this morning and she felt inexpressibly sad.

Then her gaze drifted to the biography of Lincoln her

dad had been reading, and that's when she noticed the manila envelope on the coffee table, the envelope that Orion had given her for her Dad. The one she'd chucked onto the table when Bernie had come running up to tell her about the cooler.

That was it! That was the thing she'd been trying to remember and it had been right in front of her all the time. What was it her dad always used to say about people not seeing what was actually there? There was probably nothing in it, but she wouldn't know that until she looked inside, would she? Libby leaned over, picked up the envelope, unsealed it, and took the pages out.

"What's that?" Marvin asked.

"Sweeney's and Duncan's client list," Libby said. "Orion dropped it off."

"He was here?" Bernie asked.

"That's what I just said," Libby answered.

"And you didn't say anything to me?"

"I didn't get the chance what with the cooler and all."

"Did you take a look?"

"That's what I'm doing, Bernie."

"So?" Bernie asked as Libby started glancing through the pages.

"As far as I can tell, it's a list of how much money people who invested with Mike Sweeney and Duncan lost."

"Let me see," Bernie said, and she leaned over and grabbed the pages out of Libby's hand.

"That is so rude," Libby told her.

"Sorry," Bernie said, even though she wasn't. "My God," she said as she took in the sums of money on the page. "We'd be rocking if we had an eighth of this. Hell, we'd be okay if we had one thirty-sixth. Clearly we are in the wrong business."

"Clearly," Libby said as she got up and leaned over Bernie's shoulder.

A moment later Marvin and Brandon did the same.

Brandon whistled as his eyes took in the sums. "No wonder everyone has been tipping less. If I lost that much money I wouldn't be tipping at all."

"If I lost that much money I would shoot myself," Libby said. "Jeez," she exclaimed when she came to the name on the bottom of the second page. "That's certainly interesting."

"It certainly is," Bernie said. "I'd say that's a pretty good motive, wouldn't you?"

"Definitely," Libby replied.

Brandon leaned over and took a better look. "You know he was there that night."

"What do you mean Dwyer was there that night?" Bernie asked.

"He was one of the people who was there at RJ's the night Sweeney was killed. He left early."

"Why didn't you mention him?" Libby asked.

"Because you didn't ask," Brandon told her. "I told you there were six other people there who had left earlier. You never asked me who they were."

Bernie bit her lip. "It just never occurred to me." Bernie put the papers down on the coffee table. She felt sick. She took out her cell and called Dwyer's office. No one answered.

"Maybe he's home," Libby said.

"Could be," Bernie said. "Let's go find out."

"Definitely," Marvin and Brandon said together.

Chapter 32

As Sean watched Pat Dwyer straighten out his shirt, he reflected that the man seemed out of breath. "Are you all right?" Sean asked.

Dwyer smiled and smoothed down his hair. "Fine. Just tussling with the garbage disposal. I mean what's the point of having one if every time you put something like coffee grinds or rice down it, it gets stuck?"

Sean laughed. "I've wondered the same thing myself. So where's Anne?" he asked as he took in the hallway with its white walls, lack of pictures, and plain wooden table with mail lying on it. As Sean stepped around a large, rolled up rug that had been shoved against the wall, he couldn't help reflecting on the lack of thought or care that had been put into the furnishings. Dwyer's house was like Dwyer's office, only less so.

Pat Dwyer smiled. "Anne went out shopping. You look disappointed. What? I'm not good enough for you?" he joked. "Come in. Have some coffee."

"I'll come in, but I'll pass on the coffee," Sean told him.

"I was just going to pour myself a cup. Are you sure?"

"Positive," Sean said politely. "I'm over my quota as it is."

Dwyer nodded and led Sean into the living room. "Be back in a sec. Just going to get my coffee," he told Sean as he took off for the kitchen. He emerged a moment later carrying two mugs and handed one to Sean. "Here," he said. "Try it. I make a great cup of coffee if I do say so myself."

"Perhaps in a moment," Sean said, putting the cup down on one of the end tables.

"You don't know what you're missing," Dwyer said. "And speaking of someone not being here, where's your pal?"

"Marvin? He's back in the office doing paperwork. I convinced him to let me borrow his car."

Dwyer raised an eyebrow. "That was nice of him."

"Yes, it was," Sean agreed.

"Knowing Marvin, I bet it took a fair amount of convincing," Dwyer replied.

"Enough," Sean admitted. "But I really wanted to see if I could be out on my own."

"It must feel good," Dwyer said.

"You can't imagine how good it feels," Sean said with all the emotion he could muster.

"And you used your free time to come here?" Dwyer asked. "I'm flattered."

Sean shrugged. "Don't be. I was visiting Rose and some questions about Liza popped into my head and I decided to drive over," he said, savoring the phrase *I decided to drive over*.

"You can ask me," Dwyer said.

Sean shook his head. "Thanks, but I really wanted to talk to Anne. It's always good to get a mother's perspective."

Dwyer straightened his shirt. "Then I'll tell Anne to call you when she comes in. Once she goes off shopping there's no telling how long she'll be gone."

Sean smiled. "I understand completely. Bernie's the

same way. But as long as I'm here, do you think I could see Liza's room? If it's not too much trouble, that is."

Sean noted that Dwyer seemed surprised at the request.

"It's no trouble at all," Dwyer told him after a few seconds went by. "But can I ask why?"

"It gives me a feel for the person." When Dwyer didn't say anything, Sean added, "I'm at a dead end and I'm hoping . . . well, I guess I'm hoping that something in Liza's room will give me a direction to go in."

Dwyer shook his head. "It's just a room, for heaven's sake. I'll show you if you want, but I don't see the point."

"There probably isn't," Sean admitted. He was about to make a comment about humoring an old man when he heard what sounded like a thumping coming from below him.

Dwyer shook his head. "That's the washing machine. It does that when it gets off balance."

"Ours used to do that too. We ended up having to get a new one."

"Well, I'm hoping ours will go for a little while longer," Dwyer replied.

"You know, if you're busy I can always come by another time," Sean said after a moment had gone by and Dwyer still hadn't moved.

"No, no," Dwyer said. "I'll take you up."

Sean remembered Bernie saying something about Liza's room being in the basement and remarked on it.

Dwyer hit his forehead with the flat of his hand. "Early onset Alzheimer's. It was upstairs. But then Liza moved downstairs. Something about her being free to come and go as she pleased." Dwyer frowned. "I told Anne I didn't think it was a good idea, but she always let Liza do whatever she wanted, which—not to speak ill of the dead or anything—is why she turned out the way she did." Then he pointed to Sean's cane. "Are you sure you're not going to have trouble on the stairs? They're pretty steep."

"I'll be fine," Sean assured him as he followed Dwyer through the house.

Passing by the dining room, he spotted something in the blue bowl on the sideboard that brought him to a dead stop. Dwyer, realizing Sean wasn't behind him, stopped too, turned, and followed Sean's gaze.

"Are those Anne's keys?" Sean asked. He was pretty sure they were because of the pink rabbit's foot she always carried on them. She'd explained the reason to Bernie at the shop one morning and Bernie had told him but he was embarrassed to say he'd forgotten what it was.

"Damn," Dwyer said, laughing. "So that's where they are. I had to give Anne the keys to my car."

To Sean's ear, Dwyer's laugh had a tinny sound and he noticed a bead of sweat was making its way down Dwyer's neck even though it was cold in the house.

"I thought your car was a shift," Sean said.

"It is. That's why I don't like Anne driving it. She strips the gears."

"I see," Sean said. And he thought he did. Unfortunately.

He looked at Dwyer. Dwyer stared back at him and at that moment Sean knew. He knew with one hundred percent certainty. He didn't know whether it was Dwyer's bobbing Adam's apple that told him or the faint tremor in Dwyer's hand or the sweat.

"Too bad both cars are still in the garage," Sean said.

"You can't see them from—" Dwyer said, then stopped himself, but it was too late.

"Where is she?" Sean asked.

"I told you. Anne's out shopping."

Sean heard another thump downstairs. "You should get that washing machine fixed," he said.

"I'm planning on calling the repairman on Monday. You know the builders of this place said the basement was haunted," Dwyer told Sean. "Something about one of the construction guys being killed there."

"Pesky little things, ghosts," Sean said. "Does this one have a name? Like maybe Anne?"

Dwyer forced a smile. "I'll have to ask the exorcist."

"I don't think that's what you're going to need," Sean commented.

Dwyer shook his head. More in sorrow than in anger, Sean thought.

"Amazing how things snowball," Dwyer said.

"Yes, it is," Sean agreed. "You start off small and things just get bigger and bigger."

"They certainly do," Dwyer responded.

"It might have been better if you hadn't gone to the gym all these years," Sean observed.

A smile flitted across Dwyer's face. "That's one way of looking at it," he said. "I guess I couldn't have done what I did without all that muscle. Interesting argument for not staying fit."

"Did Anne find out what you did to Liza?" Sean asked.

Dwyer took a deep breath and let it out. "Evidently Liza recorded everything. I thought I'd gotten rid of it all, but I didn't. She made backups. I came in when Anne was listening to them." Dwyer shook his head again. "And just when things were beginning to settle down too, the digital age comes and bites me in the ass."

"You know what they say," Sean continued. "If you want something done properly, do it yourself."

"I should have," Dwyer agreed. "It would have been simpler."

"So why did you do it?" Sean asked.

Dwyer smiled. "Kill Sweeney and frame Duncan?"

"Attempt to frame Duncan," Sean said.

"Because of the money, of course."

"Of course," Sean echoed.

"Don't say it like that," Dwyer cried. His cheeks began to flush. "Do you know how long it took me to amass that sum of money? Do you know how hard I've worked? How much I've given up? And to be left with nothing. Absolutely nothing." Dwyer's voice shook with rage. "And then to have Sweeney and Duncan shrug their shoulders and tell me there was nothing they could do about it. That there was no way to get my money back. To look at their smug faces. No. There was no way I was going to let that pass. None. They both deserved what they got."

"How did you get Sweeney back to RJ's?" Sean asked.

"I called him. Said I wanted to do another deal."

"And he believed you?" Sean asked incredulously.

"Sure," Dwyer said. "He figured he could fuck me over as many times as he wanted. After all, he'd done it before. But I was waiting for him. I got him in a lock, bashed his head into one of the vats to quiet him down, then held his head under." Dwyer absentmindedly rubbed his hands together. "Originally, I was going to do something else, but when I saw that fracas with the green beer . . . And Brandon never put the top back on properly. Well, when providence hands you something, you have to go with it."

"So you saw that?" Sean asked.

"I was behind the Dumpster in the alley waiting for Sweeney to leave."

"And Liza," Sean asked as he changed the position of his hand on the cane. "What about her?"

"What about her? I gave her money to put that stuff in Duncan's drink. Five hundred bucks for a minute's worth of work. She didn't even have to get it. I gave it to her. But she wanted more money once she figured out what had gone down. She always wanted more. She was a totally worthless individual. A drain on her mother and me."

"I bet her mother didn't see it that way."

"Anne never did have her head on straight when it came to that kid," Dwyer said ruefully.

"So you went to talk to Liza."

Dwyer smiled. "Yeah, I did. I told her I was bringing her her money."

"And then you put roofies in her drink and led her up to the bathroom and shot her."

"That is correct."

"You probably picked the bathroom because it was neater."

"As my mother used to say, neatness counts."

"I'm sure she'd be so proud," Sean said. "Answer me this. Why did you point me in Liza's direction?"

Dwyer smiled again. "I thought it made me look better and anyway I was tired of Anne whining about where her daughter was. I wanted some peace and quiet."

"Then why did you tip off the cops? It was you, wasn't it?"

"Who else?" And Dwyer laughed. "Impulse really. I know how much Lucy dislikes you. I thought the scenario would be amusing."

"You really are nuts," Sean told Dwyer.

"I believe the correct term is sociopathic," Dwyer said as he took a step toward him.

"Stay where you are," Sean warned, raising his cane and pointing it at Dwyer.

Dwyer sniggered. "What are you planning to do with that?"

"Come any closer and you'll find out," Sean said.

Dwyer kept coming. "Oh, that's right. I forgot. It's got a knife in it."

"A blade," said Sean, automatically correcting him.

Dwyer didn't stop. He kept coming. Finally he came up to the cane and held it against his chest. "Do what you're going to do, old man, before I cave your chest in."

"You think I won't?" Sean asked.

"I think you can't," Dwyer responded.

"You're wrong," Sean said.

"Am I?" Dwyer said.

"Yes you are," Sean said as he lowered the cane an inch while he pressed the button on the handle.

A long, thin, razor-sharp blade snaked out. Sean made a cross against Dwyer's stomach. Blood squirted out. He made another deeper cut, then pushed the blade in under Dwyer's breastbone and pressed harder, thrusting up as he went.

Dwyer's face turned pale. He dropped his hand. Sean turned the blade again. Dwyer staggered backward. His shirt was bright red with blood. Then he fell to the ground. Sean stood over him for a moment and watched Dwyer try to say something. Nothing came out.

I've killed him, Sean thought as he watched Dwyer's chest stop moving. He reached to take the cane out of Dwyer's chest, then withdrew his hand. He didn't want to touch it. Instead, Sean walked into the kitchen and called 911 on the house phone.

When he was done, he walked downstairs and found Anne Dwyer lying on her daughter's bed, gagged and trussed up with duct tape. A bruise ran down the left side of her face.

"He was going to kill me," Anne managed to croak out once Sean had removed the gag. "Liza . . ." she stopped talking. Tears ran down her cheeks.

"I know." Sean patted her on the shoulder. "I know."

"Where's Pat?" Anne asked.

"He's dead," Sean said as he began to take the duct tape off. "I'm sorry," he added.

"I'm not," Anne said.

Chapter 33

It was a week later and Libby, Bernie, Marvin, Brandon, and Sean were sitting in the Simmonses' flat having a snack. In honor of the season, Libby had wanted to make cucumber, watercress, and radish sandwiches on crustless white bread, crumpets with clotted cream and strawberry jam, and brew up some Darjeeling tea. But since everyone had wanted coffee, apple crumb cake, and cinnamon toast, Libby had gone along with that instead.

"I still don't believe that you did what you did," Brandon said to Sean after he'd taken a sip of coffee.

Sean swallowed the piece of cinnamon toast he'd been eating before replying, once again marveling as he did that such simple ingredients could yield such a pleasant result.

"You mean kill Dwyer, Brandon?"

"Yeah. Have you ever killed anyone else?"

"Nope. This is the first time. I've wounded a number of people, but I've never killed anyone."

"Do you feel bad, Mr. Simmons?" Marvin asked.

"You know," Sean told him. "I thought I would. But I don't. I'm sleeping just fine at night."

"Which is more than I can say for me," Libby said.

She, Bernie, Marvin, and Brandon had walked into

Dwyer's house a couple of minutes before the police had arrived and the images of Dwyer she'd seen had stayed with her. That could have been her dad on the floor.

"If I'd just opened the envelope Orion had given me," she began.

"Or I'd answered my phone," Brandon continued.

"Or you hadn't taken my car, Mr. Simmons," Marvin said.

Sean put his coffee cup down and glared at Marvin. "First of all, I didn't take your car. You let me borrow your car. Secondly, there was nothing wrong with my driving, and thirdly, if I hadn't gotten there when I did, Anne Dwyer would have been dead."

"And you could have been dead too," Libby pointed out. "Dwyer could have killed you instead of the other way around."

"I don't think so," Sean replied as he put a little more cream in his coffee.

"How do you get that?" Libby challenged.

Sean took a sip of coffee and put the mug down before replying. "Because I think Dwyer wanted me to kill him."

"What?" Bernie said.

Sean lifted a finger. "Stay with me, here. I've been thinking about what happened a lot and I've come to the conclusion that Dwyer could have killed me at any number of points if he wanted to. But he didn't. After all, he knew I had a sword cane. He knew what I was going to have to do when I saw Anne's keys on the table. He's faster than I am. He's stronger than I am. So he could have either run away or attacked me.

"Or for that matter not let me in at all. But he did none of those things. He basically forced me to kill him. He committed suicide by cop, or to be precise, suicide by ex-cop. Maybe he had a sudden attack of conscience. Or maybe he didn't want to die in jail. He had to know the game was up. He had to know you guys would find me."

Everyone was silent for a moment while they thought about what Sean had said. Then Marvin spoke.

"Fine," he said as he cut himself a slice of apple crumb cake. "I understand about Sweeney," Marvin continued. "Dwyer was angry at him for losing all that mone—"

"Never mind that he could have made more," Bernie interjected. "He has all of those McDonald's."

"He was losing them," Sean told her.

"Losing them?" Bernie replied. "How could he be losing them?"

Sean shrugged. "He used them as collateral for loans he took out to give to Sweeney."

"So he really was going broke," Libby said.

"Evidently," Sean answered. He turned to Marvin. "As you were saying?"

"I was just wondering what Dwyer was going to do with Anne."

"Shoot her, then roll her up in the rug and bury her and the gun in the backyard," Sean said promptly. "And you know what? It would have worked."

"A nice homey touch," Marvin noted. "Didn't Dwyer think that people would notice that his wife wasn't there?"

"No," Sean told him. "Dwyer's neighbors are snowbirds. They won't be back until the middle of April. I'm guessing Dwyer was going to tell them that he and his wife had separated and she'd moved to spend time with her brother in Arizona."

"Yeah. But what was going to happen when no one could get her on the phone?" Brandon demanded.

Sean shrugged. "According to Clyde, Anne didn't have many friends left. Most of her family was dead, except for the brother who's in a nursing home with dementia. And all of her friends were gone. They'd either moved away or died. It could have worked. At least for a while."

"That's so sad," Bernie said.

"It is," Sean agreed, thinking about how lucky he was

to have people around him that he loved and who loved him.

"And it could be years before they found her body," Brandon observed.

"Untrue," Marvin said, speaking from a professional point of view. "It's harder than you think to dig a six-foot grave around here. After three feet everything turns into clay."

"And just think what would happen if someone bought Dwyer's house and decided to remodel the backyard," Libby said, shuddering at the thought.

"I don't think he was planning to sell," Bernie said. "At least I wouldn't. I think that in this case it's a matter of keeping your friends close and your corpses closer."

"Anne is selling," Libby noted. "She listed the property with Bree as soon as she got out of the hospital."

"And who could blame her," Bernie said. "I certainly would if I were her."

"Me too," Duncan said as he came into the room. He pointed to his ankle. "No bracelet."

"Free at last," Libby said.

Duncan grinned. "I just wanted to thank you guys again before I take off. I know I said it already, but I'm saying it one more time. Thanks. Without you, I'd probably be in jail for life."

"You probably would," Bernie agreed.

"Where are you going?" Brandon asked.

"Down to the Culinary Institute. I figure it's time I got out of finance and this is always something I've wanted to do."

"I didn't know that," Bernie said.

"It's true," Duncan replied. "I did prep out at the Red Dog in Nantucket for two summers. I really liked it, but my mom was totally down on the whole culinary thing. She said you had to put in too much time for too little money."

"I think she has a point," Libby said. "It's a lot of hard work."

Duncan nodded. "I know, but I'm looking forward to it. Maybe I can intern with you guys at some point, if you could use an extra hand and you can forgive me for all the nasty things I said to you."

"We can always use an extra hand," Libby said. "Pull up a chair and sit down." And she leaned over, cut a slice of apple crumb cake, put it on a plate, and handed it to him.

"Delicious," Duncan said after he'd taken a bite.

Libby and Bernie both beamed.

"It's good to be back in the kitchen," Libby said.

Bernie nodded. "Always." She turned to her dad. "You know, I think I liked it better when I knew where to find you."

"I promise that you still will," Sean told her. And he meant it.

Recipes

The following recipes are Irish in spirit if not in fact. I've included one because the icing is green, another because it is an unusual dessert sauce made with Irish beer (although you can use any beer you want), and the last recipe because it speaks of spring.

Sarah Saulson's Grasshopper Squares

A sure hit with the kids.

Cream ½ cup butter, ½ cup sugar together. Add 4 eggs, 1 teaspoon salt, 1 teaspoon vanilla, 1 cup flour, and 16 ounces Hershey's chocolate syrup in order given. Spread in buttered 13-by-9-inch pan, bake at 350 degrees for 30 minutes. Cool completely.

Cream ½ cup butter, 2 cups confectioner's sugar. Add 4 tablespoons crème de mint (or one teaspoon peppermint extract). Add green food coloring and spread on top of brownies. Chill or freeze a short while.

Top with 6 tablespoons butter melted with 1 cup chocolate chips and spread on top. Cut into small squares and serve.

Caramel Beer Sauce

I know the following recipe sounds weird, but it tastes delicious and deserves a place in your repertoire. This sauce goes well over ice cream, pound cake, or sautéed fruit such as apples, bananas, and peaches. I don't know where the recipe comes from, but I've been using it for many years now and would like to thank the person who gave it to me.

1 cup brown sugar
2 tablespoons cornstarch
¼ teaspoon salt
½ teaspoon vanilla
1 cup of your favorite dark beer
2 tablespoons butter

In a medium saucepan mix together brown sugar, cornstarch, salt. Whisk in vanilla, beer, add butter. Cook over medium high heat until the mixture thickens.

To serve, place warm fruit and/or a scoop of ice cream in a bowl, and pour warm caramel beer sauce over top. Serve immediately.

Florence's Lemon Cake

This is the recipe my mom used to make around this time of year. In her words, "This is one of the best cakes I've ever made. It is delicious, easy to make, and keeps for weeks." What better recommendation can you have?

3 cups flour
2 teaspoons baking powder
½ teaspoon salt
½ pound butter
2 cups sugar
4 eggs
1 cup milk
finely grated peel of two lemons
¾ cup confectioner's sugar

Preheat oven to 350 degrees. Butter a 9-inch tube pan and dust it with unflavored bread crumbs.

Sift flour, baking powder, and salt together and set aside. Cream butter and sugar, add eggs one at a time, beating well after each addition. Then add alternately dry ingredients and milk, starting with dry ingredients. Beat until smooth. Stir in lemon rind. Put in pan and bake for an hour or until cake springs back.

Let cake stand in the pan for a few minutes, then invert it to get it out of pan; invert once more onto a dish. Make glaze out of ⅓ cup lemon juice and ¾ cup confectioner's sugar. (Do not heat. Just mix the two ingredients together.) Brush on the top and sides of the cake while it is still hot.